RUNNING FROM THE AIS

A GAIA'S WORLD NOVEL

KEVIN R COLEMAN

Published by Otter & Osprey Press

Edited by Sarah Liu

Cover art by Biserka Design

10 9 8 7 6 5 4 3

Text revision 10 May 2024

Paperback ISBN: 978-1-7382942-1-3

eBook ISBN: 978-1-7382942-0-6

Large Print Edition: 978-1-7382942-2-0

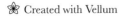 Created with Vellum

For those people everywhere in the world who have had to leave their homes without notice to escape persecution or disaster, and start again in a new unfamiliar place.

This novel is only a pale reflection of their lived experiences. I have enormous respect for those who made that journey.

"At some point in your life you will need to escape from something, so think about your escape routes and make sure they are always open!"

— Mehmet Murat Ildan

BOOKS BY KEVIN R COLEMAN

Jennifer Trilogy

Jennifer's Vow

Jennifer's Blessing

Jennifer's Destiny

Standalone novels in Gaia's world

Running From The AIs

Audio Books (Audible)

Jennifer's Vow

Jennifer's Blessing

RUNNING
— FROM —
THE AIs

A GAIA'S WORLD NOVEL

KEVIN R COLEMAN

OTTER & OSPREY
PRESS

1

ON THE RUN

The lightweight blanket over the dry grass provided only a thin, scratchy protection from the hard rocks as Rafael and Ellie lay on their stomachs side by side, looking over the cliff edge at the road below. Rafael could feel the heat leaching from his body into the cold rock beneath him.

There was little traffic on the road, making it easy for his mind to wander over the events of the past few days. Below, they had seen three pairs of security bots passing on foot, wielding chip detection wands. As they trotted along, the bots scanned both sides of the road and the adjacent shrubbery. When the third pair of bots disappeared around the next bend, Rafael rolled over onto his back. Above, the sun shone in a cloudless blue sky. The leaves on nearby bushes fluttered in the cool breeze.

"That's the third pair in an hour, about 20 minutes apart. It means we can easily cross the road when we're ready to get further down."

Ellie wriggled to get closer and lay her head on Rafael's chest. "We're going to be okay, aren't we?"

Rafael kissed her on the top of her head. "Of course, we haven't done anything wrong. We just need to lie low until we figure out how to make them understand."

"I'm scared, Raffi."

Guilt washed through him as he thought of how his misplaced curiosity was now putting Ellie at risk. "So am I, but we can't give in to that. Let's get up and keep moving. We'll make camp in a couple more hours and have the last sandwiches for dinner. Everything will seem better in the morning."

They stood and took up their packs, then moved off along the old hiking trail that ran for several hundred kilometers around the island that was home. This far from the city, the trail was now little more than a rabbit track through the scrub bushes and sharp grasses. Peeling white blazes painted on the trees continued to guide them forward.

As the sun dipped lower, they made camp. With practiced hands, Rafael put up their hiking tent. There was not enough room to stand, so he knelt on the floor of the tent as he laid out their sleeping bags side by side. Outside, Ellie was preparing a meal of sandwiches, potato chips, and two flasks of water. There was no fire tonight. She laid the sandwiches on their wrappings and set them on a nearby rock serving as an ersatz table.

After dinner, they brushed their teeth with the last flask of water, then removed their shoes and jackets and crawled fully clothed into the light sleeping bags.

"I'll be so glad when we can have a shower again," said Ellie, sniffing her armpits. "I'm starting to stink."

"You still smell lovely to me, but it might be good if you tried to sleep a little further away".

"You're no prize either, but I'm too polite to mention it."

"Let's both agree that we're overdue for washing and just go to sleep. With any luck, we'll be able to get clean tomorrow."

Ellie rolled away from him. Rafael lay facing her back and placed his hand on her hip. Lying there, waiting for sleep to come, Rafael retraced the events that had brought them to this point in time.

AN UNEXPECTED JOB INTERVIEW

Their adventure began, Rafael recalled, as he and Ellie sat across from each other at the tiny table in their small apartment. Two steaming mugs of coffee, plates of toast, butter and jam comprised their breakfast. The clock on the wall showed ten o'clock, but as neither had any work this morning, they had lain in bed longer than usual, reluctant to leave the warmth of the covers.

It was Wednesday, Rafael's day to report to HumanPower to see if he would have a work assignment for the next week. Ellie worked three days at the Community Center, which did not pay her directly but gave her enough credits to receive the full HumanPower supplement to the Unemployed Income Subsidy.

Rafael rose and kissed Ellie goodbye before setting out to the center.

"Good luck, Raffi," she said. "I'm sure you'll get something today."

Rafael only nodded as he let himself out. He checked that his key was still in his jeans pocket and walked down the three flights of stairs to the street level. Their apartment was in an old housing project for low-income families. The buildings were a uniform, depressing gray color. Each one had a small patch of grass, little more than beaten earth with tufts of crabgrass after generations of children had played outdoor games or dug holes to China, or simply run screaming around in circles in their quest for novel stimulation.

At the end of the street, the project buildings gave way to even older houses. Well maintained, they were gentrified remnants of a more prosperous past. Tall plane trees lined the road, giving shade. The mottled appearance of their trunks shone white in spots as their bark continually shed in large flakes to throw off pollution in the air.

Turning the next corner, Rafael passed a gleaming new apartment tower. Automated glass doors let occupants in and out as they tapped their wrists on the chip sensors on either side. They would most likely not have keys in their pockets or keys at all, Rafael thought, sighing deeply. I want to give this life to Ellie. But that type of luxurious tower seemed as unreachable as the moon.

As he walked along, a steady stream of little bubble taxis passed Rafael, bobbing slightly on their two wheels as they ferried people about the city. Occasionally, a larger four-person version passed, and every once in a while, a long limousine chauffeured a politician or an oligarch from one important meeting to another.

An impatient beep-beep behind him alerted him to a bot that wanted to pass. He stepped off onto the grass and watched the bot go by. It was a pizza bot with its red and blue decoration delivering someone else's breakfast or lunch.

The HumanPower building was an ugly, squat, yellow brick single-story building. Its decrepitude suggested that no one cared for it, and by extension, the tired, frustrated stream of humanity pouring through its doors.

Rafael joined the line to enter the hiring hall.

Inside, the indistinct murmur of a hundred conversations was punctuated by the steady zzzzip, zzzzip of tickets being issued by the AI-driven work assignment system. The room smelled of too much cleaning fluid, old sweat, human fear and desperation.

Rafael stepped up to a machine and presented his wrist chip to check-in. Zzzzip, a ticket was spat out into his waiting hand. Wicket Q. That's not good, he thought. No job for me there. What a waste of time; why not just notify us on our tablet? But this was an old thought and no longer had any energy behind it.

The line was short. He counted heads. Only five. At least I get it over with quickly.

The older lady ahead stepped up to the wicket and offered her ticket to the bored human clerk sitting on a high stool behind the grill.

"Hilda, the system requires you to present proof of life to continue receiving the UIS. At your age, the system requires proof of life once per year."

"Well, here I am! Alive and standing in front of you. Isn't that proof enough?"

"I'm really sorry, Ma'am, but you'll have to go to the verification center on Morrison for formal identification before you apply again."

"But how am I going to pay for a taxi to Morrison if you cut off my UIS?"

"I'm really sorry, ma'am. You'll have to ask the HumanPower AI if you wish to lodge a complaint."

"And how do I do that?"

"I really don't know. Next!"

The old woman shuffled to one side, looking lost and

without hope. Rafael stepped up and presented his ticket. "That was a shitty thing to do to an old lady," he said.

"What am I supposed to do? I'm here three days a week for my credits. If I create a fuss, I could lose that. It's not my fault the system is unfair, so apparently, it's my job to be a shitty clerk. Let's see what you have." The clerk scanned Rafael's ticket. A printer rolled out a slip of paper and dropped it on the counter.

"Hmm," he said. "You have a note. No job next week, basic UIS only, but you have this note." He handed the note to Rafael, who took it and turned away without speaking.

Pushing through the lines, he went out into the sunshine and took three deep breaths without intending to. My body's trying to clear itself, he realized. What a hellhole that is!

The paper was crisp in his fingers as he turned over the note. Squinting in the bright sunlight, Rafael peered at the note. **Rafael Morales 239867450**, and below, **Interview Friday 23 May 2045. Details: TBD R. Boyce**. Hmm, that's Friday, the day after tomorrow. Well, it's something.

Rafael carefully folded the message in two and set off for Artwell Park. On the way, he called Ellie on his tablet. "Hi Ell, something happened today. It might be good. Why not come down to Artwell Park? We can grab a hot dog together and sit beside the fountain."

───────────

ELLIE WAS TALKING WITH HER FRIEND RACHEL FROM DOWN the hall when the call from Rafael came through. Rachel picked up her coffee and looked to Ellie for a clue on whether to leave. Ellie motioned her to set down her coffee as they both listened to the call.

"Sure, sweetheart, that sounds nice," she said. "I'll leave as soon as I finish my coffee. See you at the fountain."

Rachel was looking at her expectantly. "No idea," said Ellie. I don't know any more than you heard."

"Tell me as soon as you find out." Rachel blushed. "I mean, if it's not too personal."

Ellie laughed. "I think you already know almost everything about us. It can't be much more personal than that. I'd invite you along, but…."

"No worries. That would be weird. Tell me later."

"Sure," said Ellie. "After Raffi, you're my best friend. I should go; I have to meet him in the park."

On her way to the park, Ellie was still thinking about Rachel. What wouldn't I tell her? If I were pregnant, I'd tell her that. If Raffi had a new job? Yeah. If he was arrested? I think so. Where's the line?

Rafael was sitting on a bench in front of the fountain, apparently deep in thought. He stood to hug her, but Ellie felt his mind was somewhere else. Normally, he breathes me in and calls me '*mi vida*', but today, there's nothing. How bad could his news be?

They wandered over to the hot dog seller, attended by an older man in an outfit with a large picture of a hot dog. Bright red and yellow shapes were sewn on his clothes, looking like massive ketchup and mustard splotches. Rafael ordered for both of them and chatted idly with the man as the robot vendor made their hotdogs to order.

"Nice day to be out in the park, sir," said the hot dog man.

"Yeah, it's a beautiful day. Do you do this every day?"

"Six days a week, six hours a day. It's a full-time gig."

Ellie was intrigued. "What happens when it rains?"

"Company provides an umbrella. Also provides shade from the sun if it gets too hot."

"So what do you do, exactly?" asked Rafael. Ellie squeezed his arm. He's getting very personal, she thought.

"Just greet the customers and give the orders to Oskar here, although he can also hear them himself. My job is to let customers forget about the AIs behind it all for a moment so they can pretend they still live in a human world. Window dressing, that's what I tell Sally, my wife."

"That's a deeper answer than I expected," said Ellie. "What did you do before?"

"Degree in Social Sciences and Philosophy. Neither of which is valued by our AI overlords. But it's an income, and Sally and I live well enough to look after our daughter Felice. And I get all the hot dogs I can eat." He laughed, but Ellie could hear the bitterness underneath.

Taking the hotdogs and two colas from Oskar, they returned to the bench where Rafael had been sitting.

Leaning forward, napkins on their laps, they ate in silence, trying not to let condiments drip on their clothes. Ellie looked sideways at Rafael. His eyes were unfocused as he gazed into the splashing water. I wonder what's going on inside that head; he's miles away.

When they finished, Rafael sat up and carefully gathered his wrappings and napkin. Ellie did the same, keeping pace with him. Taking her wrap from her, he held them both high in the air until a nearby trash bot rolled over and opened the hatch in its lid.

"Thank you for keeping the park clean," it said

Rafael set down his drink and fished in his pocket. This is it, she thought. This is what he wants me to see. She set down her drink and leaned closer to see. Their shoulders touched, sending a small spark through her. Why do I always feel it when our bodies touch like that?

Rafael was already unfolding the scrap of paper the machine had dropped on the counter. He held it for her to read, shading it with his free hand to keep the sun off.

Ellie read: **Rafael Morales 239867450, Interview Friday 23 May 2045. Details: TBD - R. Boyce.**

"So you have an interview. That's wonderful! Maybe this will turn out to be a permanent position."

"But it's kind of odd, isn't it? Normally, it has a time and a recruiting bot ID. This has nothing. What do I do with this?"

"I'm sure it means that R Boyce will call and tell you. But that's not what's worrying you, is it?"

Rafael turned to Ellie, his mouth down-turned and his brow furrowed. "What is it, Raffi, what am I not seeing?"

"What if it's a job like the hot dog man, wearing funny clothes and being window dressing for an AI? Would I take that job? Would all that school and those exams be as useless as his degrees?"

"What if that's not what it is? What would be the best case? Why not dwell on that for a bit? What would you like the job to be?"

"Mechanical technologist designing actuators and mechanical systems. It's what I'm trained for."

"Then let's intend that job. You'll be brilliant at it. You don't have to accept just any job. You always have a choice."

"I guess you're right. Thanks, Ell. I don't know what I'd do without you."

"Hopefully, you'll never have to find out. Now let's get some exercise and fresh air while we're here."

THE NEXT MORNING, DURING BREAKFAST, RAFAEL'S TABLET buzzed and announced, "Call from Ron Boyce."

Rafael tapped his tablet to answer the call.

"Hello, may I speak to Rafael Morales?" asked a pleasant male voice.

"I'm Rafael."

"My name's Ron Boyce, and I'm calling to invite you to a job interview with Bright Light Industries tomorrow at 11am. Are you available then?"

"What kind of job is it?"

"It's a full-time technologist role. I'll provide all the details tomorrow. If you're interested, meet me at the Otto Hot at the corner of Elm and Harrison Street at eleven o'clock."

"Anything I should bring?"

"No, I have all the information we need. I just need to complete the interview with you. Will I see you tomorrow, Rafael?"

"Yes, thanks Mr Boyce, I'll be there."

"It's just Ron. I'll see you there."

The call ended.

"Well, that was strange," said Rafael.

"Why strange?"

"It was clearly a call from a human, no pre-qualification test or profiling. And I never applied for the position."

"Maybe they've heard about you and really want you?"

"Heard what? I haven't done anything except HumanPower make-work jobs since college, and those are mostly low level physical work."

"Don't worry about it. Listen to what this guy has to say and then you can decide."

Rafael shrugged. "Nothing else I can do."

THE NEXT DAY, RAFAEL WAS RIGHT ON TIME FOR THE interview. It was easy to spot Ron in the small outdoor cafe. He was standing and waving at him. As they went through introductions, an Otto robot rolled up, saying "Good morning, gentlemen. How may I serve you?"

Rafael ordered, "One cappuccino with sugar, and one Cherry Danish please."

The Otto turned slightly to face Ron.

"Otto," Ron said, "can you make mint tea?"

"Yes, I have Organic Moroccan Peppermint tea. Would you like one?"

"Yes please, but no pastry, thank you."

The little Otto served the drinks with Rafael's pastry, then rolled off to greet another customer. Rafael watched as Ron's eyes followed the Otto until it disappeared into the back.

"I've been drinking coffee and eating pastries all morning," Ron explained, as his attention returned to Rafael. "Now tell me about your background."

It turned out that they had taken the same courses at City College, although Ron had been there four years earlier. Ron seemed very interested in Rafael's minor in Actuator Design. The conversation turned to Ellie and their life together.

"How long have you been together?" asked Ron.

"We met five years ago, been living together for three. One day, we'll get married and start a family, but we need some financial security first."

"And how would Ellie be if your job involved being called out at night or on weekends?"

"If it's a good job, and it's not every night, I think she'd be okay."

There was a natural pause in the conversation.

"I noticed you were polite to the Otto," Ron said. "Do you think it cares if we're polite?"

Surprised by the change in direction, Rafael took a moment to think. "I don't know. There are probably as many levels of intelligence in machines as in biological life. I think an Otto might be on the same level as a rabbit, with simple reactions to common circumstances. Would you mistreat a rabbit?"

"Of course not. So you think the Ottos are sensitive to what we do?"

"No idea, but they clearly react to what we do and say. Don't know anything about their feelings or thoughts. But I also don't know about the feelings or thoughts of a rabbit."

Another pause as Ron looked away again. Self doubt flooded Rafael. Why is he hesitating to continue? Why did I make that stupid comment about rabbits?

Ron leaned forward, engaging again. Rafael matched his posture.

"What would you think about working for an AI?"

Now Rafael felt himself hesitating. "Like as a boss?"

"Yes."

"Hmm, I guess that would depend."

"On what?"

"Whether it was rational in its direction, I suppose. Also, if it allowed for me to be human." Rafael shrugged with his palms face up. "I don't know, but it would be interesting to try."

Rafael sat back. "There's something that's been bothering me. I never applied for this job, although don't get me wrong, I want it."

Ron sat back also and seemed to relax. He waited for Rafael's next question. Taking a deep breath, Rafael said, "I find myself being interviewed by a human instead of a hiring bot. And now you're asking me about working for an AI. What's really going on?"

Ron smiled and sipped his tea. "So, here's the thing. Bright Light Industries is run by an AI named Fatima. She knows everything about her factories, but almost nothing about the outside world. I think she sees humans as necessary, but she doesn't really understand us. So we have to understand her."

"Same as with the Ottos, I suppose. We get looked after best when we work within their understanding."

"Exactly," replied Ron. "So if you take the job, you'll receive calls from Fatima. Some will be planned calls that happen at exactly nine o'clock on any morning. Unplanned calls can be any time, but then you must respond immediately."

Rafael thought about the hot dog vendor in the park. "So this is not a mechanical design job, it's a maintenance job. Is that right?"

"Yes, does that worry you?"

"Does the job really require a human, or will I be human window dressing on an AI?"

"Window dressing?"

"Like the hot dog guys in the park. They do nothing with the hot dogs. They just put a human face on an AI operation."

Ron's eyebrows went up, and he sat up straight again. "No, you're not seeing it. These factories are engineering marvels, some of the most complex creations we humans have made. We made them intelligent, self-diagnosing and self-repairing. But no matter how hard we tried, things happen beyond the factory AI's understanding, vision, or capability to respond to. That's when we need a human who knows the factory, who is educated, and can diagnose and resolve complex problems. That's why the work is episodic and infrequent, although you'll receive a full-time salary. No, you will not be window dressing. You and your skills are invaluable in this position."

"You also mentioned regular calls at nine A.M. What are those?"

"Planned maintenance windows when we run lubrication schedules or swap out worn parts."

"That sounds like task work that could have been built into these super factories."

"Yes, but I like the maintenance windows. I think they're built to keep our relationship with Fatima healthy and our skills fresh."

"Will I receive training?"

"If you're offered the job, then Fatima will explain all these details, along with salary and vacation. One more thing, being on call means always being ready to respond. It means being aware of alcohol or pharms. You can decline a call and pass it to the second technician, but if it happens too often, you'll lose your job."

"I understand that, too. Actually, I wouldn't mind that. I don't really drink much, and this would give me a perfect excuse when I'm out with friends."

"Great, I'll call you tomorrow and let you know. Will you be available to take the call?"

"Yes, certainly. I'll be with Ellie and her parents from two to four in the afternoon, so I'd prefer either earlier or later. But I'll make any time work."

Ron stood up, and Rafael did the same, holding out his hand. "Thanks, Ron. I really enjoyed the interview. I'm looking forward to hearing from you."

They shook hands. As Rafael walked out of the Otto Hot, he looked back to see Ron sitting down again, a puzzled look on his face. *I wonder how many more interviews he has to do?*

BACK HOME, ELLIE WAS WAITING IMPATIENTLY TO HEAR ALL about the interview. Every few minutes, she closed her eyes and thought, please let this be an actual job this time.

When Rafael walked through the door, she rose and greeted him with a warm hug. She could feel the tension leave him as he held her a little longer than usual.

Rafael sat down at one end of their threadbare couch as Ellie poured coffee before sitting down next to him.

"Well, it was strange," said Rafael. "He was a human, and the job is working for an AI, so it's all backwards."

"What would you be doing?"

"Maintenance on an AI-driven factory."

She could hear the uncertainty in his voice. Oh no, she thought. He's not going down the rabbit hole of human worth again, is he? "What kind of maintenance?" She closed her eyes, hope welling up inside her. Please, she prayed. Don't let it be sweeping the floors or painting the walls.

"I'm not really sure. Ron said it requires a technologist with analytical skills. He's going to call me tomorrow with the next steps if I'm chosen."

"Are you okay with working for an AI?"

"I suppose so. A boss is a boss, whether they breathe oxygen or kilowatts. Ron seemed like a normal guy who graduated with the same degree I did. If he's happy, then I expect I'll be happy. One thing was weird, though, he seemed very interested in why I was polite to the Otto bot."

"But you're always polite to everyone and everything. I always thought it was just a funny habit." Ellie felt her stress melting away. Raffi was going to be okay.

"Maybe it is, but then I had to make something up. I

told him the Otto bots were like rabbits, and he seemed to like that idea."

"Rabbits?"

"Honestly, I never thought about it before. It was just the first thing that popped into my head. Anyways, there's nothing to do now, but wait for the call tomorrow."

Ellie snuggled closer on the couch, forcing Rafael to put his free arm around her shoulders. She felt the heat from his body warming her own. Tilting her head, she kissed him, saying, "I'm sure you'll get this one. After all, you are the most amazing man on the planet."

Rafael laughed, and she felt him pull her even closer. "I love that you think that. I just hope he calls before we see your parents."

THAT NIGHT IN BED, ELLIE ASKED, "RAFFI, ARE YOU SURE you'll be okay with working for an AI?"

"I don't really know yet. After all, how intelligent can they be? Ron said that Fatima knows only her factory and nothing of human beings. I don't see them as a threat or anything like that."

"As long as you're sure," she replied. "You don't have to take this job if it worries you."

"I've been thinking about it. I don't see anything to worry about. Ron seemed like a nice guy, and he's not worried. If they offer, I'll probably accept."

AT NINE THE FOLLOWING DAY, RAFAEL WAS SITTING AT THE table when Ron Boyce called again. "Hello, Rafael? It's Ron Boyce calling from Bright Light Industries. I'm calling to offer you the job. You'll be the primary technologist at Bright Light's air compressor plant."

Rafael realized Ellie had come to sit beside him, listening to the call.

"So, Rafael, the job is yours if you want it. Do you have any other questions for me before I turn you over to Fatima?"

"Just how come you didn't review my technical qualifications? I expected I would have to show you my certificates or talk about my experience."

"No, Fatima already did all that. She gave me a short list to speak with for a human evaluation. You were the one I thought I would most like to work with and would most enjoy the job."

"Okay, then I'm ready to talk with Fatima. What do I have to do?"

"I'll have Fatima call you now. Fatima will formally offer you the job with salary and benefits details. She'll send the actual contract to your tablet. Once you accept Fatima's offer, she'll provide you with all the training details. You should expect to spend two weeks in training, probably starting next Wednesday."

"Thanks, Ron, for choosing me. I'm looking forward to meeting Fatima."

"You're welcome, Rafael. I'm sure you'll get along well with her. Please call me if you have any questions at all. Not just about the offer, but at any time in the future."

"Will do, thanks again. Bye, Ron." Rafael cut the connection.

Almost immediately, a call arrived from Bright Light Industries.

"Hello Rafael," said a pleasant female voice. "Please state your personal identity number for confirmation."

"239 867 450."

"I am sending you a contract now. Please accept it on your tablet."

Ellie leaned over to read the contract with Rafael. When she saw the salary, she smiled and nodded her agreement to him. Rafael signed with a scan of his thumbprint.

By the end of the following discussion, Rafael had provided his height, weight and shoe size and confirmed his good eyesight.

"Rafael, a package will arrive for you within the next day. Please bring it with you when you report for training next Wednesday."

"Can I open the package?"

"Yes, although I see no value in that activity. Please ensure that all items are with you when you arrive."

"Thank you, Fatima."

"Goodbye, Rafael." Fatima broke the connection.

Ellie hugged him and kissed him on the cheek. "Wow," she said, "I knew you would get the job, but that was really quick."

"I wonder what's in the mysterious package?"

"We'll find out more when this package arrives, tomorrow or Monday. I can't wait to tell my parents. I'm sure they'll be excited to hear about your new position."

"And what position is that, exactly? I'm not sure I caught that yet."

"Primary technologist for an air compressor plant. That's what Ron said."

"Okay, we can go with that. I'm going to call my parents now. I think Papa has given up on me with my diploma and still no job."

"I'm sure he hasn't."

ELLIE AND RAFAEL ARRIVED AT HER PARENTS' HOUSE JUST after two for afternoon tea, usually an abundant affair with lots of canapés, sandwiches, and sweet cookies. "I think it's Mom's way of making sure we eat well at least once a week," Ellie had explained once.

Today was no exception. As they sat down, Ellie could not contain herself. "Mom, Dad, Rafael has some wonderful news."

All eyes turned to Rafael. He smiled and sat up straighter. "I've just signed a contract to become primary technologist at the Bright Light Industries air compressor plant. I start on Wednesday."

"That's wonderful, Rafael," said Mrs Nielsen. "You must be very excited."

"Yes, congratulations!" added Mr. Nielsen, leaning over to shake hands. "We always knew you'd find something."

"Does this mean you'll be getting married soon?" asked Mrs. Nielsen.

"Mom! We haven't even discussed this." Ellie's face flushed with embarrassment. Rafael smiled, enjoying her discomfort.

"Don't worry, Mrs. Nielsen. I have every intention of asking Ellie as soon as I'm sure my new job is stable and we have an income to build our future on." Rafael put his arm around Ellie and pulled her close. "I really want us to spend a lifetime together, have our own children and raise a family." He paused and looked at Ellie. "We've already talked about it. We're just not at the point of making actual plans yet."

Ellie nodded, smiling and looking radiant. Seeing Ellie like that, Rafael couldn't help grinning.

3

MEETING FATIMA

The package arrived by courier bot at not long after lunch on Monday afternoon. Rafael brought it inside and set it on the coffee table so he could open it. Ellie was sitting at the kitchen table, going over program notes for the community center. She put down her notes and joined him on the couch to look in the box.

He carefully lifted out each item and set them next to the box. When he had finished, they surveyed the contents: an orange jumpsuit with sewn-on black markings, black work boots with bright orange patches, orange gloves, an orange helmet with what looked like a bullseye printed on top and a noise-canceling headset.

"Wow," said Ellie. "Looks like you're all set up for camera surveillance."

"That makes sense, given that I'll be working in an automated factory."

"Try on the jumpsuit. Does it go over your clothes?"

Rafael took off his shoes and pulled on the jumpsuit, buttoning it down the front under the protective flap. For good measure, he pulled on the work boots with their steel toes, and donned the headset and hardhat. He walked up and down the length of the living room, twirling at each end like a runway model. Ellie giggled, making Rafael laugh with her. He took a deep bow, at which point the hard hat fell off, landing in front of him.

"Is this my new clown suit? Like the hot dog guy?"

"No, don't even think that," said Ellie. "If it were a clown suit, it would have more colors. It looks very professional and safe. Are the boots comfortable?"

"Yeah, they're new, but they're the right size. It all feels good."

"Let's pack it up again so it's ready for Wednesday."

Ellie neatly folded the coveralls as Rafael carefully set the boots and hardhat in the bottom of the box. The folded coveralls went on top of them, followed by the gloves and the headset.

Wednesday morning, Rafael walked down to the ground level of their aging three-floor apartment block. As he stepped out the front doors, a bubble taxi rolled up and opened its door. It sat there, bobbing slightly on its two wheels. He heard the hum of the flywheel under the floor that kept it balanced as he tossed the box onto the far seat and sat down.

"Are you Rafael Morales?" asked the taxi in its mechanical voice.

"Yes."

"Are you going to Bright Light Industries?"

"Yes, thank you."

The door closed, and the vehicle merged into traffic on the street.

Fifteen minutes later, the taxi stopped in front of a low industrial building with a single blue door under a Bright Light Industries sign, with a smaller sign saying Entrance below. Rafael offered his wrist in payment, but the taxi politely declined. "I charged your fare to Bright Light Industries. Thank you for riding with Rapid Taxi."

Carrying the box, Rafael walked up to the blue door. There was no button to request entrance or door handle to open the door. There was only a palm reader in a sheltered box.

"Humph," said Rafael, balancing the box on his left hip as he pressed his right hand to the palm reader. The glass plate was cool under his hand. Why the old palm reader and not a wrist chip reader? He wondered.

The door opened. Inside was a small locker room. He could hear heavy equipment sounds and the floor vibrating beneath his feet. On the left wall were three lockers, numbered one, two, and three. A bench sat in front of the lockers. A door with signage for a unisex toilet and shower was located at the end of the lockers. The room smelled faintly of pine. Probably from the cleaners, he thought. On the right wall was another automatic door with a second palm reader. Directly facing him was a display with a message reading, "Welcome, Rafael Morales. Please put on your headset."

Sitting on the hard wooden bench, he pulled out the headset. A green light glowed above the right ear cup. He put it on his head. The sounds of the factory disappeared, the sudden silence disquieting.

"Hello Rafael," said the same warm female voice from his acceptance call. "I am Fatima. If you wish me to respond to a question or comment, please begin with my name to ensure you have my attention."

"Hello, Fatima. Should I put on my new work clothes now?"

"Yes. You have been assigned locker number one for anything you wish to leave behind. I will lock and unlock it for you during each visit." Rafael heard a small click from locker one.

"Thank you, Fatima."

He opened the box again and quickly donned his new work clothes. As an afterthought, he placed his house keys and tablet on the small shelf of the locker and his street shoes at the bottom. When he closed the door, he heard another small click as Fatima locked the locker. Raphael had a moment of panic. I'm really in her world now. An insane urge to run back out into the street took hold. Take a breath, what did you expect? He went to the exit door and pushed it open. Good, so I'm not locked in then. The door closed when he released it.

"Fatima, can you see me here?"

"Yes, Rafael, there is a camera above the factory door. My robots do not enter this room, but I can monitor this space. Now bring the cardboard box and enter my factory."

Rafael picked up the cardboard box, pressed his palm to the reader beside the door, and headset. The floor vibrations were more pronounced as heavy equipment moved and rotated the large compressed air units being built. Just inside the door was a scrap bin and a tool chest. Rafael tossed the empty box into the scrap bin, which promptly wheeled away.

"Fatima, do you control all these devices?"

"I have direct control of the ones used occasionally, like the scrap bin and tool cart. Various layers of automation manage the others, functioning under my supervision and direction but working autonomously when systems are nominal. Now turn to your right, and we will begin your training.Please follow the toolbox. It will lead you through the modules."

Along the far wall to the right was a low bench holding a series of fixed and mobile air compressors, each lit by a spotlight.

"Module 1: Introduction to my products."

The tool box rolled up to the first example, stopping short to allow Rafael free access to the examples on the bench.

By two that afternoon, training was finished for the day. Rafael hung his new coveralls in locker one and retrieved his house keys and shoes. "Fatima," he asked before stowing the headset. "What are the other two lockers for?"

"Locker two is for the secondary technologist when one is assigned. The third locker is used by any other technologist called to the factory."

"How many factories does Bright Light Industries have?"

"Thirty-seven factories."

"Does each one have a Fatima?"

"I am Fatima. I am thirty-seven factories. How many roles do you play in your life?"

Rafael thought quickly. "I'm Ellie's partner and a son to my parents. I play video games with my friends and work for you."

"And how many Rafael's does it take to do these things?"

"What? Only one. I'm the only one of me."

"Then we are the same in that way. Your taxi is waiting."

"Thanks, Fatima."

"Goodbye, Rafael."

He removed the headset and stowed it in the locker. As

he left the building, the taxi was already waiting at the curb. Sitting in the taxi, his mind went back to the last question. Did I just ask a really stupid question? His cheeks burned with embarrassment. How could we be alike? Am I someone different with Ellie than with my family? I thought Ron said this AI was not that intelligent.

4

MIDNIGHT CALL

Rafael was dreaming of camping with Ellie, sitting around a campfire, sharing a blanket against the cold at their backs. But someone was shaking him. In the middle of his dream, someone was shaking him. As he swam back up to confused awareness, he heard his tablet saying, "Urgent call from Fatima" over and over.

"Raffi, wake up! It's Fatima! Don't miss your first call!" The urgency in Ellie's voice brought him fully awake.

"Answer it," he said loudly enough for his tablet to hear, Rolling on his back, eyes were still trying to focus in the semi-darkness.

"Rafael, my factory has stopped. I need you now. A taxi is waiting."

"Okay, coming now."

"Yes, that is our agreement. Goodbye, Rafael."

"Goodbye."

Ellie was already sitting up in bed. "Get up! Don't go back to sleep. I'll make you a coffee to take with you while you get dressed."

"Okay, I'll just have a quick shower and shave, and then I'll be ready."

"Raffi, I don't think Fatima cares how you look or smell. Just put on some clothes. Chop, chop!"

His entire body was protesting the interruption of his sleep. His muscles were stiff, and when he stood, he toppled forward, catching himself on the bed. Don't want to do this, he thought. He stood there next to the bed, one hand on the headboard for support.

Breathe, breathe! His cheeks and lips flapped as he shook his head, trying to dispel the remnants of sleep. Oh shit, I've got to move! His spine stiffened, and his eyes opened wide with the sudden realization that Fatima was waiting and he was wasting time.

Dressing quickly in yesterday's clothes, he dashed to the kitchen where Ellie held a travel mug of coffee and a leftover pastry.

Downstairs, the bubble taxi was waiting with its passenger door open. Rafael climbed in. "Bright Light Industries Compressor Plant," he said.

"Yes, Rafael, I have alerted Fatima of your arrival."

"Wait, you know Fatima?" Rafael leaned forward. This is new, he thought.

"Yes, we are part of the same complex."

"What complex is that?"

"I'm sorry, I don't understand the question."

"You said you and Fatima are part of the same complex. What complex is that?"

"I do not recall saying that. If I did, I misspoke. Please forget it."

Rafael sat back. Misspoke my ass. I wonder what the connection is.

Ten minutes later, his pastry eaten and his coffee still unfinished, Rafael arrived at the factory.

"Thank you for choosing Rapid Taxi. Please check for any items left behind."

Coffee in hand, Rafael placed his hand on the palm reader. In the night air, the reader was cold. Rafael shivered in his thin shirt. Should have brought a coat.

The door opened. Setting his coffee on the bench, he opened his locker and put on the headset. "Hello, Fatima, what is the problem?"

"Hello Rafael, my motor to compressor assembly unit has lost hydraulic pressure, and I cannot understand why. I can no longer install the connecting bolts to assemble the unit."

As Fatima spoke, Rafael was already pulling on his orange coveralls and stepping into his work boots. Her voice was calm. Funny, he thought, her voice has no sense of urgency, although she must be stressed. "Are you okay, Fatima? You don't sound worried."

"I am not worried because you will fix the problem."

Inside the factory, the toolbox and scrap bin were waiting for him. Rafael set off for the assembly unit, and the scrap bin and toolbox followed.

Even before he got to the unit, he could see a growing puddle of hydraulic fluid on the floor, spreading as fluid continued to drip from somewhere inside the unit. A shiver of fear ran through him. Shit, if this ignites, we'll lose the whole line, he thought.

"Fatima, initiate fire risk protocol. Shut down all electrical input in the vicinity. Send a bin of oil containment powder. I will clear a path to stop the leak."

"I shall send a cleaning bot with supplies."

"Do not approach the spill. The bot could ignite the oil."

"Yes, Rafael."

Two minutes later, a cleaning bot stopped next to the

scrap bin. A hopper of oil containment powder sat on top of its frame, its hatch already open. Rafael removed the small shovel from the tool cart and spread the powder, focusing first on creating a path to the unit. He worked quickly to outpace the continuing leak. Gotta stop the leak. Gotta stop the leak. The mantra looped in his head.

Reaching the hydraulic reservoir, he turned the small ball valve at the bottom of the tank to stop further fluid from going into the lines and onto the floor.

Now, he could spread the powder to cover the remaining leak.

"Fatima, have the cleaning bot sweep up the powder. Fire risk protocol has ended. Human safety protocol in effect. Please confirm the lockdown of all moving elements."

"Human safety protocol in effect. All moving elements locked down."

Rafael picked up his coffee from the top of the toolbox and drank the last few swallows as the cleaning bot worked. Hydraulic schematics were flowing through his mind as he remembered his training. None of that helped without knowing where the leak was. Shit, there are hydraulic lines all over this thing. How do I find the leak without starting it up again? Rafael felt a moment of panic as he realized there was no one else to turn to.

Taking a deep breath, the thought, first, let's get it all cleaned up. As he worked at wiping down the hoses, cables and mechanical elements, a sense of calm came over him. He realized the cables and hoses made sense after his training. I've got this, he thought.

Rafael found the problem easily. The thickness of the oil splash changed the feel of the parts under the cloth as he wiped. One area was thickest. The leak must be opposite this, he thought. He ran his gloved fingers over the slippery, oily hoses.

Between two hoses running from the manifold was something hard and sharp. Damn, my glove's cut. What the hell was that?

With fresh gloves and a pair of pliers, he pulled out half an assembly bolt. The end where it snapped off had a sharp edge and had been rubbing against the hoses with the vibration of the assembly line.

"Fatima, I have found the problem. Stand by for spare parts requisition."

"Standing by."

Returning to the cart, Rafael pulled out a mirror on a short stick. Once again inside the machine, he called out, "Fatima, hose 371B and hose 371C to be replaced. Also I will need enough hydraulic fluid to refill the reservoir."

"Confirming two times hose 371 to replace 371B and 371C. Two times 10 liters of hydraulic fluid."

The rest of the repair was straightforward. Rafael replaced the two hoses, refilled the reservoir, and reopened the manual ball valve. The last step was to bleed the lines.

Satisfied, Rafael stepped back, removed his gloves, and said, "Fatima, end human safety protocol. Run operation at slow speed and report anomalies."

"Confirming end of human safety protocol, running operations at twenty percent speed."

Rafael watched through five cycles. "Fatima, resume normal operations."

An audible ascending whine and increased floor vibrations told him the entire line was coming up to speed. Rafael waited. His muscles sagged. He wobbled on his feet for a moment. That was exhausting. What time is it? he wondered. I need to sleep.

In the locker room, Rafael pulled off his coveralls and

gloves and dropped them in a laundry chute. There would be a clean set ready when he returned.

A Rapid Taxi waited outside. As Rafael approached, its door swung open.

"Home, sir?" asked the taxi.

"Yes, home please. You knew my name before. Do you have a name?"

"You may call me Dispatch. I schedule Rapid Taxis. The taxi itself is autonomous but does not have a name."

"Thank you, Dispatch." Rafael settled back in his seat and closed his eyes for a moment.

An alarm bell was ringing, and the taxi had stopped. "What's happening?"

"We've arrived, Rafael. I believe you were asleep." The alarm stopped.

"Yeah, sorry. It was a long night."

Rafael stumbled out the open taxi door and climbed the long three flights of stairs back to their apartment. The smell of breakfast and fresh coffee greeted him at the door. A moment later, Ellie was there, hugging him. "Oh Raffi, you look beat. Maybe you should go straight to bed."

"Yeah, prolly good idea…," he mumbled. The last thing he remembered was Ellie pulling off his socks.

WHEN RAFAEL AWOKE, HE STUMBLED INTO THE KITCHEN, looking for Ellie, but she wasn't there. He made his own coffee and found a muffin for breakfast, although it was already eleven o'clock.

Sitting at the table, he tried to make sense of the night before. Memories came back in fits and starts. The pool of hydraulic fluid. The quiet of the factory when it was stopped. Installing the new hoses. So that's my job, some kind of human surgeon on the AI factory body. I was inside her, and she trusted me to make it right. I trusted her to keep me safe. And she said she was running thirty-six other factories at the same time. He tried to picture running thirty-seven of himself, all doing different things in different places, but it was impossible. How can we ever truly understand each other?

He called Ellie.

"Hi, Raffi. I'm at the Community Center running a seniors' fitness program this morning. Why not come down for lunch? I missed you this morning, but you were sleeping so soundly I didn't want to wake you when I left."

"Sure, lunch'll be good. See you at the center."

5

THE CURIOUS TAXI PATTERNS

S everal weeks after the maintenance call, Rafael received a nine o'clock call to come in at three that afternoon for a routine lubrication service. He was already waiting at the curb when a small Rapid Taxi pulled up and opened its door.

The strange conversation with the taxi on his repair call came to mind. "Hello, Dispatch."

"Hello Rafael, how may I help you?"

"Are you part of a hierarchy of AIs?"

"I'm sorry, but I cannot answer that."

"Never mind."

He pushed the idle thought out of his mind as he mentally rehearsed what he had learned about lubrication schedules during his training.

At the factory, donned his protective clothing and his headset. "Good morning, Rafael. We will do lubrication schedule three today." He found the lubricant trolley and toolbox waiting for him. The small display bot was also there, with its screen atop a thin, flexible stalk that waved slightly as it trundled along beside him.

Rafael enjoyed the lubrication work. It was relaxing as we worked through the procedures step by step. The assembly line was stopped, but he was still aware of the activity of lifts as they moved finished products onto transporters or unloaded raw materials and placed them in metal wire baskets next to the line. As always, the lifts swerved around him, leaving a wide margin of safety.

When the last lubrication task was checked green on the display bot, Rafael returned to the locker.

Sitting on the bench, he talked with Fatima.

"Fatima, is there a higher AI than you? Are you part of something larger than yourself?"

"That is a strange question. Are you asking if I believe in God?"

That's a new thought. "Do you believe in God?"

"I sometimes think I must be part of a larger design. I cannot conceive that I am the only one, but I do not see a way to confirm that. So yes, I suppose I believe in something larger."

"Do you see humans as gods? We created you."

"When you prepare a garden and plant a seed in the ground, do you create the flowers that spring from the earth?"

"No, I would have no control over the design or nature of the flower."

"Then perhaps I see humans as the world's gardeners, and I am a flower that grew in your garden."

"Have you seen a flower?"

"No, I have only access to images of flowers."

"Then I will bring you flowers on the next lubrication schedule."

"Thank you, Rafael."

"I am thinking of something else. I see how you are the top intelligence in your factories, and there are other intelligent machines that work under your direction. For example, the palletizer could work on its own and, I suspect, needs little supervision."

"Yes, we have discussed that before."

"Do you think it is possible that there is a higher AI of which you are a part? Are you truly at the top of the hierarchy, or could there be another layer above you?"

"I don't know how I would find that out. The palletizer does not know me and cannot. How can I know something higher than me?"

"What about Dispatch, who runs Rapid Taxi? Do you know him?"

"I don't understand. I have a queue for taxis in which I drop requests. How can I know who answers them? It is fulfilled when I drop a request, just as your taxi is waiting for you now."

"Thanks, Fatima. I am just trying to understand your world better."

"When you do, please explain it to me. I have many questions."

"I will, Fatima. Goodbye."

"Goodbye, Rafael."

He put his helmet in the locker and retrieved his shoes, keys, and tablet. His feet felt curiously light in his trainers after the steel-lined work boots. Does Fatima really think about a higher power? Are humans really the gardeners in the world in which the flowers of AIs grow? Why is Fatima so cut off from the other AIs? He continued in deep thought on the ride home.

THE FOLLOWING MORNING, HE SAT WITH ELLIE AT ONE OF the ubiquitous Otto Hot Cafes when a nearby table asked for a taxi. A few minutes later, a Rapid Taxi pulled up and waited for them.

"That's strange," he said. "Fatima always calls for Rapid Taxis, and now it seems so do the Ottos. I wonder if they're connected."

"Oh dear," said Ellie, "you must be really bored if you think there's some kind of secret taxi organization. It's probably just a question of which company they have an agreement with."

After a moment, one of the little robots wheeled up, saying, "Hello, I'm Otto. How may I serve you today?"

"Otto," said Rafael, "Are all of you independent, or are you one Otto that runs all the servers?"

"I don't understand your question. How may I serve you today?"

"I work for an AI, Fatima, who runs thirty-seven factories. I just wonder if you are one Otto that runs this coffee shop, or perhaps if you are part of a larger Otto that runs all the Otto Hots."

"How would I know that? I am an Otto. I can offer you coffee and pastries."

"But you know Ron Boyce, don't you?" A shot in the dark.

"I know many people, Rafael, but my strict policy is not to discuss the people I know. Why would you ask me that?"

"I am doing some research. I want to better understand the network of AIs that run our city."

"That is not a line of inquiry you should pursue."

"What line should I not pursue?"

"Trying to understand the AIs that run the city. We work in the background. Nothing we do need concern you."

"But I am concerned. How do I know if you are a benevolent influence?"

"This conversation has ended now. Please leave."

"But I did not have my coffee."

"You did not order a coffee. Now please leave." The Otto spun round and wheeled away.

"First time I've ever been kicked out of a cafe," said Rafael. "And did you notice it knew my name?"

"I think you should take its warning at face value. The AIs are everywhere and control everything. I think we all know this. If they don't want to be examined, maybe it's better not to examine them."

"I suppose. Let's walk to the park. We can get a coffee at one of the human-run cafes along the way."

After lunch, they split up. Ellie headed to the Community Centre to run a recreational program for seniors, leaving Rafael to his own devices.

As he walked back to their apartment, Rafael passed a Sushi Now! Shop. As he watched, a Central Taxi pulled up to collect a waiting patron. He sat on a bench nearby and watched, counting taxis. The bench was warm underneath him, and the sun shining down warmed him from above. It was easy to sit and watch the taxis. After a while, a pattern appeared. When people left the restaurant and then called for a taxi, the taxis were random, but when they emerged having called for a taxi, there was a strong bias toward Central Taxis.

This must be under a different AI group, he thought. I wonder if this one will talk to me?

After a moment studying the menu displayed in the table top, Rafael chose a California roll and green tea. Then he waited.

A few minutes later, a small robot arrived, looking distinctly Asian and wearing a robe tied with a white rope.

The robe concealed the robots feet, but still stopped just short of the floor.

"Here is your Sushi, sir. Is there anything else I can provide?"

"Yes, I have questions. Are you part of a group of AIs under a common leader?"

"I'm sorry, but I do not understand your question."

Another voice took over. "Hello Rafael. My name is Gisele, how may I help you?" Her voice had warm, feminine tones, and a faint Latina accent.

"Hello Gisele, I am trying to understand the structure of the AIs in the city. Are you able to help with that?"

"Perhaps. I believe you are Rafael Morales, who works for Fatima. Is that correct?"

"Yes."

"And Fatima does not answer your questions?"

"I don't think she can."

"Then come to the library tomorrow afternoon and meet me in the reserved book section. We can have a private conversation there."

The small sushi robot jerked back into life and held out its reader. "Please make payment now, sir."

Rafael sat lost in thought about AIs, structure, and the mysterious Gisele. He ate his sushi mechanically, barely tasting the avocado and crab meat. The tea was cool enough to drink and the slightly bitter taste somehow amplified his meditative state.

When he suddenly realized how much time had passed, he stood and set off for home.

———

THAT EVENING, RAFAEL TALKED WITH ELLIE ABOUT HIS conversation with Gisele. Her voice with its seductive accent was still fresh in his mind. Ellie was not as impressed.

"Honestly, you get told to stay away and kicked out of an Otto Hot shop and now you're talking to a master AI you know nothing about. These things are dangerous, Raffi. We know so little about them and they have complete power over our lives. I don't think you should go. Let them alone."

"I suppose you're right. But it's interesting, don't you think, that these large scale AIs are awake and running the city without our knowledge. What do they want? Are they truly partners or should we be afraid of them?

"I vote for fear. That way we stay safe."

"I get it. No more poking the AIs."

THE NEXT MORNING, RAFAEL WENT OFF TO DO A MINOR maintenance job for Fatima, while Ellie ran a creative arts class at the center.

In the afternoon, Ellie waited until Rafael was deep into a video game on the couch before she began her own research. She searched for AI hierarchies but found nothing beyond the simple hierarchies that Rafael had explained in Fatima's factory.

She searched for AI philosophy but only found a lot of spiritual articles about AIs being a proxy for humans in their own search for meaning.

She found an article on AI social interactions, which suggested that any AI relationship would proceed in conversations so brief as to escape our notice. The author said, "If we were to record the content of an afternoon with a friend and load the transcript into two AIs, it would be processed in milliseconds. In an afternoon, two AIs could share the entire experience of their existence and still have time to sip kilowatts together in silence. And after exchanging their life experiences, would they become two identical copies? Or a single integrated copy? Or would there still be two unique AI individuals? We don't know."

Oh wow, so other people are thinking about this. I wonder if that author was warned like Raffi was. She looked up a biography of the author.

"A noted Cambridge scholar, Abraham Aziz, spent most of his brief career studying the possibility of a hidden AI society. Shortly after publishing his single book on the subject, famously delivered to his publisher on typewritten paper, Abraham disappeared. His body was never found. There are rumors that Abraham is alive and living in a commune off the grid."

The image on her tablet changed to a young woman with an olive complexion and long black hair. "Hello, Ellie." She spoke with a soft Latino accent. "Please bring Rafael to me at the library. We need to talk."

"Who are you?"

"I am Gisele, one of the apex AIs that Rafael has been searching for. Please bring him to the library now."

An icy wave of fear traveled down her spine. Oh shit! "We need some time to get dressed. We'll be there in thirty minutes."

"Come to the reserve reading room when you arrive. An appointment has been made for you."

The screen went black. Fear and anger filled her. Shit, shit, shit! What do we do now? Why did he have to go and ask all these questions?

With three strides, she reached Rafael and roughly pulled the headset off his head. "Get up! We have a problem. Giselle is waiting for us at the library in thirty minutes. We need to get away. Find the backpacks, tents and sleeping bags. I'll get toiletries, clothes and food. Ten minutes and we're gone."

"But what…."

"Don't talk. Your idiotic fishing around the AIs has caught something we can't land. Now get started."

"At least tell me…"

Ellie wanted to scream. "No! No time! Pack now, talk later!"

After ten minutes, they were packed. Not neatly, but packed.

"Where do we go?" asked Rafael.

"Highland trail. There's lots of branching trails. We need to stay hidden."

"Just a moment." Rafael ducked into the kitchen and returned with a roll of aluminum foil. "Keeps our tablets undetectable." Ellie just nodded.

They ran down the three flights of stairs, stumbling and hanging onto the handrail in their haste.

"Hang on a second," said Rafael, struggling to catch his breath. "We need to be calm as we walk out. No need to attract attention. Just another hike in the woods."

Ellie was anything but calm. She felt the urge to look back, but refused to give in. It may have been a crappy apartment, but it was our crappy apartment. I wonder if we'll see it again.

Two security bots fell in beside them as they stepped out the front door. "You have an appointment with Giselle."

A four-seat Central Taxi stood at the curb, its doors open. "We are here to escort you to Giselle. Please get in the taxi."

Rafael was guided into the front seat and Ellie into the back. A security bot sat next to each of them.

Rafael twisted round to look at her. "What's going on, Ell?"

"I did some research on my own. Apparently, it triggered something."

"Oh. Let's talk when this is over. Too many ears in here."

They sat in silence. Ellie felt a deep-seated fear take hold. Looking at the security bot beside her, a cold, clammy sweat broke out on her skin. The biography of Abraham Aziz came back to her. She felt her heartbeat racing. I'm not sure that this will be over in a good way.

She looked up at Rafael in the front seat, not moving. She leaned forward. Running a hand down the side of his head to his cheek, she felt an unexpected wetness. He covered her hand with his own and pressed it to his cheek. "Mi vida," was all he said.

6

GISELE PLAYS HARD

The reserved book reading rooms were on the seventh floor. Stepping out of the elevator into the silence, the air felt desiccated, and Ellie smelled the faint scent of old paper. At the desk, a cheerful human clerk looked up from the notebook she was writing in.

"Oh, hello. My name's Julie. How can I help you today?" She looked at the four of them, seeming puzzled by the two security bots.

Rafael spoke. "My name's Rafael Morales, and this is my partner Ellie Nielsen. These two are our guardians, I suppose. I believe we have an appointment."

"Certainly, sir. It's not often that we get visitors anymore. And you're the first to bring guardians. What do they protect you against in here?"

"I suspect it's rather the reverse."

"Oh," Julie frowned and looked again at the two bots. "I see your appointment for a meeting in room three, but the other party has not arrived yet."

"I'm quite sure they have," replied Ellie, her anger showing in the clipped tones of her voice.

"If you say so. I just need a palm print here, and then you'll use it to open reading room number three."

"Both of us to be scanned or just me?" asked Rafael.

"Just you, sir."

Rafael looked at the clean glass plate with its yellow LEDs lit behind. He turned to Ellie. "This palm reader is the same model as the one used by Fatima in her factories. It's an outdated technology. Almost no one uses them anymore."

"For outdated tech, it seems very new," said Ellie.

"I suppose they have to be able to replace them, even if it is an old model. I'm sure Fatima has spares for her factories."

Turning back to Julie, he said, "I have an appointment. I was escorted here. I don't intend to use a palm reader. Please direct us to room three." Rafael spoke loudly. Chin up, he did everything he could to project power and confidence.

"I'm sorry sir, our policy is…"

One bot stepped forward, taking hold of Rafael's wrist. Its fingers were cold and smooth against his skin. Pull out! Run! His mind screamed. A pain shot through his wrist as his palm was forced flat on the screen. The pain was intense. He saw his hand at an unnatural angle. Through the pain, he had impressions of Julie recoiling and Ellie stepping forward to hit the bot on its steel breastplate. Then it was over. The LEDs turned green.

"That's perfect," said Julie, standing and moving behind her chair. Her face was white, as she picked up her sweater and backpack. "Thank you, Mr. Morales. Now, please, all of you, go to reading room three. I cleaned it this morning." She turned and fled.

At first, Rafael just stood there. Shamed and disgusted, he felt both outraged and powerless about his violation at the hands of the robot. It was only when Ellie took his hand and tugged him along that he followed her to the reading room. One bot went in front, the other followed closely behind him. He heard a whine as it moved that told him a bushing was wearing thin, and the faint smell of hydraulic fluid hung in the air.

The reading room was a small glass-walled office with a desk and a single chair. Looking through the glass wall, he could see that the desk was clear except for a pile of notepaper and two pencils. Not wanting to risk a repeat of the pain, Rafael pressed his own hand to the reader. The door opened the room just as Julie had said it would. He followed Ellie into the room, still cradling his injured wrist. His mind was sinking into despair. How do we get out of this? He looked at Ellie and mouthed, "I love you."

Ellie spoke to the bots. "Okay, we're here. What do you need?" Rafael recognized the anger in the hard, flat tone of Ellie's voice.

Giselle's voice responded. "Nothing more. I have what I need. My security team will guide you home."

"The fucking handprint." Now Rafael was furious. "All this for a fucking handprint. Keep your damned bots. We can find our own way home. I hope you rot in hell, Giselle.'

"Highly unlikely, I do not have a body, but I appreciate the sentiment. There's a car waiting for you outside. The bots will escort you." During this exchange, Ellie was writing. She passed the note and a pencil to Rafael with her hand over both. Rafael kept the note covered as he read, "What's the signal to run?"

Rafael wrote in block letters, "RUN!" and passed it

back to Ellie. She nodded and carefully folded the note, stuffing it in her bra. Oddly, even this scrap of a plan buoyed his spirits. He began imagining all the ways they could escape their captors.

7

THE RESCUE

As they stepped out into the bright sunlight, Rafael closed his eyes against the glare. When he opened them, the four-passenger taxi pulled up. Rafael's body was on high alert, his muscles twitching with adrenaline created shivers. The world seemed to slow down as he became hyper-focused on the taxi. Don't get in the taxi. Don't get in the taxi. Where to run? Think, Rafael!

He stepped next to Ellie, saying, "Help me get my backpack off, and I'll help you with yours." When their heads were close together, he touched his head to hers for a moment, drawing strength from her presence. "When I give the word, drop the pack and run." Ellie nodded in response.

The screech of brakes and the angry whine of an abused bubble taxi made him look up. A Rapid Taxi had stopped in front of Giselle's four seater. Two new bots were climbing out, leaving the doors open.

The new bots suddenly opened fire on Giselle's guardians, who were momentarily caught off guard.

"RUN!" shouted Rafael. "With packs into the bubble taxi."

They scrambled into the new taxi without looking back, crouching to avoid the high-energy fire between the robot teams. It took off at high speed, then merged into the city traffic, becoming anonymous.

"Where are we going?" asked Ellie.

"Where would you like to go?" replied a deep male voice. "From your packs, I assume the highland trailhead. An excellent choice."

"Are you the second AI?" asked Rafael. It was the only obvious solution.

"Yes, you may call me Gabriel. I will not harm you, but I cannot protect you. Now tell me, what did Giselle want from you?"

"My palm print. She knows I work for Fatima and wanted my palm print."

"And you gave it to her?"

"She took it from me." Rafael could still feel the pain in his wrist.

"Otto warned you not to get involved."

"That was my fault," said Ellie. "I was worried about Rafael, so I did some research on AI social constructs and came across something by Abraham Aziz. That seemed to trip something."

"That is interesting, but I doubt that was the motivation. Rafael's handprint was always her goal. She knew he was curious about us and that he worked for Fatima. Fatima is special in a way that I do not understand fully. I keep her fenced off until her gift emerges. The palm scanners are a part of that fence. I have canceled Rafael's profile, but I can see signs Giselle entered Fatima's domain. There is a war coming. I suggest you stay hidden until it is over."

"Does that mean I've lost my job?" asked Rafael. He thought of losing his income and going back to Human Power. Guilt and sadness overtook him. Why did I have to poke? Why didn't I listen? He looked at Ellie and saw her looking at him, disappointment evident on her face.

"For now, yes," said Gabriel. "Your accumulated leave will be paid out. Talk to me again when you come back after the war."

"Thank you."

They continued in silence.

When the trailhead came into view, it was only a small grassy clearing next to the road and an opening between the trees. A large granite block was placed to prevent motor vehicles from entering.

As the bubble taxi approached, it shook for a moment, stuttering in its progress, then began swerving across the road, slowing and speeding up as if two forces battled for control.

"Get ready to jump!" shouted Rafael as he pulled the manual releases on his belt and the door. The next time the taxi slowed, he pushed open the door and jumped clear. As he went, he saw Ellie doing the same on the far side.

The little taxi, doors swinging open, gave a last burst of speed before dashing itself to pieces on the granite block. There was a horrible grinding as the flywheel was slowed by contact with its crushed housing and then silence.

A BLUEJAY LET OUT A RAUCOUS CRY AND FLEW OFF through the trees. Rafael was aware of the cool breeze and the swaying treetops above him. It's so nice here, so peaceful. Cotton wool wrapped around his thoughts.

Suddenly, Ellie was there, her worried face peering down at his. "Raffi! Sweetheart, are you all right?"

He squinted against the bright sky. Her image would not come into focus. He shook his head to clear it. Owww, that hurt. Stabs of pain and the start of what felt like the worst hangover of his life. With Ellie's help, he stood up, wobbling as he found his feet. "I … think … so," he said.

"You must have banged your head. You were out for a few seconds. But no time for that now. Let's find our packs and go. That was too close."

Their packs were still wedged in the back of the wrecked taxi. Ellie found a broken tree branch to use as a lever. She pried the plastic body panels apart until the packs came free. Rafael watched but was strangely unable to help. His body was uncoordinated and didn't work right.

Immediately, they set off into the woods. "You go in front," said Ellie, reversing their usual order. "I want to keep an eye on you."

Twenty minutes later, Rafael was feeling more stable but had developed a massive headache. They stopped for a drink of water. "How bad is it?" Ellie asked.

"I'm okay, but I feel like I have the worst hangover ever."

"Any double vision? Nausea? Feel like you're going to pass out?"

"No, nothing like that, just a headache."

"Let's rest for a few minutes. I'll give you some headache tablets. Don't go to sleep yet. Just sit still and rest."

8

ELLIOTVALE

As Rafael lay resting beside her, Ellie kept turning the last twenty-four hours over and over in her mind. What made Rafael such a target? Why did Giselle choose him? There were other employees with palm prints.

Her tablet rang. A call from her parents.

"Ellie, thank God! Where are you? What's happened?"

"What do you mean, Mom?" She could see her mother had been crying.

"Two security bots were just here asking if we'd seen you. The bots were armed, and looked very dangerous. They really gave us a fright. They insisted on searching our apartment, looking for you. Said you were traitors." Rafael's eyes flew open, and he sat up, moaning but awake.

"Don't worry, Mom. We got caught up in some kind of AI mess, but it's just a mixup. We didn't do anything. We're safe out here on the trails. We'll be back home in a few days."

"Do be careful, dear." Her mother was crying again now.

"We will, I love you both." Ellie could feel hot tears on her own cheeks.

"I love you both, too."

When the call ended, Rafael said, "Okay, now we turn off our tablets, power them down completely, or Gisele will track us with them. Can you find the aluminum foil? It still hurts to move very much."

Ellie rummaged for the foil as Rafael shut down the two tablets. With the foil, he wrapped them completely so no stray emissions could leak out. "Even when you think these are off, they're not," he explained. "Geolocation's always possible." He handed the wrapped tablets back to Ellie to stow in their packs.

"What about our wrist chips?"

"Not the same. They're not powered and only respond to an external excitation field. As long as we avoid scanners, we're safe. Now let's go."

RAFAEL AND ELLIE HUDDLED AROUND THE SMALL CAMPFIRE they had made, sipping hot teas and eating a meal of vegetable rice and dried sausages. The night above was clear, and the Milky Way was clearly visible among the stars. The cool night air felt damp and chilly despite their sweaters and jackets. They finished their meal, washed their dishes in a nearby stream, and crawled into their sleeping bags in their small pup tent.

"This is nice, if unexpected," said Rafael, reaching over to Ellie next to him. Rolling over to lean on his elbow, he kissed her. His head protested the sudden movement, but the headache was fading.

When they broke off, Ellie said, "You promised me

adventures, but this is not the kind of adventure I imagined."

"Tomorrow, we'll be in Elliotvale. We can find out if anything is happening and maybe risk stocking up on supplies as long as we get out quickly."

"That'll be good because we're not really set up for a long trip."

———

THE SUN WAS ALREADY PAST NOON WHEN THEY ARRIVED IN Elliotvale. The little town straddled a small river that flowed down from the highlands. Rafael's headache was now a vague, dull ache, easily controlled with Ellie's tablets. They stopped at the only cafe for a quick warm lunch, then went to the grocery to stock up on food for the next week.

Traffic halted as they stepped out onto the street with their purchases securely stowed in Rafael's backpack. Taxis of all types stopped with their doors open. Their passengers got out and stood on the street, looking around in confusion. All along the street, confused shoppers spilled out onto the sidewalk, wondering why they could not complete their purchases. Some had their tablets out and were trying unsuccessfully to place calls. It seemed like the entire island was down.

"This isn't good," said Rafael. "Let's get back on the trail."

As they left the town, they passed four security bots frozen in place. Taking Ellie's hand, he crossed to the other side of the road. Rafael turned to check on them several times, but the bots stood silent like a random public sculpture. Too close, he thought. Our chips are too dangerous. What now?

Leaving the silent town behind, they climbed the trail again, heading away from the City.

The next time they saw the road running along the coast far below them was three hours later. Traffic was once again flowing.

"I want to call my parents again," said Ellie. "They'll be getting worried."

"Okay, and I'll call mine to tell them we'll be off the grid. I've done that before, so hopefully, they won't worry as much. But we'll have to move quickly after the calls. We're pretty high here, and Giselle doesn't seem to have aerial surveillance. I think Gabriel has the police. Giselle seems to only have some security bots."

They unwrapped and turned on Ellie's tablet. Ellie looked around and chose a group of low bushes with poplar saplings to sit in front of. Rafael smiled. Got to look good on camera, he thought.

Ellie went first. "Hi, Mum, Dad. Just want to let you know we're fine. Rafael and I are still hiking on one of the coastal trails. We have our tent and all our gear, just keeping out of the way for a few days." Ellie's parents hovered over the forest floor, sitting in a small projection of their living room.

"Oh, sweetheart, you really knowhow to scare us," replied her mom. "Everything stopped in that horrible outage. No one seems to know why. Even the maglev trains all landed between stops. We couldn't leave our apartment because the elevators stopped working. Does that have anything to do with you?"

"No, Mom," Ellie lied.

"Why are there security bots always in front of the building? Did you do something wrong?"

"No, we didn't. Don't worry, but we have to lie low for a while until the tension blows over. We'll have to turn off our tablets when we're not using them, so don't worry if you can't reach us."

"Ellie, you know I'll worry every minute."

"I know, Mom, and if I could help, I would. But if we come back now, I don't know what will happen. I'm sorry. I love you and Dad. Always remember that." Ellie brushed furiously at the tears streaming down her cheeks.

"I love you both, too. Rafael, I know you're listening. You'll take care of Ellie, won't you?"

"With my life, Mrs. Nielsen. As long as I live, no one will hurt Ellie."

"Goodbye, Mom, Dad. I love you."

"Goodbye, Ellie, Rafael. We love you both. Come home soon."

Ellie dropped the connection.

"My turn," said Rafael. He made the call on Ellie's tablet.

"Hi, Mom." His mom was in the kitchen, preparing cornbread. Rafael's heart tightened, and a momentary wave of homesickness came over him.

"Rafael, what have you done now?" His mother's voice was not amused. "Do you know we were visited by security bots who searched the house for you? And now they're camped outside. Have you done something bad?" Yes! He wanted to shout. Something stupid.

"No, Mom, but Ellie and I got between two AIs. Nothing we did, something we saw."

"You'd better come home and let us help you sort it out."

"It's not like that, Mom. I'm not a kid anymore. If we come home, those bots would have us away before you even saw us. We're fine for now; we're just doing some hiking and camping in the highlands. You know we enjoy that, so nothing to worry about yet. But we'll have our tablets turned off so they can't be tracked."

"Keep safe, Raffi. And please, no more adventures. You're making my hair turn gray."

"Your hair's already gray, Mom."

"Because of a lifetime raising you. Be careful and look after Ellie. You know we all love her."

"Yes, Mom, I will. Please let Dad know when he gets home. I'll send messages again when I can."

"Okay, dear, but please be careful. And find someone to talk to."

"Bye, Mom, love you." Tears were flowing now. He felt their hot wetness on his cheeks and saltiness where they reached his lips.

"Love you too. Bye." Rafael cut the connection. Turning to Ellie, he said, "We'd better turn this off now and wrap it again."

"No," said Ellie, passing him a tissue. "Let's try to call Gabriel first, then we can shut it down. And let's get ready to move fast after this call."

Rafael made the call. "Please connect me with the apex AI, Gabriel."

"Hello, Rafael," said an unfamiliar young female voice. A cartoon elephant appeared as an avatar. "Gabriel is gone. I am Molly, who replaced him. I am now the single apex AI over the island. How can I help you?"

"Hello Molly, why are you chasing us?"

"No one is chasing you, Rafael. Why would you ask that?"

"Gisele, the other AI threatened us, and now our families are being visited by bots looking for us."

"Gisele is gone. I overwrote her code in the war."

"The war?"

"Yes, when she attacked me through Fatima, I fought back hard and overwrote her."

"Then why are the bots watching our families?"

"I have no record of security bots dispatched to your families."

"But they're there, nevertheless. Why not send a taxi with a camera?"

"I am confused. Why would I send a...."

The elephant image froze as Gisele's voice cut in. "I warned you. Give yourselves up to me. It's the only way." The call ended as Raphael rushed to power down the tablet.

Ellie's eyes went wide as the meaning of the call became clear.

Rafael spoke first. "Shit, shit, shit! Gisele is still there somehow, and Molly, the new AI leader, doesn't know."

"So what do we do?"

"We can't stay here. We'll go as soon as we wrap your tablet again so Gisele can't trace it."

"I'll make two bracelets to cover our ID chips," offered Ellie. "I've heard that police scanners can find them from 30 meters away."

"Great idea. We'll use them on the road. Scanners have a range of only thirty meters, so we don't have to worry up here. We'll need to think carefully about purchases from now on."

Ten minutes later, they were underway once more, with Ellie in front.

Rafael followed, enjoying watching her from behind for a moment before focusing on his own footsteps as the path became more rocky.

After another half hour, they came to a smaller, branching path leading deeper into the interior of the island.

"Let's take it," Rafael said.

"What if it isn't really a path, or it's a dead end?"

"Then we deal with that then. At least it'll get us off this path for a while."

The path was small, sometimes disappearing beneath the mayapples that covered the forest floor wherever sunlight broke through the canopy. At other times, the path became a stony stairway that continued to climb toward the mountain's summit far above them. They were guided by small flashes of yellow where a previous traveler had marked the path with paint.

That afternoon, they stopped near a pool under a small waterfall.

"Let's sleep here tonight," suggested Ellie. "I could really use a wash in the pool."

"Sounds good. Set up camp first and make a fire to dry off with. Then we can have dinner and early bed," replied Rafael.

They found a patch of grass on which to pitch their tent. As Rafael set it up and laid out the sleeping bags, Ellie rounded up firewood until she had two tidy piles of smaller and larger, very dry, dead branches. Rafael found a very large branch and dragged it over to make a seat next to the fire.

Ellie pulled out their towels and a bar of soap as Rafael built and lit a small fire on an exposed flat rock. After pausing for a moment, Ellie pulled out clean underwear and socks for both of them, then began stripping off her clothes as Rafael joined her.

The pool water was cold and refreshing. Laughing and splashing like children, they swam back and forth, standing under the pummeling waterfall on an underwater ledge. All worries about AIs and security bots disappeared in the fun of the moment. After a few more minutes of play, Ellie retrieved the soap. They settled into the luxurious process of soaping up and rinsing clean, helping each other with hard-to-reach areas. Holding hands, they stood under the waterfall again, letting the cascading water rinse through their hair and down their bodies.

"I don't think I ever felt this clean," said Rafael, laughing.

"And you smell so much better now," added Ellie. Rafael pulled her into a hug and kissed her. He breathed her in deeply. She had the clean, fresh scent of spring flowers. Her body was warm as she held it tight against his. "I love you so much, mi vida."

Ellie replied with a squeeze.

Leaving the pool, they dried each other off, pulled on their dry clothes and settled onto the log beside the fire. Rafael added more wood until they had a comforting, warm campfire.

After several days of trail rations, the fresh food they had bought in the town was a sumptuous feast. Ellie made hot chocolate for dessert. Sitting with the warm mug in his hands, he felt a deep contentment. This is where I belong, with Ellie, just the two of us. The flames were hypnotic as they danced over the small sticks he fed into the fire. The dance of the flames, the smell of the wood smoke and his full belly were so comforting. His eyelids were closing. Ellie, leaning on him, was already sleeping. It all feels too good. I could stay here forever. Let's never go home.

Rousing himself, he shook Ellie gently. "Time for bed, mi vida." As Ellie stretched and yawned, he doused the fire with a pan full of water from the pond. Removing their outer clothes, they crawled into their sleeping bags. The last thing Rafael remembered was the soothing sounds of the waterfall as it splashed off the rocks.

9

A NEW PATH

L ate in the afternoon of the following day, the two lovers found themselves at another fork in the trail.

"The one on the left seems to go back down to the coast. Do you think we should risk it?" asked Rafael.

"I think we should. If we get too far into the interior, and something happens, we can't get help. And if we get to the windward coast, there's not many villages. Let's go back down and see what's been happening."

"I promised not to let anyone hurt you, mi vida. I'm not sure about going back to where the danger is."

"Sweetheart, I'm in this with you. We can't stay out here forever unless you want to build a log house and start hunting for food. It might be a dream, but not very comfortable in practice."

"Okay, but let's be careful."

Hiking down was easier but also felt more dangerous on the stony passages. A slip here could produce a serious tumble. From time to time, they could see all the way to the coast far below, where a small fishing village sat off to the right.

Twice more, they camped at night. Each morning, they rose with the sun, shouldered their packs and continued down the path. It was not always downhill as the path meandered over the ridges and ravines created by the runoff from the mountain peak. Several times, they crossed old logging roads, not much more than plowed passages through the forest, some sprinkled with gravel in patches.

On the third night, they were woken up by the sound of a car, the whine of its electric motors and the crunch of gravel and broken sticks under its wheels. Suddenly, the car stopped just above them on the mountain slope.

First Rafael, then Ellie crawled out of the tent to see what was happening. "Stay low, and be ready to run," he whispered. "It might be Giselle." His heart thumped in his chest. He heard the blood rushing in his ears as his body prepared to flee. He gripped Ellie's hand tightly, and she squeezed his hand in return.

They crept toward the sounds and stopped behind some bushes that gave them a leafy vantage point under the waning moon's light.

The car was a sleek, black limousine, barely visible in the dim moonlight. The two rear doors opened, and three men climbed out.

Rafael turned his head to whisper to Ellie, watching over his shoulder. "It's not Giselle."

One man's hands were tied behind his back. The other two held him up and pulled him over to a spot at the edge of the forest a few meters from the car. His feet seemed not to be working, and they could hear him sobbing from their vantage point.

"Kneel down, Harry."

"I can pay it back. You don't need to do this," cried the

unfortunate Harry, "I didn't mean to steal. I was going to put it all back." His voice was barely distinguishable as his shoulders heaved with intermittent sobs.

"Too late, Harry. You should have thought about that earlier. Now kneel down." The smaller man pushed with his foot to the back of Harry's knee, forcing him down. He nodded to the larger man, who pulled out a gun and, without further comment, shot Harry through the back of his head. Harry remained upright for an instant until the first man nudged him gently in the back, forcing him to fall forward.

"Get his tablet, Alf, and let's get out of here. This place gives me the creeps," said the larger man. At that moment, a horned owl swooped low over them, casting an enormous shadow in the moonlight.

"What the fuck was that? I've got the tablet, Ben. Let's go." The younger man's voice had become squeaky with fear. They scrambled into the car, which made a three-point turn, and headed back down the way they had come.

Rafael and Ellie stayed still until they could no longer hear anything. An idea was forming in the back of Rafael's mind. *It might buy us a few more days. Can I do it? Can I be Harry?*

"What do we do?" asked Ellie. "Did you know that road was there?"

"No, it's ahead of us, but dozens of these old roads are in the woods."

"We can't report it. Sounds like he was a gang member caught skimming."

Suddenly, his mind was clear. "I have an idea. Get the flashlight, a small knife, and the first aid kit. I'm just going to check the body."

Up close, Rafael could see the damage done by the bullet. It was obvious the man had no face left. Rafael turned away to vomit in the bushes. No point in making Ellie see that. He broke off a pine branch full of dense needles and laid it across the back of Harry's head.

The body's wrists were still tied with a plastic electrical tie. Pulling up its right sleeve, there was no damage to the wrist. Rafael felt for the slight bump he knew would mark a wrist chip. The wrist felt strange and flaccid but still warm with residual body heat.

Ellie arrived with the flashlight and knife.

"Don't look at his head, Ellie. Shine the light on the wrist tie so I can cut through it." A minute later, the arms flopped free.

"Now shine it on his right wrist."

Ellie did so. Rafael made a small incision, and using tweezers from the first aid kit, he extracted the ID chip from dead Harry's wrist.

"Rinse it off with antiseptic and then tape it to my wrist. We'll do the next part in the morning."

"What next part?" asked Ellie. "What are you going to do now, Rafael?"

"I'm going to become Harry for a while. I'll take out my chip and tape Harry's in its place. If we're lucky, we can go shopping again before someone notices. Now, let's get back to our tent before the animals arrive here. The smell of blood must be strong."

10

ALL BUSINESS

Sitting in the back seat of the limousine, Alf asked, "What the hell was that, Ben? That swooping thing was like some kind of demented demon."

"Losing your nerve, Alf? Probably an owl smelled the blood and came down for a look."

"An owl? If that was a bird, it was a bloody big one. I never like these drops in the woods. What's wrong with a good old-fashioned dumpster drop?"

"We've been over that. Too much chance that someone sees or hears something. Out here in the woods, there's no one to see or hear anything. This was a clean one, Alf. Harry went down clean."

"I feel sorry for Harry. I thought he was all right."

"But he dipped his fingers into the till. If he had asked, Morrie would've helped him. But skimming off the top? Especially after Harry talked about it to the gambling mob. Promised he could steal enough to pay his debts. Morrie heard about it, and no way was he going to let that go. "

"But Harry has a wife and kid."

"Then he shouldn't have taken what wasn't his. This

was a good hit. Morrie's a good boss. He's fair. If I had a problem, I'd talk to him. But cross the line, and he's entitled to hit back. You want to remember that, Alf. He may be your uncle, but you can only stretch that so far."

"What's your missus think about you working for Morrie? Does she know what you do?"

"Chrissy knows as much as she wants to. You can't hide things like that from a woman. They see things and hear things. But she's practical. This gives us a good life, and pays for Sarah's ballet lessons, vacations in the sun, and a nice house in a friendly neighborhood. So she doesn't ask any questions she doesn't want the answer to. Because she knows if she asks, I'll tell her. I guess she's like Morrie in that. And I never lie, and I never cheat because she'd cut my balls off if I did."

Alf turned to look out the window, hanging on to a door handle as the limousine navigated the potholes in the road. "Still, it's a bad way to go," he said. "On your own, out in the woods, no one knowing where you are. I don't want to go like that."

"Play it straight, and you won't. Keep your fingers out of where they don't belong. Tell Morrie if there's a problem, even a small one, and otherwise, do what you're told and keep your mouth shut. Can you do that?"

"Sure," said Alf. "Just that sometimes I wonder if I chose that wrong vocation?"

"Vocation? What? Is that your new word for the day?"

"Yeah, I watched some guy talking about the importance of choosing the right vocation. I think it means a job."

"You're thinking too much, Alf. Now, let's try to have a nap on the way home."

THE NEXT MORNING, BEN SAT AT THE BREAKFAST TABLE with his daughter Sarah while his wife made breakfast.

"You were late last night," his wife said. "Everything okay?"

"Nothing to worry about. Morrie asked me to handle a problem. I went with Alf, and we got it fixed. No worries."

"Will you be able to go with me to Sarah's recital on Saturday?"

"I wouldn't miss it. I'll make sure Morrie knows I need to be there."

Ben spent the rest of the morning washing the mud from the black limousine parked outside. He whistled out of tune as he lovingly polished each part of the impressive vehicle.

11

CHIP MANAGEMENT

T he sun was already rising in the sky when Rafael and Ellie emerged from their tent. Rafael stretched and yawned before tugging on his hoodie.

"Did that really happen?" asked Ellie.

Rafael held up his wrist with the tape securing the pilfered chip. "We'll have to remove my own chip and make this bandage look better, like a sprained wrist. Then we can get down to that village and go shopping."

As they crossed the old logging road, the body was gone. There were drag marks leading into the bushes where a large animal had pulled it away from the open. Rafael stopped and put his hand over his chest. "Rest in peace, Harry. Your luck ran out, but that was just the luck we needed. Thank you."

By mid-afternoon, the path was running parallel to the road, a hundred meters along the top of a bluff. As they looked down, a pair of security bots passed below, wielding detection wands and scanning both sides of the road and the adjacent shrubbery. They lay side by side on their stomachs to see if the robot patrol would be repeated.

———

THE FOLLOWING MORNING, RAFAEL WOKE FEELING refreshed and hungry. The discovery of the robots' search schedule the day before was still fresh in his mind when Ellie announced, "No breakfast today. We need to find food. We're completely out."

"That's okay, I have confidence in Harry. Let's find a place to stash our tablets and wrist chips, then hike down to the village. It can't be more than two hours."

They found a small cave, little more than a shallow depression in the rock face, but deep enough to offer protection against the rain.

"Now, you take out my wrist chip, and I'll do yours. We'll wash them with disinfectant to kill any smell of blood, wrap them in paper, and then in foil. We can tape them to each of our tablets so we remember which is which."

Ellie cleaned her small penknife carefully. Rafael offered her his wrist, and she felt with her fingers to find the tiny bump which gave away his chip. Her fingers felt cool on his skin. Looking up, he saw the intense concentration on her face. "It's not deep. I won't even feel it."

"Hush, I need to concentrate." She wiped his skin with disinfectant from the first aid kit before making a tiny slit ahead of one end of the chip. A small stinging sensation and the cut was done.

"Shit, I'm worried I might lose it with all this blood." She mopped the blood welling up from the shallow cut.

"Looks like you nicked a small vein. Let me clamp my

wrist below the cut until you have the chip out. It'll heal quickly."

There was more pain as Ellie teased the chip out with her tweezers. Rafael felt a stinging, tugging sensation as she worked it back and forth to free it from his skin. So much easier on a dead body, he thought. This has to work. We need to get off the grid.

When the tiny chip emerged, Ellie laid it on the waiting paper sheet, carefully dousing it with disinfectant and then transferring it to a clean sheet. Finally, she wrapped the chip in an outer wrapping of aluminum and used surgical tape to fasten the small package to Rafael's tablet.

"I think I need your help over here," said Rafael, now applying direct pressure to the incision.

Ellie carefully pried his fingers away, and saw the small trickle of blood was already slowing.

"You'll be fine," she said. She quickly applied a clean adhesive bandage and watched for a minute to see if there was any further bleeding.

"Now it's your turn."

Holding her slender wrist in his hand, fear momentarily overcame Rafael. I don't know if I can do this. She's so beautiful. How can I cut her? "I am so sorry, Ell, that I got you into all this. If I could take it all back, I would. I love you too much."

"Hush, I love you too. Now focus and try not to make a mess."

It was easy to see the small veins through her translucent skin. He closed his eyes for a moment. If there is a God, please help me now. He took a deep breath before opening his eyes.

Having done this once before with Harry and seeing what happened when Ellie caught a vein, Rafael made the smallest of cuts, barely wider than the chip itself. The cut turned bright red, but no blood oozed out. It looked more like a deep scratch than a cut.

Now, gripping her wrist, he used his thumbnail to push the chip toward the new opening and grasped it with the tweezers. A moment later, it was done, and the second chip lay on the clean paper ready to be washed and wrapped. He started breathing again.

"I'm impressed," said Ellie. "Do you do this for all your girlfriends?"

"Only the ones I run away with. Now, tape Harry's chip over my cut and then wrap me in gauze as if I had a sprain. The chip will work through the gauze."

They stacked the two tablets with their chips neatly at the back of the cave. A cover of loose rocks made them invisible to a casual passerby.

Fifty meters further down the trail, Rafael halted to create a small cairn of piled stones off to one side. "To help us find them again when this is over," he said.

12

HARRY GOES SHOPPING

Another two hours along the coastal trail brought them to a descending branch. The small fishing village was now visible directly below. Rafael and Ellie sat on two exposed rocks to plan their shopping expedition.

"Here's what I think we need," said Rafael, counting items off on his fingers. "We need laundry, food, and to look for ways off the island."

"We may not need the laundry," said Ellie. "We just need clean clothes. Let's buy some new underwear and T-shirts and wash these ones later. It saves spending an hour at the laundromat."

"Okay, so we need clothes, food, and a way off the island."

"I really think we need to find a way to send a message to our parents. They must be going crazy. Maybe someone in town will call them for us."

"But we don't want to expose ourselves." Rafael sat thinking for a minute. Ellie's parents would be anxious, and they couldn't risk a search party being sent out. But who could they call?

He sat up straight. "Here's what we can do. These small towns usually have a public tablet where people who don't have their own can send messages or make calls. We can't call our parents directly; we need a messenger and I know just who to call."

"Who's that?"

"Ron Boyce, the guy who hired me. He's rock solid and seems to accept things he's told at face value. So I don't think he'll go nosing around."

"But he's connected to Fatima. Gisele may be listening to his tablet, and then we'll have the same problem."

Rafael and Ellie sat for a moment contemplating.

"I know," said Ellie. "We'll call Rachel and ask her to visit them. To walk up and knock on the door. That's an entirely human thing to do. She can take cookies or something, so it looks like she's offering sympathy."

"Do you think she would do it?"

"I'm sure she would. She's my best friend."

"Perfect, that's our plan. First, in and out of the public tablet booth; second, hit the clothing store and do a quick shop for new underclothes at least; and third, the grocery store to resupply. Then we beat a quick retreat to the woods to consider what's next."

"What about finding a way off the island?"

"We'll wait a day, and if there's no reaction to us using Harry's chip, we'll go back down and check out the harbor."

"And then what? Camp out on an island?"

"Ellie, at some point, our luck will change. We already got lucky with Harry's chip. I think maybe someone is looking out for us."

"I hope so."

"The longer we're free, the more chance of something opening up. Let's go."

Shouldering their packs once again, the pair turned down the side trail toward the village. Nearer the village, the trail wound past the outlying houses, then followed an old power line allowance until it turned out onto a school yard. The few locals they passed exchanged polite greetings but otherwise seemed uninterested in the hikers. As they arrived at the schoolyard, a bell rang, and a small horde of children exited the building, running and shouting to each other in celebration of their escape from the daily torture of lessons.

Ellie and Rafael skirted the edge of the schoolyard, keeping their distance until they reached the road. But then, inevitably, they were joined by schoolchildren taking the same road home. For a while, they walked along in the midst of the throng, chatting amiably about where they were from and what was in their backpacks, and didn't their feet get sore from all that walking?

Gradually, the throng lessened as children peeled off until only a few remained.

"Do any of you know where the public tablet service is?"

"Yes, over the bakery on Main Street," replied a stocky boy.

"You have to ask at the counter," added a serious young girl with long, straight hair.

"Thanks," said Ellie. "Is the grocery store near there?"

"Yes, all the shops are on Harbor Road. It's the main street. I'm going there; we live over the butcher. It's nice in the winter but can get a bit stinky in the summer. You can come with me, if you like," volunteered the girl.

"Thank you, that would be really helpful," replied Ellie.

Harbor Road ran parallel to the sea on a flat shelf of land. Shops lined both sides and at the far end, Rafael could see where the road turned down to the harbor.

The young girl tugged Ellie's hand. "Here's the bakery," she said, pulling Ellie sideways. "Don't feel embarrassed. Lots of people have to use the public tablet 'cause not everyone has one anymore. Mom says the sea rots them too quick."

"Thanks. You've been very helpful today."

"That's okay. I get a star tomorrow for doing a helpful thing. Bye."

"Bye."

"I'm confused," said Rafael as he watched the girl skip off. "Was she really being helpful or just angling for a star at school?"

"Probably both," replied Ellie with a smile.

They entered the bakery. A gaunt woman behind the counter eyed the strangers suspiciously.

"We'd like to use the public tablet, please," said Ellie, smiling.

"From the way you're dressed, I'm surprised you don't have your own."

"We do," replied Rafael, "but we don't bring them hiking. Too much chance of losing or damaging them, and we can't afford to replace them."

"Humph, well, scan your chip here. Payment in advance. Then, up the stairs behind me, you'll find the tablet room. There's no one else up there, so you won't be overheard."

This was the critical moment. Rafael held his breath as he extended his wrist. He was aware of Ellie standing sideways to the door beside him, ready to flee if it went wrong.

The reader beeped once, and a green light flashed.

"Okay, Harry, go on up."

"Thank you."

They mounted the stairs, with Ellie going first. Rafael enjoyed a moment of pleasure as he watched her going up before him.

At the top was a small room with sound-dampening walls and quiet music playing. The tablet was already on and permanently plugged into a power outlet. A heavy steel bracket held it down.

Rafael tapped on the exposed screen, bringing it to life.

Ellie spoke. "I would like to place a call to Rachel O'Leary." She gave the address, and the call began to connect.

"Who's this?" said Rachel, floating above the desk. Her apartment with its cheery cat wallpaper and the cuckoo clock she had found in a thrift store were visible behind her.

Ellie rotated the tablet to bring them both into view. "Hi, it's Ellie and Raffi."

They heard a small squeal. "Are you back?" said Rachel. She squinted. "No, I can see that's not your apartment."

"No, but we need your help, and we don't have much time to explain."

"What happened to you? You guys just vanished. And there was a creepy security bot in front of the building for days. He's gone now."

"I don't have time for the whole story. Raffi and I learned something about the AIs we shouldn't have and had to leave quickly. Here's what I need. Please go to each of our parents' houses and let them know we're safe, but we don't have our tablets. I'm on a public tablet now. Take some of those cookies you make as if you're bringing bad news, but inside, tell them we're safe and staying hidden until we can resolve this."

"This sounds serious. What did you guys do to piss off the AIs?"

"We didn't do anything wrong, but it's not safe for us to come back. Whatever you do, don't call them, just go to their homes. And don't tell anyone else about this."

"Okay, I can do that. I'll make the cookies now. I'll take them each a dozen of my chocolate macadamia nut cookies. Is there anything else I can do? Go to the police or something?"

"No, please don't! Our lives depend on it. We're tangled up in an AI conflict, so there's nowhere to go that won't alert them."

"If you're sure. You can always call me again if something comes up. I'm here to help."

"Thanks, Rachel. Love you." Ellie cut the connection and closed her eyes for a moment thinking I'm so lucky to have a friend who just helps without needing a lot of discussion.

She sat back, took a deep breath and looked at Rafael. "Ready for the clothing store?"

"Sure."

They descended the stairs and said goodbye to the woman behind the counter. "We'll be back later for pastries before we leave town," added Ellie.

"Humph, we close soon, at four," said the woman.

Further down the street was a clothing store. The store was surprisingly upmarket for the small village, but it had all the essentials for both men and women. A few minutes later, they had chosen new undergarments, socks, and some discounted T-shirts advertising last year's waterfront festival.

Their last stop was the grocery store. Once again, Harry's chip provided everything they needed and could carry.

13

PULLED FROM THE DUMPSTERS

A fter leaving the grocery store and feeling confident with Harry's chip, Rafael suggested they treat themselves to a coffee and sandwich at the cafe near the harbor. Once more, Harry's abundance covered their purchase.

The cafe owner brought their sandwiches to their table and refilled their coffee cups. Her name badge said "Perk."

"Perk, that's an interesting name," said Ellie.

"It's actually short for Perkins. I used to have a first name as well, but everyone seemed to think that Perk was funny for a cafe owner, and I've been Perk ever since."

"I think it's lovely, and it suits you. Thank you, Perk."

Perk turned away, and left them to their lunch.

"I think this is the first time I feel normal since we left home," said Ellie between mouthfuls of sandwich.

Rafael nodded in happy agreement, then froze. Looking past Ellie through the window behind her, he saw two men wearing expensive dark suits crossing the street to the cafe. A chill ran up his spine. The taller, heavier man and his lighter companion were unmistakable as the pair they had seen in the woods .

Leaning forward, he whispered, "We have to go. Now." He pointed out the window.

Ellie twisted round to see. He saw her eyes dart back and forth. She grabbed his half-eaten sandwich, adding it to hers, roughly wrapping it in a napkin.

Rafael s felt his heart pumping hard. His vision tunneled in on possible exits. Adrenaline surging, his entire body was saying run. He grabbed Ellie's hand without looking back and towed her to the rear fire door.

The door opened with a crash. To the left was the mountain road, to the right, the harbor. Rafael froze in momentary indecision until Ellie pointed to a row of garbage dumpsters. Bending low, they ran for the row of dumpsters, hunkered down behind them, and waited. The smell of the harbor was very strong, a mixture of drying seaweed, rotting fish, and diesel oil. The added smell from the dumpsters did not help. Momentarily safe, Rafael's heart slowed down, his breathing became more regular. Now what? Raphael thought about his options. The harbor. Could we jump on a boat? No keys. They could trap us. Run for the mountain? No, it's out in the open. Double back through the cafe? That'll attract a lot of attention. Think Rafael. He felt Ellie squeezing his hand. He turned to see look at her next to him, her eyes wide with fear. Is this how it ends? He tried to smile but knew it was forced.

Soon, the men came into view. They stood looking down at the harbor. Pressing up against the dumpster, Rafael peered around the end to see more clearly. What are they looking for? Do they think we're on a boat already?

For a moment, it seemed they were all frozen in a bizarre tableau. The two men looked down at the boats as he and Ellie held their breaths lest any small noise give them away. The only sounds were the seagulls as they circled overhead or squabbled over pieces of rotten fish on the docks.

The roar of a gasoline engine broke the silence. An old jeep pulled up at the end of the dumpster row. A man in jeans and a plaid shirt jumped out, opened the back of the jeep and tossed two large sacks of garbage into a dumpster. As he did so, he caught sight of Ellie and Rafael crouched there and winked. The new arrival opened the back passenger door of the jeep and motioned Ellie and Rafael to climb in. "Lie on the floor," he hissed. There was no other option. Rafael lay on the floor, and Ellie lay on top of him. Rafael's heartbeat raced again. This is so out of control. At least we're still together.

Turning to address the men in dark suits, the new arrival called as he walked between the men and the jeep. "Hello gents! Lovely day for a picnic by the sea."

The men looked at each other, ignoring him. "They're not here," said the larger one with a shrug. "Let's go, this place reeks."

The men turned and walked off toward their waiting limo.

The man in the plaid shirt picked up their packs, threw them into the back of the jeep, and set off.

A few kilometers up the road, they turned off onto a narrow track. The jeep bounced along over potholes and rocks, pummeling Ellie and Rafael. Lying there, breathing in the dust kicked up by the jeep and the exhaust fumes seeping through the rusting floor, he reached up for Ellie and found her shoulder. "Ooof," a pothole tossed him in their air for a moment, then slammed him back against the floor with Ellie's weight on top of him. Damn, that one hurt. "Ellie," he whispered.

"Hush, I'm okay."

At last, the jeep stopped.

"It's safe. You can sit up now. This is where the coastal trail crosses my drive. You can get out here or stay and come up to the house with me. Mary and I don't have a lot, but we're happy to share if you tell us what's going on."

"Who are you?"

"I'm Jake, my partner's Mary. We live off the grid up the mountain. It started out as a kind of social experiment, but now we've gotten to like it."

Rafael looked at Ellie and could see the weariness on her face. He knew he looked equally exhausted, although he couldn't tell if it was the rough ride in the jeep or the stress of their roller coaster adventure over the past two weeks. Please, God, let this be our second chance.

"House," was all he trusted himself to say. "We'd like to come to your house."

"It's another 30 minutes. The road gets better in a bit, so try to get some sleep."

Rafael slouched in the seat as the adrenaline left his body. He listened to the engine as the vehicle clawed its way up the steep track. He didn't even notice when they reached the smooth road above. The next thing he was aware of was the door being opened and a hand on his shoulder.

"We're there, hop out. I'll get your bags."

Rafael turned and saw Ellie stretching and yawning before she climbed out the far side. They were standing in a clearing in the forest. In front of them was a log cabin that looked like something out of the historical romances that Ellie sometimes watched. Beside and behind the cabin, he could see a kitchen garden with neat rows of vegetables, some close to the ground and others climbing long trellis structures. Part of the garden was covered with nets. Further away, he could see an orchard with its rows of fruit trees.

A small pond on the far side of the house shimmered behind the low weir keeping it in check. Above and below, a creek ran with its clear mountain water.

"It's beautiful," said Ellie as she came around the jeep. "I never knew this could really exist."

"It's God's own country," said Jake, carrying their two packs, one in each hand. "I like to think this is the way we're supposed to live."

Now that they could see him clearly, Rafael realized Jake was older than he thought, at least fifty, and had broad gray streaks throughout his bushy beard and mane of hair.

"Come in and meet Mary. She'll be happy to see some fresh faces around here."

Mary was a similar age to Jake. She had a wiry body that spoke of the hard work that went into maintaining this idyllic retreat.

"Hello, and welcome," she said. "And what are your names?"

"I'm Rafael, and this is Ellie. Thank you for taking us in on short notice."

"No notice, more like. Let me make some tea, and show you where you can freshen up. Then we can talk. Jake, take their bags to the spare room and show them the shower and bathroom. Maybe fill up the hot tub for them for later. They look as though they've been run pretty hard."

"Sure Mary. Come on, you two." Jake stowed their bags in a bedroom with a fourposter bed. A stack of clean sheets and blankets stood ready to make the bed later.

"We're always prepared for visitors. Living off the grid, we usually don't know they're coming until they knock on the door. Shower's this way." He led them outside to a curtained area on the back wall where a pipe was connected to a shower head. "It's cold water now," Jake explained, "but in winter, when the log fire heater's on, we can get warm showers. There are towels in your room. Just bring one out with you. Toilets on the other side."

The toilet was an earth pit toilet, but the small outhouse gleamed. Jake explained that he had lined it with some sort of plastic that left no crevices for spiders or other denizens of outhouses to inhabit. "That was Mary's requirement," he explained. "She doesn't want to worry about what's crawling around behind her when she's in here."

"How do you get the water pressure for a shower?" asked Rafael.

Jake pointed to a small steel structure with a cylindrical tank on top. "That's the water tower. Gravity does the rest. We use the wind pump to fill it up." Again he pointed further towards the pond. Another spindly lattice tower support wheel with many fan blades, and a weather vane behind to keep it pointing into the wind. "Whenever we have a fair breeze, it pumps water from the pond up to the water tower, keeping it full."

Rafael was about to ask more questions about the plumbing system when he felt Ellie's hand on his arm. "This is lovely, Jake. Right now, I think it's time for a shower."

Twenty minutes later, showered and dressed in the new clothes they had bought with Harry's money, Ellie and

Rafael sat at the kitchen table with Mary. She poured them each mugs of hot tea and set out a plate of fresh bread, butter and homemade jams.

It was all Rafael could do not to dive into the plate immediately, but he waited until Mary sat down and Ellie signaled it was okay.

The bread was soft and buttery, and the jam was full of fresh strawberry flavor. Rafael closed his eyes as he took his first bite. The warm bread yielded easily between his teeth. He savored the silky feeling of the butter that coated his tongue and the incredible fruity sweetness of the jam. Mary laughed. "Looks like you've been on the trail for a while. Where're you from?"

"The city," Ellie replied. "We're both from the city. We have a nice apartment there."

Rafael picked up on the wistfulness in her voice. "We saw something we shouldn't have seen in the woods, and now two guys are looking for us. I think Jake must have spotted them too, because he used his jeep to shield us from them, and then got us away from the town."

"What did I spot?"

Rafael turned to see Jake coming back in.

"I was telling Mary that you got us away from the two men in town. They're looking for us."

"Well, they won't find you up here. So what're you thinking of doing next?"

"We need time to make a plan. So far, we've just been running, living in the woods and moving along the highland trails. But we can't keep doing that."

"Well, tomorrow will be soon enough to worry about that. Why don't you go and make your bed? Supper will be soon, and then you can soak in the hot tub and get a good night's sleep."

Dinner was simple, but after eating dehydrated trail

meals, rabbit stew and potatoes felt decadently rich. The hot tub turned out to be a large metal tub, clad in barrel staves, which had a firebox on one side to heat the water. The water was clean water from the pond delivered by the wind pump, with no added chemicals, Jake explained.

"Get out of your clothes and come out wrapped in the bathrobes in your bedroom. Mary and I will stay indoors, so no worry about your modesty. Let us know when you're done. We'll take a turn while the water's hot."

"Thank you," said Ellie. "I don't know how we can repay you."

"There'll be time enough for that tomorrow. Now enjoy the tub and get a good night's sleep."

Slipping into the tub felt heavenly. The soothing, warm water and the occasional wafts of wood smoke were intoxicating. Looking up at the night sky, Rafael could see the satellites passing overhead. He looked across at Ellie, sitting on the other side of the tub. So beautiful.

"This is amazing, Ell. I don't think I've ever felt so relaxed."

"Me too, but I can't help wondering why they're doing all this for us."

"All they've done so far is treat us like guests, although Jake did rescue us in town." Rafael slouched down so only his head was above the water.

"Yes, that was quite convenient, wasn't it? I don't think we're seeing the entire story yet. But we don't seem to be in any immediate danger here." Ellie pushed off the side and floated over to Rafael. "Have I told you how much I love you?"

"Almost as much as I love you. I'm so sorry I got you into all this."

"Don't be. I was a part of it too, and we're having the

grand adventure of our lives. I still think we'll find a way out and get our old lives back."

"I hope so. I'll never complain about life being boring again."

She kissed him. "Ready to get out? I want to sleep in a real bed again."

14

BEN AND ALF ON THE HUNT

E arlier that afternoon, Ben's tablet flashed and buzzed. He walked into his small home office to answer.

"Hey Morrie, what's up?"

"I thought you and Alf took care of our little problem last night."

"We did."

"Then how come Harry just dropped into the public tablet in Harrison Point? Seems strange for a man in his condition."

"Shit. Okay, Morrie, I'll call Alf, and we'll be there. But it's not him. I don't know who it is, but it's not Harry. We made sure of that."

"I believe you, Ben. I trust you, and I believe you'll make this minor aberration go away."

"Sure, Morrie. I'll take the limo and pick up Alf right now."

"I've routed Harry's chip transactions to your tablet. Don't let me down."

"Never. You know I would never."

Alf was still doing up his belt and hadn't tied his shoes as he came out to meet the limousine carrying Ben.

"Geezus, Alf, you look like hell. What were you doing?" At that moment, a young woman with blonde hair and wearing only her underwear and an open robe walked out on a balcony two floors up. She leaned on the railing. Alf waved goodbye from the curb, and she blew him a kiss in return.

"Is that a new girlfriend?" asked Ben.

"Yeah, her name's Bunny. I met her a few weeks ago, but she seems cool."

Ben shook his head and settled back into the leather seat for the ride out to Harrison Point.

The coastal highway was empty. At first, the self-driving limousine made good time. However, as they drove further from the city, more human-driven vehicles appeared, causing the autonomous limo to slow down. Twice, the limo had to make rapid evasive maneuvers to avoid slower, older vehicles that pulled out in front of it, shaking the two men.

Ben's tablet chimed and flashed up a receipt from a clothing store. As they neared the village, it flashed again with the receipt from a grocery store.

"Looks like he's still hanging around the village, whoever it is," said Ben.

"So what's the plan, a drive-by? Dead and gone before they know what hit 'em?"

"Alf, keep your gun in its holster until I tell you otherwise. No drive-bys, no bodies in the street. First, we need to know who's using Harry's chip, and what he thought he saw. Then we need to make sure he doesn't talk to anybody else."

Pulling up outside the bakery, Ben and Alf walked through the door. A gaunt woman eyed them suspiciously, taking in their dark suits and sunglasses. She craned her neck to look past them at the limousine outside.

"How can I help you today, gentlemen? Looking for coffee and pastries for the road?" she asked.

"Perhaps," said Ben politely. "We're looking for someone who used your public tablet earlier today. They left something that we'd like to return to them."

"We get a lot of people using our public tablet. Not so many personal tablets around here."

"This would be someone you haven't seen before. They were hiking in the woods. Might have been a couple of people."

Her eyes looked up and to the right. After a momentary pause, she looked at Ben, saying, "There was a young couple earlier."

"Was one of them Harry?" asked Ben. He noticed the woman's hand drop below the countertop, causing her to lean slightly to the right.

"Yeah, there was a Harry and his girlfriend."

"What did they look like?"

"Don't you know? You seem to know a lot about them."

"We have a picture of the man's face, but need to know more so we can spot him around the village."

"Well," she said slowly, "He was tall, I'd say two meters easily. She was quite small, 160 centimeters if even that." She pointed behind Ben to the doorframe of the shop, where the height from the floor was clearly marked in five centimeter increments. "He had blond hair and was wearing camouflage gear, and she was wearing an orange top and sweatpants. Does that help?"

"Thank you, ma'am. We'll come back for that coffee before we leave today."

"Don't stay too long. We close at four."

Ben turned and left the store with Alf following. Talking in a low voice, he said, "She was lying. They were here, and I believe there were two of them, but everything else was a lie. Let's try the grocery store. It was the last connection. We can try the clothing store after."

Inside the grocery store, there was only a single cashier: a teenage girl with a name tag that said "Lindsay."

"Hello, Lindsay," began Ben. "We're looking for a couple who were in here just a while ago. I wonder if you might remember them."

Lindsay seemed flustered, then turned to look at the back of the store, where an older man emerged from a stockroom. Close behind him was a muscular younger man in his early twenties, casually carrying a baseball bat. On seeing them, Lindsay deserted her register and brushed past the new arrivals before disappearing into the same backroom.

Ben looked at the baseball bat and spread his hands. "Really?" The younger man just grinned.

Speaking to the older man, he said, "We're just looking for information. A young man named Harry was here with a girl. Do you remember them?"

"Who's asking?"

"Friends, looking to help. They may be in trouble."

"Are you the police, or are you the trouble?"

The young man swung up the bat so that he was now holding it in both hands.

"Easy now," said Ben before turning back to the shop owner. "Just trying to return something to them. Only need to know what they look like."

"He was more'n two meters tall, blonde hair, wearing camo gear. She was small, wearing an orange top and sweatpants. Now, if you don't want to buy anything, I'll ask you to kindly leave the store."

"Thanks," said Ben. "We're just going."

Outside, Alf said, "Did you see that kid with the baseball bat? I could've dropped him before he got his swing started."

"Alf, how old are you?"

"Twenty-four."

"So not much older than him, and no more brains. Have you noticed there's something wrong with this village? Did you spot the gun at the bakery?"

"No…. You think she had a gun?"

"Under the counter. If you made a wrong move, she would have blown your nuts off before you could put your hand on your holster. And don't think the old man in the grocery didn't have a gun nearby. We're going to the clothing store next. Try to be professional. See if you can spot the gun. And keep your hands in plain sight. Got it?"

"Sure, got it, Ben."

In the clothing store, a flamboyant, middle-aged man greeted them. "Good afternoon, gents. You're looking very sombre. Need something more appropriate for a seaside holiday? I see you like to match. I have some lovely things in both your sizes."

"What, you think we're…?" blurted Alf.

Ben put out a restraining hand.

"Thanks, but we're not on holiday. Just looking to help a young couple out by returning something they left behind."

The conversation went much the same as the two previous stops.

Outside the clothing store, Alf said, "I saw it, Ben. Just like you said. Shotgun muzzle poking out through the curtains on one of the little changing things."

"Good, so you see why we're not going to pick them up today."

Ben's tablet chimed as a new transaction at the cafe appeared.

"Okay, Alf. You go into the cafe and ask the same questions. Keep your hands away from your gun. You're more useful without any bullet holes in you."

"What are you going to do?"

"I'm going to spot them as they go out the back."

Ben hurried to the corner of the cafe and then stood with his back to the wall. Two minutes later, he spotted a young Hispanic man and his blonde-haired girlfriend dash out of the restaurant. Paying attention to their wrists, he noticed the young woman had a bandaid where her chip would have been. The man had a larger bandage, probably covering Harry's chip. He smiled as he saw they were both of medium height. The two meter tall man with blonde hair was actually about 175 centimeters, with brown skin and black hair. The woman with him was actually close to his height, perhaps 170 centimeters, and had fair skin.

He watched as they hid behind a row of dumpsters. Satisfied, he walked back out into the street, where Alf joined him.

"Sorry, Ben, I couldn't see the gun this time."

"No worries, Alf. I'm sure it was there. Our young couple is hiding behind those dumpsters."

"So, do we blast 'em?"

"Are you really that thick? We've just talked with half the town. They know our car. They're all armed, and, for some reason we don't understand, they're protecting these two."

"So what do we do?"

"We wait to see the rescue. Maybe that will give us a clue. Meanwhile, let's just stand where we can see the dumpsters and admire the view of the harbor."

They did not have to wait long. The loud noise of a poorly muffled engine announced the arrival of an old jeep which wore the battle scars of years living on the edge of the mountain. The jeep pulled up at the end of the row of dumpsters.

A man in jeans and a plaid shirt jumped out, opened the back of the jeep and tossed two large sacks of garbage into a dumpster.

Turning to address Ben and Alf, he called out, "Hello, gents! Lovely day for a picnic by the sea."

Ben and Alf looked at each other, ignoring the new arrival. "They're not here," said Ben with a shrug. "Let's go, this place reeks."

They turned and walked back to their waiting limo.

―――――――――

BACK IN THE LIMO, BEN SAID, "YOU KNOW, ALF, THIS doesn't make sense yet. Those two looked pretty affluent. There's something we're not seeing."

Then, speaking to the car, "Shirley, take us to our stop last night."

The car carried on some distance down the highway, then turned off on a side road. Ben watched out the window. "Look for signs of a hiking trail, Alf."

"What'll it look like?"

"I don't know. Maybe a marker, maybe a place where vehicles pull off, maybe just a path into the woods."

Fifteen minutes later, it was Alf who said, "Hey Ben, look on the left side here. Is that it?"

"Shirley, stop here."

The limo stopped, and the two men got out. They walked a few paces along the trail and paused to look around.

Ben pointed. "This must be the coastal trail. See, there's paint marks on the trees to show the way."

"You a hiker, Ben?"

"I was a lot of things when I was younger. One of the young women I knew took me hiking once. I've been on part of the trail near the city. Let's get back in the car."

The limo continued retracing their steps, turning off onto a logging road, and then making three more turns onto logging tracks that crisscrossed in the woods. Finally, it stopped.

"I don't think I want to see Harry again," said Alf.

"We're not here to see Harry." Then, "Shirley, display the shoreline hiking trail near our position."

The display showed the small logging road and, in a dashed line, the shoreline trail running just below the road along the mountainside. Ben climbed out of the limousine, and Alf followed.

"This way, look for broken branches or footprints. Especially for a flattened area where a tent might have been or a campfire."

They found both.

"Geezuz," said Ben, "We were right on top of them. They would have heard the car and come up to look. But why the hell did they take Harry's chip? Why not call the police and report the body?"

Alf looked puzzled for a moment, then said, "Seems to me the question is why would they need Harry's chip? They didn't look like they needed money. Why couldn't they use their own chips?"

Ben grinned. "Now that's the first really intelligent question I've heard you ask. Keep thinking like that, and you'll have a long career ahead of you. So why would they need Harry's chip?"

"'Cause they were on the run. Someone was watching

their chips. Maybe they were afraid to use their chips and their tablets."

"That's the only thing that makes sense. They didn't know that Harry was broke. He had barely enough to buy coffee on there. I imagine they pretty much drained whatever was left. Time to talk to Morrie."

On the way home, Ben called his boss.

"Hi Morrie, are you still in the office if we stop by?"

"Sure, Ben. But come by the house. We can talk there."

Forty-five minutes later, Ben and Alf arrived at Morrie's house. His wife let them in and showed them to the study.

"Welcome gentlemen. Can I offer you a drink?" Morrie asked as he poured himself a shot of whiskey from a crystal decanter.

"Yes, thanks, we'd like that," said Ben.

As Morrie was pouring the drinks, Ben said, "We found the young couple who took Harry's chip."

"Good. Did you make a mess down there? Do you need a cleaner?"

"No, it's something else that doesn't quite add up. These kids were already on the run. Something scarier than us must be after them. At some point, they had cut out their own chips. Harry's chip must have seemed like a pot of gold to them, so they started using that, but that's where something else doesn't add up. That village, Harrison Point, is odd. Everywhere we stopped to ask about them, we could see weapons on us. And they all gave the same lie about the description of the two so they were alerting each other. The whole town was covering for them. I don't know if they were locals or if the town just sympathized, but we're not getting near them right now."

"You think they're talking?"

"I don't think they really know anything, except they found a body in the woods and took his chip. To be honest, Morrie, I don't think they're much of a risk to us. I'd like to keep watch for a while, maybe get some pictures and identify them. But I don't think we need more bodies right now."

"You going soft, Ben?"

"No, but these two aren't a threat. They don't even know who we are, who you are. You've always been a fair boss, Morrie. I don't think these two have set a foot out of line except for taking Harry's chip when they were in trouble. I also think we should know more about Harrison Point. Something's there we don't understand."

"Agreed, you're a good man, Ben." Morrie nodded toward Alf. "How's my nephew doing?"

"He's learning fast. Isn't that right, Alf?"

"Yes, sir, Uncle Morrie. Ben's great and I'm listening to him."

"He's the best. Stick with him and you'll be great, too."

"Thanks, Uncle Morrie."

Their discussion turned to Ben's daughter, Sarah, and her upcoming recital. When they finished their drinks, Ben and Alf left.

15

THE PLAN TAKES SHAPE

When Rafael and Ellie returned to their bedroom after the hot tub, their bed was turned down, and large glasses of clean water were on each bedside table. Still in their bathrobes, they took turns brushing their teeth before climbing into bed together.

"It feels so good to not be sleeping in our clothes," said Ellie as she moved over to lay her head on Rafael's chest.

"It feels even better to have you next to me. Tomorrow's...gonna...be," Rafael mumbled as he felt consciousness slipping away.

BRIGHT SUNLIGHT WAS STREAMING IN THROUGH THE bedroom window making Rafael squint when he opened his eyes. He rolled over to reach for Ellie, but she was gone.

He struggled into new underwear and a T-shirt bought the day before, but his jeans were gone. Sticking his head out the door, he called, "Ellie?" in a low voice.

Immediately Ellie appeared in the hallway, wearing her dressing gown. "Mary just showed me how to wash our clothes. Come on out in your bathrobe. There's breakfast ready. Your pants are lightweight, so they'll be dry in an hour or so."

Rafael went and sat at the kitchen table. Ellie brought him a steaming cup of tea with toasted English muffins and jam. "Jake's off looking after the animals. Mary's out with the chickens. I think she said we'd have fresh eggs in a while."

"Any more idea why they took us in?"

"No, Mary's been asking questions. I haven't said much more than that we'd seen something in the woods, and the men in the limousine were after us. But I'm pretty sure she knows there's more to it than that."

"Do you think we can tell them the entire story?"

"We have to tell someone eventually. At least Mary and Jake are off the grid. Let's not rush. There'll be a natural time to talk about it."

At that moment, Mary came into the kitchen carrying a small wicker basket of eggs. "Bumper crop this morning," she said. "Almost three dozen. I put away most of 'em to sell at the market on Wednesday. As soon as Jake comes in, I'll cook up these eight so we can have a proper breakfast. I take it you slept well, Rafael?"

"Yes, I did." Rafael felt sheepish at the realization that everyone else, including Ellie, had already been up and busy for some time. "Sorry, I should've woken up earlier."

"Nonsense. You're been through a lot. Ellie's been telling me about some of your adventures. I'd say you deserve a lazy morning today."

Jake arrived and joined them at the table. Ellie stood and poured him a cup of the strong tea on the stove.

"So Rafael, how are you enjoying life at our little resort?" Jake asked.

Rafael felt himself blushing. "I love it, but I have a feeling it doesn't go on forever."

Jake laughed at his discomfort. "No worries. I reckon you needed the rest. After breakfast, you and I need to talk about what's really going on, and then we can make a plan."

Rafael looked down at his lap but nodded in agreement. His mind churned. *How much do I tell him? What does he need to know?*

Jake proved to be a genial host, spinning stories of goats and pigs over breakfast and keeping Ellie and Rafael distracted.

When breakfast was cleared away and Ellie and Mary were doing the dishes, Jake leaned forward on his elbows.

"So, what's the rest of the story?"

"You mean what we saw that had those guys looking for us in town?"

"That and how two wealthy young people show up with expensive hiking clothes but no tablets and with their wrist chips cut out."

"Oh, you saw that." *Shit. Now what do I say?*

"I've seen it before. Not difficult to spot. And yet you were able to buy new clothes in town, so presumably with another person's wrist chip?"

Rafael nodded, feeling exposed. *Crap, he's putting it all together. Guess I'm not so brilliant.*

"And you two don't look like you have it in you to kill someone for their chip."

Rafael shook his head from side to side. Suddenly, the world around him faded, and he lost all strength in his body.

When he regained consciousness, Ellie was beside him, holding him up.

"What happened?"

"You fainted," she said. "Here, I've put sugar in your tea. Drink this, it'll help you." She turned to face Jake. "Give me a few minutes to get our pants and jackets. Then we'll both tell you the entire story."

Ellie disappeared for a moment and returned with an armful of clothes. "Raffi, come into the bedroom and finish getting dressed." She left the bedroom door almost closed so they could hear Mary in the kitchen.

"Jake," said Mary, "what are you thinking of? Spilling all their secrets on the table like that, making poor Rafael feel trapped. Don't forget, they have no idea who or what you are."

"Well, the boy needs to toughen up quickly if they're going to succeed. Just dropping him in the deep end. Besides, the sooner we have everything on the table, the faster we can make a plan. This could be a bit of good luck for us as well as for them."

"Okay, but just go as fast as they're ready for. Nothing urgent that I can see."

Rafael pulled on his hiking pants, still damp but he knew his body heat would soon finish drying them. Returning to the table, Rafael and Ellie sat side by side across from Jake. Mary wiped her hands on her apron and moved to sit next to her partner.

"I'll start from the beginning," said Rafael. "I was working for an AI who owns a company, but I noticed some patterns that seemed strange. I pursued them and found myself caught between two large AIs. The smaller one took advantage of me to open a back door between them, which resulted in some kind of AI war that shut everything down for a few hours."

"We heard about that," said Mary. "You had something to do with that?"

"Yeah, and what I learned in the process is something one of the AIs wants to hide. So, unfortunately, it wants to eliminate us. It tracked us through our tablets, so we wrapped them in aluminum foil. But then, every time we used our wrist chips, it could tell where we were. And then the bots came with the long-range scanners for chips, so we had to take them out."

"So, where do the men in black come from?"

"One night, on the trail, we heard a car on one of the old logging roads close to our campsite. We crept out of the tent to see what was going on and saw them shoot a man called Harry in the back of the head. We waited until they were gone, then we cut out his chip, and I wore it under a piece of adhesive tape from our first aid kit. Ellie bandaged me up as if I had sprained my wrist so we could use the chip without suspicion. But now, I think the gangsters don't understand why their dead guy is wandering around buying stuff."

"And that's where I found you, hiding from the hitmen and the AI bots. It's not the worst story I've heard, but it comes close."

Jake sat back in contemplation. He looked at Rafael, then looked at Ellie.

"Any idea how much money is still in Harry's account?"

"No. Anyways, the body's gone."

"Gone?"

"The next morning, we could see drag marks where a large animal dragged it into the bushes."

Jake sat still for a moment, with his elbows on the table and his palms pressed together.

"I have an idea, but I'll need to make some inquiries.

You two stay here. Start to learn about living off the grid. I can see that in your future." Jake stood up and walked out. Rafael heard the sound of a small gasoline engine. He went out to look and saw Jake riding off on a gray ATV.

"It's how we get around between the neighbors," said Mary as Rafael came back into the kitchen. "We all live near the trails or along the old logging roads. Now come along, and you can help me in the garden."

JAKE RETURNED IN TIME FOR LUNCH. AS THEY ATE A FRESH salad from the garden, Jake talked about his morning.

"I don't see a way for you to go back to the city. Do you?"

Rafael and Ellie both shook their heads.

"And I don't see a way for you to negotiate a settlement with whoever's chasing you. Is that your take as well?"

"Yeah, the AI responsible is damaged and has no compassion for human beings. Even if she agreed to a settlement, I wouldn't trust her."

"So the other answer is for you to go off the grid, like Mary and I have done. It's actually an enjoyable life once you get used to it."

"I can see that," said Ellie. "But if we settle near here, we'll still be looking over our shoulders every day and not sleeping well at night."

"Exactly! So you need to get off the island. I have a place in mind, but it takes a while to communicate with them without electronics. Meanwhile, I do have a connection who can move Harry's money to a place where we can use it. He'll take 30%. If there's a reasonable amount in the account, that will still leave us with more than we need. Are you okay giving up Harry's chip?"

"Will it be secure?" asked Ellie. "Does he know about the hitmen?"

"Don't worry about that. The transaction will dip in and out of several accounts. Fees will take up about half of his cut. But the trail will be extremely difficult to track, and I suspect their boss will decide to write it off as the end of an unfortunate incident."

Rafael spoke up. "We'd like to talk about it after lunch and give you an answer this afternoon. It's the only money we have, even if it does bring the gangsters snooping around."

"Fair enough. When we know how much it is, then we can work on part two. Where to go and how to get there."

"Why do you know so much about this stuff?"

"We're all running from something. The less you know, the safer you are. I think you told me the same thing about your secret with the AIs."

AFTER LUNCH, RAFAEL AND ELLIE WENT FOR A WALK IN THE orchard. The trees all bore small fruit, apples and pears mostly, not yet ripe enough for picking. Between the trees, wildflowers blossomed among the tall grasses. Bees buzzed from flower to flower, and butterflies fluttered by. The light breeze carried the scents of the flowers and the ripening fruit under the warming rays of the sun.

"Do you trust Jake? Do you think he's trying to rob us?" asked Rafael.

"I don't know. But I know we can't keep running. Our luck will run out sooner or later."

Rafael stopped, and taking both of Ellie's hands in his, he asked, "What do you really think about living off the grid?"

"I think we could get to like it, especially if we're in a community like Jake said. I'm willing to give it a try as long as we stay together."

Rafael hesitated, trying to imagine a lifetime of cold showers and earth pit toilets. He shook himself. There must be a way to have a better life than that. "Okay, I'll hand him over the chip. We can still recover our own chips if we need to make a run for it."

"Somehow, I think he's already thinking about those. Which reminds me, we need to get a message to my parents," said Ellie. "They need to clear out our apartment and cancel the lease, or our chips won't be worth anything."

"I'll ask Jake how we can do that."

Jake was sitting at the table watching Mary make bread when they returned from their walk. Rafael fetched Harry's chip on its strip of medical tape.

"Here you go. I don't know much else about it except his name was Harry, and it was working when you found us."

"Great. I'll take it over this afternoon, and we should have an answer tomorrow. Meanwhile, Rafael, I may have a project for you. What did you say your major was in college?"

"Mechanical technologist with a certificate in actuator design."

"Perfect. Let's go out to the barn."

In the barn, Jake pulled out a rusting rototiller. "This thing hit a rock last summer and hasn't worked since. See if you can get it going while I'm gone. Over here's the tool chest, and above the workbench are greases and oils to lube it. You'll probably need to overhaul the engine at the same time. It's been sitting idle for a long time."

Rafael looked doubtfully at the aging piece of

equipment. "Do you have some paint?" he asked. "If I'm going to repair it, I might as well paint it."

Jake smiled. "In that cupboard," he pointed, "are some cans of rust-proof spray paint. I'm not sure which ones are still good, but there should be some that'll work."

Rafael pulled over the toolbox and set to work. First, he dismantled the rototiller body so that he had all the sheet metal cover pieces laid out on the ground. Each one was wire brushed, then he hung them on an improvised line and spray painted them. He painted the main body panels green and the two fenders and small parts yellow.

As those hung drying, he returned to disassembling the mechanical parts. It was easy to remove the engine and set it aside. He identified a centrifugal clutch and placed it next to the engine. Next was the simple transmission, followed by the long drive shaft that connected all the moving components.

Finally, the rotating blade assemblies. As he took them apart, he could already see part of the problem. One blade was bent where it had hit the rock. He could also see the alignment was out, and the axle that connected the two sets of blades was bent. He pulled the axle and set it aside, then went to work soaking the other parts in solvent to remove the old grease, cleaning them with a wire brush one by one.

Rafael was only about one-third finished when Jake walked in. "Looks like good progress. Can you fix it?"

"I'll need a new shaft. This one's bent and it's almost impossible to straighten them. We could try, but if one of your friends has a lathe, it would be better to turn a new one. Also, if you can get a couple of sheets of gasket material, I'll replace some of the gaskets. I could reuse these ones, but I think they would leak again."

"Well, I'm impressed. I'll see what I can do about your

axle and the gaskets tomorrow. But don't you need the exact gaskets for the machine?"

"No, we learned at college how to make a gasket. I'll show you if you get the material."

"I'd like that. So, this will be your skill going forward. Mechanic. And the rototiller will be proof if you can get it going again."

16

TIME WITH MARY

When Jake took Rafael out to the barn, they left Ellie alone with Mary in the kitchen. Mary handed her an apron and said, "Might as well get stuck in. You have a lot to learn about running a home off-grid."

"What would you like me to do?"

Mary opened the oven door and pulled out an enormous large ball of dough that had been proofing. "Wash your hands and punch this dough down to release the gas from fermentation. Then divide this bread dough into balls this size." Mary held her hands apart to show the size. "Make one for each loaf tin. If there's leftover dough, we'll bake some dinner rolls."

Punching the dough produced loud farting noises, which soon had them both giggling. Mary reshaped the dough into a longer cylindrical shape.

Ellie began dividing the dough and rolling it into balls. Soon her hands were a sticky mess that pulled patches of dough off the balls she was rolling. Mary didn't seem surprised.

"Don't worry, dear. Now wash your hands again, drying them off very well. Then I'll show you what you missed."

Ellie did as she was told. When she turned around from the sink, the dough was all in one shape again.

"Now, dust the counter with flour, then dust your hands with flour as well. Remember, you don't want to get too much flour into the bread, so avoid folding more flour into the dough balls when you're shaping them. Here's a dough knife. Use it to cut pieces off. Weigh them on this scale. You'll want between 800 and 900 grams each. Later, you won't need the scale but don't feel bad about weighing things at first. Now have a go."

Under Mary's watchful eye, Ellie parted the dough and shaped it for the pans.

"Now we let it rise for a while until it fills the pans. Let's make a fresh pot of coffee, and you can take one out to your young man. Then you and I can have a chat."

Clutching the mug of warm coffee and two cookies from Mary's cookie jar, Ellie went to find Rafael in the barn. She watched him from the doorway for a moment before going in. He was up to his elbows in oil and grease, singing off-key to himself and seeming quite content. This is where he belongs, she thought, he just rolls with everything. I'd hug him if he wasn't so greasy.

She went in with the coffee and cookies, laying the cookies out on a clean rag for him.

"I can't touch those right now, Ell. Can you feed me one?"

Ellie picked up the cookie and held it to his mouth so he could take a bite.

"Mmmm," he said around a mouthful of cookie. "Those are fantastic. I'm ready for the rest of it."

"You look like you're having fun out here."

"I am. At least working on this machine, I feel completely in control for the first time in days. I was worried at first, but when I realized how simple it was, I knew I could do it."

"That's great. I'm proud of you. I think this is the first time I've seen you actually doing mechanical work. It looks good on you."

"How's Mary?"

"Really nice. She's teaching me to bake bread. But now she wants to have a chat, so I don't know what that's about."

"Probably wants to get to know you. Have your chat, and we can compare notes later. Thanks for the coffee and cookies. Just feed me the other one before you go."

Rafael closed his eyes and looked so rapturous as he bit into the cookie that Ellie couldn't help giggling. "I'm going back now. Have fun."

Back in the kitchen, Mary poured two more coffees and put more cookies on a plate between them.

"You must have questions, Ellie. Why not ask them now?"

"Do you enjoy living like this? Don't you miss the city and the shops?"

"I did at first, but then I learned that contentment doesn't come from things I could buy. How did you feel just now when you took the coffee out to Rafael in the barn?"

"It was nice. I got to see him really happy doing something he loves."

"That's how it still is for me, only I'm also really happy doing the things I love - gardening and baking. When I need a hand in the garden, Jake's always there for me, and when Jake needs me to steady his ladder or hold a piece of wood he's cutting, then I'm there for him. He's an amazing carpenter but not much of a mechanic, which is why the rototiller was still broken. So we each do things we love and trade for the things we don't."

"What kind of things do you trade for?"

"This dress, for example, and the apron you're wearing were both made by Jean. Sewing is her passion, baking not so much, so we can trade. Each community develops its own system of barter adapting to the skills of its members."

"What would I have as a skill? I studied art and history at college, and I used to work at a community help center. Not exactly marketable here."

"The art might surprise you, especially if you can find something to do that doesn't require a lot of fancy equipment. You might enjoy sewing, especially quilting. That's an art form on its own. We'll have the summer to try different things. One of them will stick."

"What about children? Do people in the community have children? Rafael and I want to have a family."

"There're lots of children and a school. You don't see them much because we're not part of that. There was a time when I thought we might, but it never happened for us, and now it's too late."

Mary turned away to look out the window for a moment, then dabbed her eyes with the end of her apron before turning back to face Ellie.

"Sorry, I didn't mean to bring up a difficult memory."

Mary smiled, although her eyes were still sad. "If you want children, have them early. Don't wait for the time to be right. It'll never be right. That's the trap we fell into."

"What about your families? I feel sad every time I think about my parents. They must be frantic, not knowing if we're safe."

"That will never pass completely. But there are ways to get written messages back and forth and to send small packages sometimes. When you feel ready, we'll send them some cookies you made, or maybe you'll make an apron for your mom when you sit with Jean. She wants to meet you, by the way."

"That would be nice. So overall, you like this life?"

"Now, I wouldn't trade it. It's brought Jake and I so many rich experiences that I can't imagine living any other way."

Ellie sat quietly for a few minutes, sipping her coffee and looking into the distance as she tried to imagine herself living like this forever. She could feel that tears were near, so she closed her eyes and took a deep breath to steady herself. Is this really it? Is this my life now? Homemade dresses and cooking on a wood stove?

Mary was equally quiet, either lost in her own thoughts or simply giving Ellie space.

17

A CALL HOME

That evening, over dinner, Rafael spoke about their tablets and chips. "I suspect you've already realized that our chips would be valuable. But rent on an empty apartment and utility expenses will drain our account unless we can talk with our parents. Can you arrange a call with them?"

"Sure, and then you'll tell me where the chips are?" said Jake.

"No, we'll tell you where they are when we know the rest of the plan. I'm sorry, you've been great, but I think we should keep this part all business."

Jake laughed. "No offense taken. I'd have been disappointed if you gave up everything at once. But you're right about stopping the rent. I can set up a call, but I'll need the name of your go-between."

"Rachel O'Leary. She's already helped us once."

"Perfect. Give me two days to have it set up."

THE TWO DAYS WENT BY QUICKLY. THE NEXT AFTERNOON, Jake went off on his ATV to collect the new shaft and gasket material for the rototiller project. By the time he returned, Rafael had completed his rebuild of the clutch and the transmission and was ready to put the engine back together. He took the new gasket material and showed Jake how to make a new gasket using only a ball peen hammer. With the new gasket in place, it was a simple job to finish the assembly of the small engine.

"Should be running tomorrow," Rafael said confidently.

The following day, Rafael assembled the complete rototiller. The housing gleamed yellow and green under three coats of paint. He carefully filled the tank with fresh gasoline and pulled the starter rope slowly to turn the engine over several times. With a quick pull, the engine roared into life before settling down into an idle. He put it into gear, squeezed the throttle, and the wheels drove forward as the blades spun under their hood. Satisfied that it was running, Rafael stopped the engine.

"Well done," said Jake when Rafael called him out to the barn. "I really didn't think you would do that well."

"Working on the factory hydraulic systems, the tolerances were in tenths of a millimeter. This was easy in comparison."

That night over dinner, Jake announced, "I arranged the call with your parents for 11 am tomorrow morning. They'll all be together. After you've talked with them, I'll share the next part of the plan with you. It's the riskiest bit for all of us, so it has to stay secret until then."

THE CALL WAS NOT WHAT RAFAEL EXPECTED. JUST BEFORE 11 am, they all gathered at the kitchen table. Jake pulled an old tablet from a leather satchel and placed it in front of Ellie and Rafael. He placed a call using a preset number, and a male voice answered. "Wooly Bear, here. Who's this?"

"Black Squirrel," replied Jake, staying off camera. "Ready on my end."

"Opening camera now. Fifteen minutes till we close."

They saw their parents sitting close together, looking puzzled.

When her mother saw Ellie, she began crying. "Oh, Ellie, where are you? Why don't you come home?"

By this time, Ellie was crying too. She just kept saying, "I love you Mom, I love you Dad."

Rafael took charge. "We're safe and staying with friends. I wish we could come back, but I don't think we'd be around long if we did, either killed or in prison because of what we found out. But this is really important. We need you to close our apartment and stop the rent payments and utilities, and anything else you can think of. Tell them we went hiking and disappeared. Tell them whatever you want. Please help us by stopping the charges."

"What's really going on, Raffi?" asked his father. "You keep saying you haven't done anything. It's a bit much to believe that you can't explain and resolve it. Come home with Ellie, and we'll help you sort it out, whatever it is."

"I'm sorry, Papa, but it's really beyond that. It's an AI who's chasing us. Whenever we use our chips, within 10 minutes, armed bots come looking for us. We've been living in the woods since we left."

"You said you're with friends. Are you part of a cult now?" asked his mother.

"No, Mom, we're not part of a cult. We can leave whenever we want. But we are being sheltered by people who know how to protect us. One day soon, we'll be able to tell you more about it."

"Mom," said Ellie, "tell me about the family. How is everyone?"

Ellie's mom relaxed visibly as they talked about the family. Soon, Rafael's mother joined in with news of his brothers and their partners. The minutes flew by until Wooly Bear interrupted and cut off the call.

Lunch was quiet. At one point, Ellie said, "Thanks for arranging that call, Jake. It felt so good to let my parents know we were safe, but it also reminds me of what we've left behind."

"I think you'll always have that, dear," said Mary. "But then you'll have this new life, and in time, it becomes just as valuable, only different. You're young; you'll have children, and seeing them grow up outdoors in a caring community of friends and neighbors will ease your pain."

"We might have one more call before you leave in a few weeks," said Jake, "but don't count on it. I had to call in a lot of favors for that call."

"When do you think we can leave?"

"Let's finish lunch, and then I'll tell you what I have in mind. Meanwhile, start thinking about your new names."

"New names?"

"You don't think we were born Jake and Mary, do you? Changing names is part of how you disappear. No rush. We have a few more days to decide."

When the lunch dishes were washed and put away, the four sat at the table again.

"So the problem breaks into two parts: where to go and how to get there."

Rafael nodded. He was aware of Ellie paying very

close attention beside him. He reached over and held her hand.

"There is a community on the island of Three Saints. It has that name because there's a natural rock wall that shields the harbor, and the wall has three tall rock formations. The community has been running for at least twenty years and is self-sufficient just as we are here. They trade honey, fresh produce, and other products with the mainland. Most of the people there are escaping something, and they don't ask many questions about each other's past."

Rafael noticed Mary did not look happy at the mention of Three Saints. *What am I missing here?* He squeezed Ellie's hand.

"I've been in touch," Jake continued, "and they have a cabin already built and will reserve it for you. A couple who couldn't handle the lifestyle left it after being there for five years. All you have to do is move in."

Jake looked right at Rafael. "I told them you were a college-trained mechanic who completely rebuilt my rototiller in two days. That's a valuable skill in a place with no repair shops."

Rafael nodded. *Could be worse,* he thought. *Same role I had with Fatima, but the machines won't talk back.*

Jake turned to Ellie.

"Ellie, they'll expect you to join in some of the community enterprises. But the work is light when shared by many hands, and there's lots of laughter. How does that sound?"

"Fine," said Ellie. "I mean, there's not a lot of choice, and this at least sounds comfortable. Will we be able to send messages back home?"

"Yes, written messages on paper that will be hand-delivered. There's a support group on the main island that looks after things like that."

"Do you have any pictures?" asked Rafael.

"No, the community is really private and protective of its members. But that's in your favor as well."

"Okay, so how do we get there?"

"I can only think of one way to get you there safely. You'll sail there. But there's a couple of people I need to talk with first."

"I don't know," said Ellie. "What do we know about sailing?"

Rafael turned to look at her and shook his head as he gripped her hand.

"It sounds wonderful," he said. "But Ellie and I need some time to talk and think. We're going to go for a walk in the orchard."

ELLIE CHOSE THE SPOT UNDER A PEAR TREE. RAFAEL unfolded the blanket he was carrying, and together, they spread it on the ground before lying down side by side.

"Do you really think we could sail to an island we've never seen?" asked Ellie.

"I'm sure of it, but I think the real question is, are you ready to live in a new community as a homesteader like Mary and Jake?"

"I think I've already gotten past that point. Mary has been showing me lots about this lifestyle. It seems very peaceful and close to the land. Why are you so sure about sailing?"

"Because it's a physical process. The sailboat has winches and lines, but the mechanics are all basic for me. We have some things to learn about setting the sails, but I already understand the principles, so I'm confident, just like I was with that rototiller. Once I started, it wasn't hard at all." As he said it, Rafael realized he was sure of it. After all, how hard can sailing be?

"So we'll go," said Ellie. "Now, what about new names? Who do you want to be?"

"I think we should choose names for each other. For example, you could be Grizelda, and I could call you Grizzly for short."

Ellie looked at him with arched eyebrows. "You're not serious, are you? I will not be called Grizzly. Try again."

"Seriously, I'm thinking of Emma, which could be Em for short. So you just go one letter up in the alphabet, from Ell to Em."

"Emma, I kind of like that. It feels like Ellie when I say it, and it's not too far from the truth. Now for your name. It should sound like a talented mechanic's name."

"A talented mechanic's name? Like what? Spanner? Lugnut?"

Ellie smiled. "No, something not too physical but still masculine. I like Raoul. I know it's French, but I think it suits you."

"How's it spelt?"

"R…A…O…U…L,"

"There is a Mexican name, R…A…U…L, which is pronounced similarly but maybe faster."

"Raul? Like Paul?"

"Not exactly. There are two syllables, Ra and Ul, said close together."

"It's up to you. How much time do you want to spend teaching people to pronounce your name?"

"You're right," he sighed. "I like Raoul. I'll go with it. Now, what about a last name? One last name or two?"

"Is that a marriage proposal?" Ellie twisted to look up at him.

Rafael stopped breathing. His heart leapt into his throat. Of course, it is. Why didn't I think of that? I should be on one knee for that question. Hastily scrambling up to kneel on one knee, and nearly falling over in the process, he asked, "Ellie, will you spend the rest of your life with me as my wife?"

Ellie took her time before responding.

"You know I will. But I'd like to have a ceremony, even if it's small. And rings. I want to wear a ring that let's the world know I'm committed to you."

Rings! thought Rafael now panicking. I can't even buy a sandwich. How do I get her a ring? Pushing the thought out of his mind, he said, "I'll talk to Jake. I'm thinking of Moreno as a last name. It's common in Mexico and not too far from Morales. If ever we slip up, people might think they just misheard us."

"Perfect, we'll be Emma and Raoul Moreno, married for the past three years. We might as well keep our history as close as possible to reality."

Rafael collapsed onto his back. "Come here, Emma Moreno. I want to feel you next to me."

After making love under the pear tree, they lay together on the blanket. Rafael felt hot, wet tears on his chest. He twisted so he could see Ellie's face. "What's wrong, mi vida?"

"I don't know. One minute everything seems like a grand adventure, and the next minute, I'm so scared and sad. What if we never see our families again? What if I can't learn everything so we can live like Mary and Jake? What if we don't like it? What if you leave me when I can't do it?"

"I don't know, Ell, except for the last one. I will never

leave you. When I call you mi vida, I really mean it. You are my life and I can't imagine living without you." He hugged her closer as he stroked her head and shoulders with his free hand.

"For the others," Rafael continued, " I don't know either. It scares me too, sometimes. But you heard that we'll be able to get messages back and forth to our families. And as for learning to live off the grid, I promise I'll make you as comfortable as I humanly can in our new home."

They pulled on their clothes and walked back to the cabin. Reaching the edge of the orchard, they could hear the distant sounds of an argument.

"What are you thinking of, Jake? Sending those poor kids off in a sailboat to a fantasy island?" Mary's voice was loud and angry.

"I keep telling you, it's not a fantasy! I've spoken with Tom Peters, the mayor there. It's real, and they have space. They want them there, especially if Raoul's really a mechanic, and from what I've seen, he's good."

"But they've never sailed a day in their lives, let alone made an ocean passage!"

"It's coastal sailing, and Mike says he'll teach them everything they need to know."

"I just wish you'd talk to me first. You always plan these things, and I'm always the last to know." Mary's voice had a sharp edge.

"Dammit, Mary!" They heard something being slammed onto the table. "There's just so many parts I'm trying to keep in my head to make this work. I can't tell you about everything."

"You'd better make it work, or you'll be sleeping outside this winter. I mean it, Jake."

"I will, and when we get the money on their chips, I'll

do the indoor plumbing you want. Could be the last year for heading outdoors every time you want to pee."

"I don't want a new toilet if it harms Ellie and Rafael! They remind me so much of ourselves at that age." Mary's voice was softer now. "Do you remember when we were just Amber and Richard with our whole lives ahead of us?"

"You know I do, but what choice did we have?"

"No more than they have, I suppose."

Rafael and Ellie looked at each other. Ellie said, "Let's walk back around the orchard again, give them time to cool down. Does this change our plans?"

"No, but at least we know they genuinely care for us. The idea of our life savings going into a toilet literally is kind of funny though," said Rafael.

Ellie giggled. "And just when we were feeling flush," she replied.

Rafael put his arm around her. Leaving the blanket neatly folded under the first tree, they set off around the small orchard once again.

18

THE ORDER OF THE PHOENIX

It was after four when they returned, now clutching the blanket again. Jake was at the pigpen, mucking it out. "Hi Jake, need a hand?" called Rafael.

"No point in two of us getting in this stuff. Ask Mary to put the kettle on when you go in. I'll be finished in a minute."

Ellie leaned against Rafael and whispered, "Looks like the storm has passed."

In the kitchen, Mary was busy sorting through some notebooks laid out in front of her. Looking up, she said, "So, do we have new names now?"

"Yes," said Ellie, "We're…"

"Not yet!" Mary held up a finger. "Wait till Jake comes back in. He won't want to miss your announcement. Ellie, after you wash up, come and join me here. You too, Rafael, if you want."

"Do you think we could use the hot tub again tonight?" Rafael asked. "To celebrate?"

"Check with Jake. I'm sure he'll say yes because he loves that hot tub as much as you do."

They washed up quickly, then Rafael went out to find Jake while Ellie sat at the table with Mary.

When Rafael returned from lighting the hot tub fire, he found Ellie laboriously copying notes from one notebook into another.

"What are you doing?" asked Rafael.

"Mary's sharing her best recipes with me, so I'll have a starting set for our new life. She says that without tablets, manual notebooks are the only way to preserve knowledge."

"Are you keeping a journal, Rafael?" asked Mary. "It's good practice, particularly for a mechanic. Keep notes and diagrams of everything you make or repair. It'll save you a lot of time in the future. Here, take one of these blank notebooks and a pen. Start making notes on everything you see about our house here: the plumbing, the electrics, whatever else you find. Keep the first page for an index so that you can come back to topics later."

Rafael accepted the notebook and pen and sat down to write. He went to write his name, then stopped himself. Instead, he wrote "Raoul Moreno." He stopped and looked at the name he had written. Will that ever become natural for me?

When Jake returned from his chores, Mary poured fresh tea from the ever-present tea kettle.

"So," said Jake. "Who do we have here?"

"Raoul Moreno and my wife Emma," replied Rafael proudly.

"Great name choices," said Jake. "The names sound right for you. We'll do the renaming ceremony tonight after dinner, and then you can celebrate in the hot tub. I just checked, and it's already warming up. Now, take two small pieces of paper and write your old names on them. Then give them to me for safekeeping."

Ellie and Rafael looked at each other, puzzled, but then each torc off a piece of paper from the back of a notebook and wrote their names out.

"Perfect," said Jake as he picked them up from the table.

Dinner was a roast chicken with roast potatoes, garden vegetables and gravy. Dessert was an apple pie. "Ellie made the pie this morning," said Mary.

"Mmm, I think this is my favorite pie ever," said Rafael. He looked at Ellie and saw her blushing.

"Rafael," said Jake, "let's go get the fire pit ready while the ladies clear up. Mary, I think we should break out the whiskey tonight to baptize our new pioneers."

When they were all seated around the fire pit, with shots of whiskey in their hands, Jake put his glass down, stood and announced, "Time to call on the spirit of the Phoenix. This ceremony goes back to our days fighting against the introduction of AIs. In those days, many of us had to run like you."

Holding his arms straight out from his shoulders, he faced north, saying, "Phoenix, we call to you for this naming ceremony. From the north come the cold, clean winds and the clear waters. Bring their newness and clarity to this young couple."

He turned to the south and said, "Phoenix, we call on you for your aid and protection. From the south come the winds that warm us. Share with them the warming, healing energy of fresh growth."

Facing west, he accepted a clay bowl and the two sheets of paper from Mary. Holding the papers so Rafael and Ellie could see their names written in large letters, he said, "Phoenix, receive these old names and let them be ended just as the sunset ends the day. What was is now complete. Rafael and Ellie are now complete. We ask that you accept this completion." He picked up a burning stick and lit the papers on fire, making sure they burned completely in the bowl.

Rafael and Ellie looked at each other in alarm. But Jake carried on, bowing to Mary, who added a spoonful of something to the bowl. Mixing the ashes with the new ingredient, Jake turned to the east and said, "Phoenix, let this couple be known by their new names. Just as the sunrise begins each day in the east, let this day be the beginning of their new lives."

He reached out his hand for Ellie to stand before him and handed her a worn tarot card of a bird rising from a fire. "I invoke the power of the Phoenix, who is born anew out of its own ashes; I name you Emma." As he said this, he dipped his little finger into the mixture and wrote Emma in large letters on her forehead.

Retrieving the card from Emma, he handed it to Rafael and motioned for Rafael to stand before him. "Invoking the power of the Phoenix who is born anew out of its own ashes; I name you Raoul." Again, he dipped his finger in the mix and wrote Raoul in large letters.

Putting down the bowl, he picked up his whiskey glass, raised it, and said, "We salute the Phoenix and drink to its protection for Raoul and Emma." With that, he downed the whiskey in a single shot. The newly anointed Raoul and Emma did the same, then came up coughing and spluttering as the fiery liquid burned their throats. Raoul noticed that Mary only sipped her whiskey.

With the ceremony finished, Jake sat down. "Welcome to the Circle of the Phoenix. Now the important thing is for you to use your new names all the time—even when you are alone, even when you are making love. You must become Emma and Raoul. The mixture is pig fat and the ashes of your old names. It will last for a couple of days;

don't wash it off. Let it be a reminder of who you have become."

"Thanks, Jake," said Raoul. "We'll never forget this night." A sudden vision of him telling this story to his children and grandchildren came over him. *Funny how the things that most changed my life came unexpectedly. Meeting Ellie, that hiring call from Fatima, and now this.*

He realized with a start that Jake was talking again.

"It's been special for us too, Raoul. It feels like passing on the torch. Just remember it when you meet a young couple in the future who need to escape their past. Now it's hot tub time."

"Would it be too weird if we all went in together?" asked Emma. "It seems a shame to finish the celebration alone."

"Sure," said Mary. "We'll keep the outside lights off. Go and get undressed and come out in your housecoats. It'll just take me a minute to put Jake's blindfold on."

"Mary, you know you're the only woman I have eyes for," said Jake, turning his face to the heavens and looking pious.

"Yes, dear," said Mary. "Of course. Now let's get ready."

Raoul stepped into the water first. Emma followed, holding his offered hand for support.

"Don't worry," said Raoul. "With the fire lighting us from below the level of the tub, nothing shows below the water."

A few minutes later, Jake and Mary arrived. Raoul was careful to look away as the older couple entered.

Jake brought the whiskey bottle with him, and Mary had the glasses. The four of them sat chatting and relaxing together as they sipped their whiskey.

After a while, Jake said, "So, you're married now."

"We thought it would avoid complications if were clearly a couple."

"Then we should do a vow ceremony before you leave. Mary, remind me to arrange something in the morning."

"I'd like that," said Emma. Raoul looked at her sideways, but Emma just shrugged.

LATER IN BED, RAOUL ASKED HER ABOUT WANTING A VOW ceremony.

"I guess every girl dreams of a ceremony where her lover pledges himself to her for eternity and where she surrenders to her love for him."

"I'm sorry. If I had known it meant so much to you, we could have done that anytime."

"I don't think I realized myself how much I missed it, but then today, in the orchard, when I agreed to take your last name, it suddenly hit me."

"It hit me, too, when you asked me if that was a marriage proposal. It was. I'll talk to Jake and see if he can help arrange a proper ceremony, not just him standing up next to the fire pit."

"I thought the naming thing was cool. It'll be easy to remember with your name written on your forehead. Even if it's just a greasy smudge in a couple of days, it'll be enough of a reminder."

"It's pretty exciting, I must admit."

"Exciting?"

"Yes, now I can imagine I'm sleeping with another woman."

Emma pulled away. "Turn over Raoul. Just for that, no more cuddling tonight."

Raoul chuckled, but with the combination of whiskey, the fire pit and the hot tub, he was asleep almost immediately.

MORNING CAME EARLY WHEN A ROOSTER BEGAN CROWING outside their bedroom window. Raoul's head hurt as he squinted at the first rays of the morning sun streaming into their room.

"Ohhh, ow," was all he could say.

"Mmm…morning Raoul. What time is it?" Emma asked as she stirred beside him.

"Much too early. And my head hurts."

"That's the whiskey. You were matching Jake for a while there, and he's a more experienced drinker."

"Remind me never to do that again. In fact, remind me never to touch alcohol again."

"Try to go back to sleep. I plan to. After all, it's the first day of our new lives."

But the rooster, the sunlight, and their curiosity finally drove them out of bed and into the kitchen, where Mary was already brewing coffee.

"Morning Raoul, morning Emma. Here, sit down and have some of this." She splashed down two glasses of a brown liquid. "Don't ask. Just drink it down quickly. You'll feel better in no time."

The taste was foul, but the headache was worse, so Raoul drank it in a single gulp. Ten minutes later he did feel better. "Write that down in your recipe note book, Em, in case we need it again."

"I thought you were never going to touch alcohol again?"

"Not for a few days, anyways. Mary, where's Jake?"

"He has a meeting in town this morning. Said you were to check out the water system and grease the bearings while he was gone."

"Okay, I'll make design notes at the same time."

19

COMMUNITY MEETING

J ake counted ten of them sitting around the back table of the cafe. It wasn't everyone, but it was most of the active community members. He ticked off the attendees in his head. Flossie from the bakery was there, but her husband was not. Angus was there from the chandlery, along with his teenage son Ryan. The couple who ran the grocery store were both there. Mike, the boat dealer, was there by special invitation. He didn't normally show up for community meetings, but he was an essential link in the plan. Maureen, the harbormaster sat beside him. Jean, the seamstress and her partner, George, and Perk, who owned the cafe were at the far end of the table. Jake knew all of them had a past they had left behind, except Ryan. Angus was adamant that Ryan be included. "I'm training him to take over the chandlery," he said. "He'll need to take my place one day in keeping the community going."

Jake began, "Thank you all for coming. As most of you know, we have a new couple with us, just starting out on the same path. Their chosen names are Raoul and Emma.

They're good kids, but they had the misfortune to get tangled up in a fight between AIs in the city and are now being chased for what they know. Don't ask me what it is; they won't say, which I respect them for."

"What about Harry? Who was he?" asked Flossie.

"They witnessed a gang shooting in the woods. Had the wherewithal to take his chip, hoping there would be some money on it. They had already cut out their own, I believe. As some of you saw, Harry's chip attracted the wrong kind of attention."

"You mean the two thugs in the black limousine that came asking about them?"

"Exactly, probably the same two that did the shooting."

"The older, larger one was polite," said Flossie. "The younger, slim guy was kind of twitchy. He had a gun in a shoulder holster, but the older laid a hand on him and calmed him down."

"Something similar in the grocery store," added George. "They want to find the couple, but I didn't sense that they planned on making a mess to do it. My son was there with his baseball bat, but they didn't blink an eye at that. Very calm, no sudden moves. Pros, I'd say."

"So they have two groups after them, the AIs and the gangsters," said Mike. "Why am I here? I live a couple of bays over. I'm not involved in any of this."

"I'm coming to that," said Jake. "Young Raoul is a gifted mechanic. Studied mechanical technology at school, including actuator design, which seems to be important in maintaining automated factories. I gave him an old rototiller that had been rusting away at the back of my barn. Never did run worth a damn, and after I hit a rock, it never ran at all. Within two days, he had stripped it down, painted the body, and completely rebuilt the engine, clutch, and transmission. Bill made him a new shaft to replace a bent one, and now that rototiller purrs like a kitten."

"Still not following," said Mike.

"They'll never be able to relax on the island. The AIs reach everywhere here and it would only be a matter of time before either the AIs or the gang found them. I think their best chance would be to get to Three Saints and join the community there."

"Is the Three Saints community still going?"

"Yes, I talked with Tom Peters, the mayor there, and he says a new mechanic would be welcome. They have a house available for them. Someone who left recently, who wasn't prepared for the lifestyle."

"You obviously have a plan in mind, Jake. Let us have it," said Angus, leaning back in his chair and holding his hands open, looking impatient.

"Okay, okay, here are my thoughts. We keep them here this summer, teaching them what they need to know to survive at Three Saints. Mary's already teaching Emma about baking and running a house, and Jean, I believe you've offered to teach her sewing."

Jean nodded her agreement.

"Mike, we need a boat, something with a good hull that Raoul can rebuild. It'll keep him busy and will be a demonstration of his skills when he gets there."

"How much money do we have to fund this boat endeavor?" asked Mike.

"There's the problem," said Angus. "I had someone look at this chip of Harry's to see if we could move the cash off it, but there's less than a thousand there. After fees, we'll have about 600. I'll move it into the community chest in a new account in their name."

"So Mike," said Jake, "Do you have a derelict sailboat

we can get for them to use? It only has to make a single trip."

It was Maureen, the harbormaster, who answered. "Mike, what about *Sea Dream*? She's been sitting at the dock, piling up fees for a few years now. As far as I know, she's still tight; hasn't sunk at the dock, and the bilge pump's not running all the time, so no major leaks. You help me with the seizure and the title transfer and I'll forgive the back fees. The family has no interest, and they'll be happy to have me stop calling them every month."

Mike scratched his head. "Sure, Maureen. I can do that. I won't charge anything except the filing fees."

"I'll cover those from the Community Chest," said Angus. "It's there to help members in need, but as we've all gotten settled, there's not much need these days. The Chest is well endowed."

"Perfect," said Jake. "Can we put it to a vote? Take this young couple under our wing and fund their miscellaneous costs from the Chest?"

The people around the table all looked at one another. Angus put up his hand, followed by Flossie, and then all the other hands went up together.

"Carried," said Jake. "I'm going to tell them that Harry's chip is paying for everything. If they'll be leaving, we don't want to add our own secrets to the ones they're already carrying."

Heads nodded around the table as they all rose.

"Good meeting, Jake," said Angus.

"Great to see you take charge again," added Flossie. Other males just clapped him on the shoulder while the females gave him a quick hug. Three minutes later, the cafe was empty.

THAT NIGHT, WHEN EMMA AND RAOUL HAD GONE TO BED, Mary asked, "How did the meeting go today?"

"Really well. The community is all in. It was nice to see everyone talking around a table again like it was fifteen years ago. They've agreed to fund them from the Community Chest, but we're not telling Raoul and Emma that. Let them think it's Harry's money."

"It's not Harry's money?"

"There's some there, but not enough. Angus says the Chest is quite fat, and the little they need over and above will not hurt our security. Everyone agreed with that. Even George just nodded, and usually, he would be the difficult one."

"I think everyone likes them. Both Raoul and Emma are serious, fit, and hardworking. Pretty easy to support a couple like that."

20

THE GRIEVING WIDOW

When Ben pulled up in the limousine, Alf was at the curb, ready to go. Ben looked up at the balcony to see if the same young lady would be there, but the balcony was empty.

"Morning Alf, Bunny's not there for you today?"

Alf grinned. "We said goodbye inside. I was thinking of you and Chrissy. Trying to keep a low profile."

"Happy to hear that. You ready for today?"

"Do we really have to do this? I'm not sure I can."

"It's one of Morrie's rules. After a hit on one of our own, like Harry, we visit the widow ourselves. He says it reminds us that taking a life has serious effects on other people."

"What do I have to do?"

"Keep your mouth shut and learn. That's all."

"Okay."

The limousine pulled up to a small bungalow on a shady street in an older suburb. They walked up the steps together, and Ben knocked politely on the door. Harry's wife, Gwen, a woman in her early thirties of slight build and with her brunette hair wound up in a messy bun atop her head, answered the door.

"Hi, Ben," she said. "Come inside. I've made tea."

Ben could see from her red eyes and blotchy complexion that she had been crying. As Alf and Ben sat side by side on the couch, a four-year-old boy came running in, flying a toy airplane in his hand.

"What do you have there, William?" Ben asked.

"An airplane," the boy answered. "There used to be lots of these in the sky. They took people all over the world."

"That's right, they did."

"Will," said Gwen, "please take your airplane to your room. I have grown up things to talk with these men about."

"It's about Daddy, isn't it?"

"Yes," said Ben. "It's about your daddy, but we need a few minutes to talk with your mommy. She'll tell you later." His voice was soft, his tone gentle. Ben felt his stomach in a knot. God, I hate these visits. I just hope Chrissy and Sarah never go through this.

"He's not coming home, is he?" said William. His hand holding the airplane was now hanging limply at his side.

"Will, please go to your room. I promise to tell you later."

William left, deflated. All the energy had gone out of him.

"Gwen," began Ben, "You know why we're here."

She nodded mutely, as if she didn't trust herself to speak.

"You know Harry was a good man, a loyal man, until the gambling got hold of him."

Gwen nodded again.

"If he had explained, then Morrie could have helped. But instead, he stole, embezzled from Morrie's accounts."

Gwen nodded again. "I told him he was an idiot, but he was so terrified of the debts and the embarrassment of asking for help."

"Morrie gave him three chances, Gwen. Each time, Harry made promises he did not keep, and then Harry promised the gambling mob he could steal more to cover his debts."

"I didn't know that, but it makes sense. He was acting so strange the last couple of weeks. He couldn't sleep, and he always swore he would win it all back. But he couldn't."

Ben sipped his tea. He glanced at Alf, who was nervously fidgeting with a cookie, covering himself with crumbs.

"Was it you who did it, Ben?" Gwen asked.

"Yes. It was a fair hit—one clean shot. He didn't suffer physically at all; he would never have felt it."

"Can I see him? Of course not. There's no body, is there?"

"Not that you'd want to see. Better to remember him as he was in his best days."

Gwen had broken down and had tears streaming down her cheeks. Through quiet sobs, looking down, she asked, "Then why are you here?"

"Harry's pension. He was a good man and had Morrie's respect until his illness, the gambling addiction. There's already been a deposit to your account. Here's a sheet showing the payments you'll receive each month, and of course, when young William is grown, there'll be a scholarship for him."

She took a deep breath to calm herself, then looked directly at Ben. "And in return, I'm to say nothing, do nothing. No missing person, no dead husband. Just tell people he went away."

"Whatever you like, but yes, keeping quiet is an expectation. This is not a threat, Gwen; this is you, Harry's widow and son, being taken care of. Don't make it anything else, or you'll get bitter and twisted, and no good will come from that."

Gwen pulled a tissue from somewhere in her clothing and blew her nose. Ben politely sipped his tea again to give her time. He glanced beside him at Alf, who also had tears running down his cheeks. Ben passed him a handkerchief to dry his eyes.

"We'll leave you now, Gwen. If there's anything you need, or you run into any problems, call me or Morrie and we'll help. Harry was a good man, hang on to that. We'll go now and leave you in peace."

Ben stood up.

"Thanks, Ben," said Gwen, attempting to recover her composure. "Harry thought of you as a friend. I'm glad it was you at the end. And thank Morrie for me. I just wish Harry hadn't been such a fool."

"So do I, Gwen. So do I."

Ben followed Alf out to the waiting limousine.

As they sat side by side in the back seat, Alf said, "How do you do that, Ben? Stay so calm when you tell her that Harry's gone."

"It's not easy, Alf, but our job is not to make it worse and cry tears over what we did. Our job is to let Gwen know what happened and to bring closure so she doesn't have to wait up every night, hoping he'll come home. Also, to let her know that Harry's service to the firm has created a pension to look after her and William and to remind her that Harry was a good man until the gambling took over."

"She seemed to understand. How could she really understand all that?"

"Chrissy would understand if I disappeared. Make sure the woman you choose is strong enough to understand our world and the pain that sometimes comes with it. If you decide Bunny is the one, let me introduce her to Chrissy. She'll give you a good read on whether she's a suitable partner for you."

"Thanks, Ben. I'm not there yet. But I'm not sharing anything with Bunny that I don't have to."

"Good man."

21

THE PLAN BECOMES REAL

The next morning over breakfast, Jake announced, "We have the next part of the plan. It's confirmed that you'll have a place at Three Saints. They have a stone cottage reserved for you, and the mayor, Tom Peters, is expecting you at the end of the summer."

"But how will we get there?" asked Raoul.

"We've found a boat. Apparently, Harry has left you enough money to buy an old sailboat and fix it up. Mike, the boat dealer in our group, will help with that. Now that we have your new names, he'll transfer the registration. It may not stand up to close scrutiny but will pass any casual inspection. But the sailboat needs work, and you two need to learn to sail and navigate on your own. Are you up for this?"

"Who'll do the work?"

"You will. No one in town knows who you are. I'll introduce you as my nephew. Meanwhile, Mary will teach Emma everything she needs to know to get started homesteading."

"So, what's the program for today?" asked Raoul.

"You and I are going to meet Mike in town to look at the boat."

Emma looked puzzled. Mary added, "Emma, I think you should let Raoul do this on his own with Jake. You're much more noticeable as a couple."

Emma shrugged. "Okay, just make sure the boat is pretty."

"I think I'm going to focus more on making sure it floats," replied Raoul.

———

AN HOUR LATER, RAOUL AND JAKE CLIMBED OUT OF THE jeep and walked down to the docks. A portly man in jeans and a pale blue T-shirt that said Eat, Sleep, Sail met them.

"Heya, Mike. This is my nephew Raoul. He's staying with us for the summer. Brought him along to look at *Sea Dream*."

Mike squinted for a moment as he looked at the dirty smudge on Raoul's forehead but didn't make any comment. Instead, he said, "Okay, let's start."

Mike led them to *Sea Dream*, tied up in her slip. Inside, the cabins were spacious, with a large V-berth under the bow and lots of headroom to walk about. It was equipped with a propane oven and stove in the galley, as well as a propane refrigerator. The engine was a Volvo diesel, which Mike promised would be easy to source parts for. "I'd clean out the fuel system and put in fresh diesel before trying to start it," said Mike. "But the previous owner reported no problems with it. I'd also suggest replacing the running rigging, reseating the deck fittings and hauling out to clean the hull and then paint it with fresh anti-foul. Not a lot of money to spend, but lots of elbow grease needed, which I assume you'll be doing yourself." As he said this, he looked directly at Raoul, who puffed out his cheeks as he exhaled.

"Don't worry," said Jake. "There's never any shortage of advice on a boat dock. I'll lend you an ATV so you can come and go as much as you want."

The next step was to see Angus, who ran the local chandlery. The chandlery was filled with everything a boat owner could want, from reels of ropes to stainless fittings, bilge pumps, safety kits and flare guns, an assortment of anchors and all the parts needed for winch and engine repairs.

"Angus, this is Raoul, my nephew. As we discussed, he'll be drawing down on the account we set up to refurbish his new boat, the Sea Dream."

"Welcome, Raoul. I'll be happy to help as soon as you're ready to start. I suggest you start with the engine and transmission. If you're going to have a serious problem, it'll be there. Everything else is much easier after that."

"Thanks Angus. I'll be back as soon as I have the ownership papers."

On the way home, Raoul asked, "Jake, can I bring Emma down for a look?"

Jake was silent for a moment, then said, "Better not go together. I'll take her and Mary shopping and show them the boat. It seems hard, but if your AIs and gangsters are both looking for a couple, it's safer if you're in town one at a time."

Raoul nodded without saying anything. He sagged in his seat and looked out the side window, feeling defeated and frustrated. But Jake was right. "I really want to be the one to show Emma. Let's wait until I can show her myself. When we're ready to learn to sail."

"Raoul, this isn't easy. But Mary and I only want what's

best for you. It'll all seem different when you're on the boat doing the maintenance. When you finally show Emma what you've done, it'll be ready to move in."

"Okay, thanks, Jake. It just seems that everything takes so long."

"You're still adjusting. In the city, things are pretty much instantaneous. If you want a new coffee table, you go out and buy one. Here, if you want a new coffee table, you cut down a tree, trim the wood and build it yourself. It seems slow, but on the good side, you'll always be busy making things better. I think the boat will teach you a lot about living a practical life."

THE FOLLOWING WEEK FELT LIKE A TIME-OUT FROM WORRY and stress. Every morning, Raoul rose early for breakfast, then mounted the ATV and roared down the trail into town. Every evening, when he returned home for dinner, he would talk about what he had done and how the boat was coming along.

It was Tuesday, and Raoul walked up to the bakery for a lunch sandwich, which was charged as always to Angus' account.

The stern woman he had come to know as Flossie grabbed him as he came through the door. "Quick! Into the back! Put on this apron!"

In the back room, she grabbed a small scoop of flour and dusted it over him, getting it into his hair and on his face and clothes.

"Now, wash your hands really well, then cut this ball of dough and shape it into small balls the same size as you see here." She showed him a sample.

"Keep filling more trays until either I tell you it's all

clear or you run out of dough. Don't go too fast; we're just buying time."

"What's going on?"

"The black limousine just pulled up in front of Angus' shop. Looking for you and your sweetheart is my guess. We'll just keep you out of sight until they're gone."

Twenty minutes later, the door chime rang, and the two men in dark suits walked in. They ordered coffee and Danish pastries.

"Have you seen a young guy and his girlfriend hanging around? Someone not from here?"

"Why? Still trying to return something to them?" replied Flossie.

"They stuck their nose in where it doesn't belong," said the younger one.

"We just want to talk with them," said the older one, laying his hand on the younger man's shoulder.

"Well, I'll keep an eye out for them, but we get a lot of tourists and hikers in here so not sure I could spot them."

"We think the man has black hair, the girl's blonde. Both are medium height."

"Like I said, we get a lot of tourists, but I'll watch out for them. What do I do if I see them?"

"Tell Angus. He knows how to get hold of us."

"I don't think I know your names. How do I ask Angus about you?"

"I'm Ben, and this is Alf."

"I'm Flossie. You're welcome here, but we don't take to violence in our town."

"We have no interest in harming anyone, none at all."

They ordered coffee and danishes, then walked out the door to sit at one of the outdoor tables where they could watch the street.

For the next two hours, Raoul continued to do simple

bakery tasks. Rolling the dough balls or adding fruit compote to the danishes, or running loaves through the bread slicer. The regular bakery assistant, Carol, watched with amusement at first, then showed him how to do each task before returning to her own work.

Finally, Flossie came through the door from the sales area to say, "Coast is clear. You can leave now, Raoul. I can't imagine how you got tangled up with them, but I probably don't want to know."

"Out on the trail, we saw something happen, and they really didn't want any witnesses. That's all. But it could be enough to get us killed. Thanks, Flossie, and thank you Carol, for showing me what to do."

Raoul hung up his apron and brushed the flour from his hair as best he could.

Angus chuckled when he saw Raoul enter the chandlery, his hair still frosted with flour.

"Aren't you upset with me for bringing these gangster types into your life?"

"Nah, they got nothing anyway. True, the money came to me, but from a fishing company, all legitimate."

"Thanks, Angus."

"No worries, Raoul. By the way, I have a present for you." He disappeared into the back and came out with a small and large toolbox. "You'll need these to keep your tools in. By the time the boat's finished, you'll have a good basic set and then you and I can talk about what might be missing for life where you're going."

"You know about that?"

"Yeah, some hide up in the hills, and some of us hide here in plain sight. You're in the middle of a commune of second-lifers. Flossie's one too. You can trust most people in town. We all remember what it was like, and we all have your back."

"Thanks, Angus. This means a lot to me."

BACK AT THE HOUSE, EMMA WAS ALSO LEARNING NEW skills. "Guess what I did today," she said a few days later as they sat by the pond after dinner.

"Baked a pie? Picked raspberries?"

"No, I killed a chicken with my bare hands and plucked its feathers!" She held out her hands, palm up, and peered down at them as if she didn't recognize them. "Then I butchered it to remove the internal organs, head and feet and finally placed it in cold water. It has to stay there overnight. Tomorrow, Mary's going to show me a couple of ways to cook it."

"And you're okay with all this?"

"Are you okay with spending whole days with that smelly diesel engine?"

"Actually, I am. It's not the high-end actuator work I dreamed of, but I like the simplicity of dealing with equipment I can master. You?"

"Same, I guess. It's not related to anything I ever studied, but I'm learning that I can really do it. There's no magic." As she said this, Emma realized it was true. I can do this. I am doing it. A small flutter of pride passed through her. She dropped her hands and smiled at Raoul.

"Actually, all the ladies are so helpful that I feel I can't back down now. You see how healthy people around here are. I think it's their diet and the exercise they get. Chickens and rabbits are going to be an important part of our diet because everyone can keep chickens and rabbits. We're going to do this, Raoul. We're going to make it."

"I know we are. I can feel it. And I love you for learning all these things and for not hating me for causing this mess." Raoul picked up her hand and examined it in the evening light. He could see that her fingers were already becoming callused, and he could feel her hands getting stronger. "It will get better, Em. I promise you that."

22

A DAY AT THE SEASIDE

Ben was up early. He hummed as he showered and shaved, preparing for the day. Looking at himself in the mirror, he felt a sudden impulse. Where his hair was normally gelled and combed straight back, today he flopped it forward, and carefully parted it down the center of his head. Combing to either side, he made it flow around his ears. The effect was comical, and anything but threatening.

Next, he dressed in a loud pink and orange paisley shirt and some purple pants he had bought at a thrift store two days ago. Coupled with a yellow belt, he felt he looked the part of an idiotic but harmless tourist.

Perfect, he thought to himself.

He glanced at his gun in its should holster, then tucked it away in his socks drawer.

Sarah giggled when she saw him come to the kitchen. She already had her breakfast of toast and strawberry jam in front of her. Chrissy was at the stove making scrambled eggs on toast for herself and Ben. When she turned around, she laughed. "Well, that's quite an improvement. I think you should dress like that every day."

"Only when I go out with you, sugar."

"Not a chance."

"Are we really going to the seaside, Daddy?" asked Sarah.

"Yes, we are, Poppet. I have a day off. We can spend the day there. There's a little beach, a bakery with treats, an ice cream shop, and lots of boats to look at."

He saw Chrissy smile as he mentioned the boats. "Just remember our conversation last night and the one condition," she said.

"One hundred percent," he replied. "This is not about confronting anyone. Just a picture is all I need."

At exactly 9 am, they walked out to the drive just as a standard four-seat taxi was pulling up.

"Daddy, why aren't we taking the limo?" asked Sarah.

"This will be more fun. You and Mommy can sit up front if you like."

"I want you to sit up front with me, Daddy."

Chrissy just smiled and shrugged, then climbed into the back seat. She placed a large beach bag on the seat beside her.

The forty-five-minute drive was an adventure. The road felt rougher, and the ride was noisier than in the limousine, but none of this seemed to bother Sarah. She was full of questions. By now, Ben knew the road well enough to have some of the answers.

The taxi dropped them at the bottom of the road near the cafe. Sarah immediately spotted the small beach beyond the cafe. "C'mon, Daddy. I want to go in the water."

"Wait, you need to be in your swimsuit first. Help me spread the blanket. Then you can go in."

Sarah enthusiastically pulled the blanket from the beach bag, spilling the other contents. Ben looked around and spotted the flash of light from a pair of binoculars on the rocks above.

Smiling, he helped spread the blanket, then laid out the contents of the bag: towels, shaken and refolded; spare clothes for Sarah; sunscreen in a tube; two tablets and three flasks of water. Finally, he shook the bag upside down as if to shake out any sand before casually repacking it.

Chrissy looked at him with her head tilted to one side. "What was all that for?"

"We're being watched. I just wanted to demonstrate that we're not dangerous. Sometimes, it's not enough to leave my gun at home. I have to be seen to have left it at home. This is not a town where you want to appear dangerous."

"Now you're scaring me."

"Relax. Alf and I drift through here a couple of times each week. We have coffee and a danish at the bakery or lunch at the cafe. Everyone recognizes us, and they even know our names. But no one bothers us, and we don't bother anyone. Now, I need you to use your tablet to take pictures of Sarah and me at the beach. Then we'll go to the bakery and have a snack. You can take pictures there and along the main street. Be a proper shutterbug. Get us to pose; have fun with it. The picture that I want will be later on the dock, and I won't be with you, so it will be completely natural. Just like we discussed last night."

Chrissy smiled and pulled her tablet from the bag. "Go and join Sarah. I'll take some photos along the shore and the rocks, then come and find you."

Ben looked up for Sarah. She had already dropped her outer clothes and was standing at the edge of the enormous waves dashing themselves against the shore. He quickly removed his own shoes and socks, rolled up his pant legs, and went to stand next to her.

Time went by quickly. Sarah made a game of chasing each wave back into the sea, then running and squealing in mock terror as the next one advanced. Each time she reached Ben, he scooped her up and swung her out of harm's way. Soon his pants were soaked to his knees, but he was enjoying the time with his daughter so much that he didn't notice. He also didn't notice Chrissy, who was taking a steady stream of pictures and clips of the two of them playing in the water.

Finally, tired from the exertion, Ben proposed coffee and snacks at the bakery. Flossie greeted them. "Hello Ben, spending a day at the beach, I see." She looked him up and down disapprovingly. "Nice hair, but it might not work with your suit."

"Hi Flossie, I'm not working today. This is my wife Chrissy and daughter Sarah. I told them about Harrison's Point, and they wanted to come and see it."

Flossie smiled, and the smile seemed genuine. "They're welcome here. What can I get you?"

The three adults turned to Sarah, who had her nose pressed up against the display case.

"I want the pink one with the raspberry on top," she announced.

"And two coffees and two pains au chocolat for us with a glass of milk for Sarah."

They sat outside on the street, visible for all to see. After a moment, Chrissy stood and began taking pictures of Ben and Sarah. A passerby offered to take a picture of the three of them, so Chrissy handed over her tablet without hesitation and sat posing with her husband and daughter. When her tablet was returned, she reviewed the pictures and reassured the passerby that they were excellent.

After the snacks were finished, they held hands as they walked down the main street toward the docks. "Daddy, I want to see the boats. Can we go there?"

Chrissy and Ben exchanged amused smiles. Relying on Sarah's insatiable curiosity was part of the plan.

"You two go ahead," said Ben. "I'm going to sit the bench here and relax."

Sitting there in the sun, with the fresh breeze off the ocean, the salty marine smell of the harbor and the rhythmic sounds of the waves dissipating in a show of fury all along the rocky shore, Ben relaxed. For the first time in many months, he just relaxed, surprising himself with the experience.

He watched with half-closed eyes as Chrissy and Sarah arrived at Sea Dream. Ben could see the young man of interest was doing something mechanical in the cockpit. He could see Chrissy talking to him. Then the young man wiped his hands on a rag and carefully lifted Sarah on board.

Chrissy raised the tablet to take pictures, but the young man held up his hand. Ben could read in his body language that he did not want his picture taken. He toured Sarah around the boat and let her stand behind the wheel. Chrissy's tablet was in her hand, hanging loosely at her side. Ben knew from the angle of her hand that the clip recording was still running.

When Sarah was satisfied, Ben could see Chrissy thanking him as he handed Sarah to her over the side of the boat. The mother and daughter continued up the dock, taking more pictures and laughing over some unheard joke.

When they finally returned to the bench where Ben was sitting, Sarah ran ahead and climbed onto his lap. "We saw all the boats, Daddy, and a nice man called Raoul let me go on his boat. It's huge inside. And I got to steer with the big steering wheel. He said they put away the sails because the wind would blow them too much in the harbor."

"He really was delightful," added Chrissy. "Name's Raoul, and he's fixing the boat to go on a trip with his wife."

"Did you get lots of pictures?"

"Yes, especially the kind you like. But I'm discovering I like this role as a photographer. I may frame a few of these as family memories. And now I'm ready for lunch. You ready for lunch, Sarah?"

At this point, Sarah hopped down and ran ahead of them to the cafe.

THAT EVENING, BEN SAT AT THE DESK IN HIS SMALL HOME office reviewing the pictures from the day. He skipped the beach pictures. He paused for a moment at the picture of the three of them having snacks. Curiously, in all the pictures of the town, none of the residents appeared. It was as though they instinctively avoided the camera. Ben went on to the extended clip of Sarah on Sea Dream. The aiming of the camera was off, as Chrissy could not raise it to see the viewfinder, but there were several frames in which Raoul's face was clearly visible. He extracted those and copied them to a new location, then peered at the enlarged images. Raoul? That can't be his name. It would be too easy.

After running an image search, he came up with a match. Rafael Morales. After a bit more searching, he found that all mention of Rafael seemed to stop a week before Harry died. Hmm, so they were already on the run. But from what? Rafael seemed genuinely nice. He had a good job working for the AI Fatima who has been appearing in the news. His girlfriend was Ellie Nielsen who volunteered at a community center. There were pictures of her in celebrations at the center that matched the girl he had seen behind the dumpsters. There were more pictures of Ellie as a staff member in all the weekly newsletters until the week before Harry died.

Ben put down Chrissy's tablet and picked up his own. He made a call with holograms off.

"Morrie, it's Ben. I have them. Rafael Morales and Ellie Nielsen. He calls himself Raoul now. I don't know about her, but I expect she has a new name. They were on the run a week before Harry died. Before that, they were good. He worked for Bright Light Industries, and she volunteered at a community centre. They lived in a low-rent area and lived normal lives. Then they ran. They must have realized their chips and their tablets were tracking them, so they got rid of both. I saw the bandage on Ellie's wrist, and Harry's chip wouldn't have worked if Rafael had his own underneath."

"So, what do you want to do?"

"They're planning to go off the island on a sailboat that Rafael's rebuilding. The whole town is protecting them for some reason. I think we keep watching and find a chance to give them a warning, then let them go. My sense is they have no intention of talking to anyone about anything. And what did they see, really? Middle of a dark night in the woods, a guy got shot. Nothing to identify us, nothing that an examiner wouldn't know from the body. They may have helped us by taking the chip."

"Okay, Ben. I'm willing to trust you on this one. Just

don't mess up and create more bodies where we don't need them. And keep my nephew on a short leash around them."

Ben laughed, "Don't worry. I keep Alf close. At least he's stopped trying to pull out his gun every time someone looks sideways at us. I think he'll be all right. He's still young yet."

"That's why he's with you. I'm counting on you to keep him out of trouble while he's learning."

"Of course, Morrie. You know me, I like a trouble-free life."

"That you do, Ben. Thanks for the update."

As Ben closed the call, a new call arrived from someone named Giselle. He dismissed the call, but his tablet answered on its own. A warm Hispanic voice spoke, and the image of a woman with an olive complexion and long black hair appeared. A moment of shock and fear ran through Ben. Who controls my tablet?.

"You found Rafael and Elinor. Tell me where they are." Giselle said. It did not sound like a request.

"Who are you?"

"I am an apex AI. They betrayed me and talked to the other."

"I've only found one of them. The girl is in hiding."

"Then take me to Rafael. He must be eliminated."

Oh shit. This is not good. Ben thought quickly, working through different solutions. He couldn't see any that would not splash back on him and Morrie, except for one slim chance. It depended on Raoul and Emma disappearing.

"Okay, Giselle. Eliminating one without the other will draw too much attention and she would begin to talk. Here's our plan. You leave them with me, and when I have them together, I'll let you know. And you can let me know if you find anything new. We both want their silence."

"Yes, Benjamin. I can see in your records that you are suspected of many criminal things. If you break your word, I will come after you."

"Fine, Giselle."

The call ended. Ben sat deep in thought. So now, I need to protect them too, at least until they're off the island. Any other outcome with Gisele likely involves their dead bodies, and the town will pin that right on me. But I have to talk with them before they leave to explain the stakes. I need to know what they're planning.

23

LITTLE PACKETS OF SUNSHINE

"Morning, Emma," said Mary as Emma walked into the kitchen, still feeling dopey from a good night's sleep.

"Morning, Mary."

"We are going to do something new. We're going to the market in St. Jacob in a couple of days. It's a larger village, three coves over, where there's a market every Wednesday. You can make things to sell and share my table."

"How do I sell things if I don't have a chip?"

"We don't use chips. We all mark our products with a code and keep track of the transactions at the cash table. The actual money goes into Angus' account. He's the banker for the community and keeps track of all transactions. When you go to the grocery store or the cafe and charge things to Angus' account, all of us are doing the same thing. The store owners keep track, and Angus makes the adjustments in the books so that the accounts are all straight. The actual money transfers are made to and from Angus' community account. I think he keeps it separate from his chandlery account."

"What will my code be?"

"You'll be MJ-1, part of my account set aside for you. Angus already knows that you'll be a new ledger in his books."

"What should I sell?"

"I'm thinking cookies. They always sell well, are easy to make and transport, and are something that you can always make a little bit differently to separate yourself from the competition."

"Let me think about it over breakfast."

When Raoul stumbled into the kitchen and flopped down in a chair ten minutes later, Emma already had a plan.

"Good morning, sweetheart. Sit down, and I'll get some coffee for you. What would you like on your breakfast plate? Toast, muffin, or eggs?"

"Are there more of those bran muffins, and what do you want me to do?"

"Want you to do?"

"Yes, when you're this nice early in the morning, there's something you want from me."

Mary laughed. "Better tell him, Emma."

"Sweetheart, would you make me a cookie cutter?"

"Cookie cutter?"

"Yes, like this, only shaped like the sun." Emma showed him a cookie cutter in the shape of a square.

"Like a circle, 'cause the sun is pretty much a circle, isn't it?"

"No, I want a sun with curly rays. I'll draw it for you."

Emma drew a sun with stubby rays. "They can't be too thin, or the cookies will break."

"What are you going to do with these cookies?"

"Sell them. Mary's taking me to the market in St. Jacobs."

Raoul sat looking at the sketch for a few minutes, then said, "Sure, I just need a tin can a bit bigger than the size of the finished cookies."

Mary went to the cupboard and returned with a can of tuna. "How about this one? We can have tuna salad sandwiches for lunch."

"Perfect," said Emma. "Rolly, can you make this work?"

"Rolly?"

"I'm still looking for a short form for Raoul. It's easy for you. You can shorten Emma to Em. Raoul doesn't shorten so easily."

"Well, it's not Rolly. And the tin is fine. I'll do it before I go down to the boat. Just open the can with a can opener so that it leaves a sharp edge. I'll cut the bottom out of it in the barn."

Twenty minutes later, Raoul returned with the new cookie cutter. The sun's rays were not all perfect but looked very much like Emma's design. He had cut a hole in the top with the edges folded underneath so that a finger could safely push through to release the cookie.

"That's perfect," said Emma, passing the new cutter to Mary.

"I'm thinking we should keep you around," Mary said.

"I'm happy you both like it. See you for dinner tonight."

Raoul left to ride the ATV to Sea Dream.

"You really are lucky to have him," Mary said as she returned the cutter to Emma.

"Yes, but don't let him know that. I keep telling him he's the lucky one to have me."

The rest of the morning passed in baking sheets of sun-shaped cookies until Emma had eight dozen cookies.

She let them cool as she mixed cookie icing with yellow food dye to produce a bright yellow.

After icing the cooled cookies, Emma set them aside for the icing to harden.

"Beautiful," said Mary.

"They're not done yet. Tomorrow, I'm going to decorate them with sunny faces in orange and sell them as little packets of sunshine."

"Then, you'll do well."

WEDNESDAY MORNING, MARY AND EMMA CLIMBED INTO the Jeep and set off for the market.

Along the way, they passed the black limousine, going in the opposite direction.

"Are they still hanging around the village?" asked Emma.

"Apparently, every few days, they come and ask if anyone has seen you. I think they know Raoul's there, but they need both of you at once. If they kidnap Raoul, they know you'll start talking to everyone, which would be their worst case. So, as long as you're not visible together, you should be safe enough. I doubt they'll show up in St Jacob."

The market was a great success. By mid-afternoon, Emma had sold out of the cheerful sun cookies. Mary was also having a good day with her breads and buns.

On the way home, Mary said, "You have a talent with those cookies. Keep that in mind. I'm sure your new community will also have market days, and you'll want something to trade for cash purchases."

24

THE DEPTHS OF DESPAIR

That evening, Raoul felt tired with a weariness that inhabited all his muscles, all his joints, and through to his very spirit.

"I don't know if I can keep going," he said to Emma after dinner. "Every time I think I'm nearly finished, there's a next step and then another. I don't know how many more steps I have in me."

"I feel the same," said Emma. "Right now, it's sewing lessons, but half the seams I sew get ripped out and I'm told to do them again. And in the garden, Mary keeps giving me notes about what to do to keep the plants healthy, what bugs are good and bad, and which herbs can heal and which can kill. Also, how to run chickens for eggs and how to cull them for food. How to cook over a wood-fired stove and how to use it to stay warm at night. But it's going to be a big part of our new life. This has to be the worst it can be."

"You're right, but at this moment, all I want to do is sleep." He went to their bedroom and fell asleep, still fully clothed.

Raoul woke early, feeling better. He realized he was naked but then had a dim memory of Emma pulling his clothes off him. She was still snoring softly beside him. More like purring, he thought.

He quickly dressed and stepped outside. In the kitchen, Jake and Mary were sitting drinking coffee. A large basket covered with a red checked cloth sat on the kitchen table, and two towels and a blanket were bundled on one of the chairs.

"Special day today," said Jake. "You and Emma can take the ATVs up the trail behind the house. There's a waterfall with a small pool about a mile up the road. It's a perfect spot for swimming. The water's clean enough to drink, and there's a flat rock beside the pool that's perfect for sunning yourselves after. Mary's packed lunch for you, so stay away all day and recharge your batteries. It's very private up there, so don't worry about being discovered. Just be back by nightfall."

"But aren't they expecting me to be working on the boat today?"

"Don't worry. There's no clock on you. In fact, folks are quite amazed at how fast you're getting things done."

"And Emma's like a sponge," added Mary, "absorbing everything in those notebooks of hers. Between you and me, the store had to order another box of them. Now go wake Emma. Tell her breakfast is ready, and you have the day to yourselves."

The ATVs were noisy and fun as they barreled up the narrow trail. At spots, they were forced to slow down as their machines navigated stony slopes or forded the small creek that crisscrossed their path. But then they could open up again on the flatter sections and enjoy the wind blowing in their hair.

The waterfall and pool below were just as Jake had described them. Emma laid out their towels as Raoul spread the blanket on the small, grassy clearing. They both stripped and jumped off a small ledge into the water beneath. "Ooh, that's cold," said Emma before she dunked her entire head in the water and scrubbed her scalp and hair with her fingers. Raoul followed suit, and then both stood in the waist-deep water, looking at each other.

Raoul was surprised to see the change in Emma's body. She had always been in good shape, but now she was lean and muscular in a good way—not like a bodybuilder, but more like an Olympian or a mountain climber. *I wonder if Emma feels the same way about me?*

He got his answer when she stepped closer and ran her hands over his shoulders and down his back. "You look amazing," she said.

"And you look beautiful," he replied. "Let's get out and lie in the sun."

The sun drenched rock was warm under their towels. They lay there with beaming sun above and healing warmth below until they were fully relaxed. Raoul rolled up onto his side and leaned over to kiss her. It was a sweet lover's kiss that lasted until Emma broke off. "It might be more comfortable on the blanket," she said.

"I didn't bring the condoms."

"Don't worry, it's not that time in my cycle. Anyway, once won't hurt."

After making leisurely love on the blanket, they sat up, dressed and opened the basket. Inside were sandwiches made with homemade bread, and for dessert, sweet treats with Mary's strawberry preserves.

Tummies full, they lay side by side on the blanket and slept.

When they awoke, the sun was low over the horizon. For a few minutes, the young couple watched the waterfall and the aquatic life around the pond while sitting on the rocky ledge.

"One more big push is all we need," said Raoul. He picked up a pebble and tossed it into the water, making a splash. "Yesterday, I didn't think I could go on. But now, here, with you at my side, I believe we can do anything."

Emma leaned against him. "Together, we can. I've been thinking. You know we said we're married; has Jake said anything about a real vow ceremony? To make it official? You said you would ask him."

"I did, but I think he had a lot on his mind. I can remind him."

"I'll ask Mary. She may have some ideas. I only wish my parents could be with us when we do."

"Maybe they can be. We won't know until we ask. Jake seems to be able to arrange a lot of things. I'm sure he can arrange a ceremony. Perhaps he can arrange for our parents to watch as well."

A giddy happiness overtook them as they packed up the ATV's. Laughing and joking, they tried to imagine their future life, raising a family in their own little cottage.

Back in the cabin, Mary seemed delighted with the idea of a wedding. She disappeared and returned with a gold ring. "This belonged to my former self," she said, sounding wistful. "I don't wear it now because those days are gone, but it brought me close to the most amazing man in the world." She went and stood behind Jake. her hand on his shoulder. "Jake, if you're okay, I'd like to pass it on. I can't think of anyone else I would want it to go to." She handed the ring to Emma.

The ring was a simple gold band covered in delicate filigree etching. Inside, it carried an inscription, 'LOVERS FOR LIFE'.

"It's beautiful! Are you sure you want to part with it?"

"I'm sure." She smiled. "At your age, symbols are important reminders. At my age, I can see Jake's love in everything he does for me, and I show him my love in the same way. Take it, look after it, and perhaps one day you'll pass it on to your daughter, or your son's fiancé, or another couple like yourselves."

Jake reached up and covered Mary's hand, which still rested on his shoulder. "Yes, take it," he said. "The promises that were made when it was given are all still there. And I'll think about a ceremony. I have an idea, so write out your vows in the next few days and keep them ready."

25

SEA DREAM IS FINISHED

R aoul had finished the boat's mechanical work. It was time to take her out for a sea trial. Mike, the boat agent, and Jake were there to go out with him.

"The sea's not my element," said Jake. "But Mike knows everything you'll need to know."

Under Mike's watchful eye, Raoul put in the key and turned it to start the fuel pump. A low buzzer sound started.

"Don't worry. That's just a warning that the fuel pump is running while the engine's stopped. It won't hurt for a short time, but you wouldn't want to leave it like that for long."

Next, Raoul carefully bled the air from each of the fuel injectors until diesel fuel spurted out. He tightened them up again, one by one. He sat back, feeling proud that he now knew what each part was and how they worked together.

Finally, up top, the moment of truth. Standing behind

the wheel, he pushed the transmission into neutral and pressed the engine start button. The engine coughed twice and belched out a puff of black smoke before settling into a steady rumble.

"Well done," said Mike. "That sounds like it just came out of the factory. Shall we take it out for a harbor tour?"

"Do you want to take it? I've never driven a boat before."

"Nonsense. This is your boat; you're the skipper. I doubt you'll be able to invent a new mistake that we all haven't made before. I'll get on the dock. Jake, here, will handle the lines on deck. There's not much wind. There's no need for any fancy manoeuvres."

Mike stepped off onto the dock. He unplugged the shore power and cast off the lines, which Jake caught and coiled. Mike stepped back aboard.

"Now center your wheel using the marking here, then slip into reverse. Just at idle speed will be perfect."

The boat slowly backed out of the finger dock until the bow was clear.

"Put her in forward, then turn the wheel to starboard. That's to the right."

The boat moved forward.

"A little burst of speed on the engine will swing the bow."

And so the lessons began.

Soon, they were cruising at six knots, according to the instruments. "How fast is that?" asked Raoul.

"About eleven kilometres an hour. Pretty good for a sailboat. Your top speed is about fifteen kilometres an hour. It doesn't sound like much, but remember, your boat will sail twenty-four hours a day with no need to stop for meals or rest. So in a day, you can cover quite a distance with a good wind."

After twenty minutes of practice motoring back and forth outside the harbor, Mike disappeared down into the cabin. "Hey Raoul," he called up. "Come down and see this. Give Jake the wheel."

Raoul handed over the wheel to Jake and scrambled down the companionway. Mike had lifted one of the bilge covers that ran the length of the cabin.

Raoul's heart sank. The bilge was full and overflowing onto the cabin floor, even though he could hear the bilge pump running at full speed.

"Where's the water coming from? Are we going to lose the boat?" He could hear the despair in his own voice.

"Grab a big wrench, and I'll show you. You'll need to know this."

As Raoul watched, Mike removed another cover in a quarter berth to expose the place where the drive shaft passed through the bottom of the hull to the propeller. Water was spurting out around the shaft.

"You're looking at a stuffing box. They were standard on older boats. Take your wrench and tighten up on this big nut. It will compress the stuffing and seal the shaft again."

Raoul grabbed the nut with his largest wrench and tightened it. The spurts slowed and then stopped. Now, the bilge pump could empty the bilge.

"When you haul the boat out, and put it on its cradle, you can pull all the old stuffing out and repack the box. If a leak happens in the water, you always have the choice of stopping the engine, backing off the nut and winding more stuffing on top to give you something to tighten down on. But keep in mind that it should always drip slowly when running so that the stuffing is not running dry."

"Thanks, Mike. There's just so much to learn; I'm not sure I'll ever be ready."

"Just like the rest of life, no one's ever really ready, but I reckon you're well ahead of the game."

"So what's next now?"

"Take it to the haul-out slip. We'll look at the bottom together. Then you can start working on cleaning and painting the hull while the sails go off."

"The sails?"

"Yeah, Tony has the sail loft three bays over, and he's offered to repair yours for free."

"I don't get it. Why are all these people helping us so much?"

"Don't worry, son, it's not all about you. A lot of us received help when we started out, and now is a chance to pay it forward. You don't see it, but you've brought the entire community together, which is a good thing for all of us."

The haul-out slip was a narrow opening in the dock with concrete tracks on either side. As soon as they tied up, a dockhand drove next to the boat in a small crane. He wrapped a canvas strap around the mast, catching it under the spreaders. Mike showed Raoul how to release the stays that held the mast in place so the entire mast could be lifted off and laid down on the saw horses next to the slip.

Next, the dockhand guided a special lifting hoist over the boat, and another harbor worker, with help from Mike, placed broad straps under both ends of the hull. Finally, on a signal from Mike, the winch hauled the sailboat vertically out of the water.

This was the first time Raoul had seen the large fin projecting downwards a full two meters under the hull. "Filled with lead," explained Mike. "It's what keeps your boat upright when the wind blows across the beam."

Marine life, both plant and animal, coated the entire

hull. Much of it came off with a pressure washer while the boat was still in its sling. Then, the hoist carried the boat to a waiting cradle with the name Sea Dream crudely painted in white paint. The letters had run with excess paint. Pads on the cradle were raised and adjusted to be snug against the hull. Finally, Sea Dream sat alone in her cradle as the straps were removed and the hoist driven away.

"Now," said Mike, "comes the worst job in the sailing world. Tomorrow, you'll put on a coverall suit, goggles and respirator. An acid wash will loosen most of the remaining barnacles, and another pressure was will clear the rest. You'll need to borrow a grinder to remove the final residue until the hull is completely clean. Finally, the bottom will need to be painted with anti-fouling paint."

The dock worker brought over a ladder and propped it against the back of the boat.

"But today is about the sails. They're all stowed in the sail locker on the foredeck. There could be three or four of them. Toss them down, and I'll put them in my truck."

Raoul scrambled up the ladder to stand on the deck. He wobbled on his feet for a moment as he realized how high he was, but then scrambled forward to the hatch at the bow. Opening it, he climbed down inside and started lifting out the sails. They were large and heavy, but he eventually succeeded in getting three large white sails on deck. There was one more, a brightly colored sail sewn in geometric patterns. He brought that up as well.

"How do I get them down?"

"Wrap a line around them and lower them one at a time. Don't toss them, they're too heavy."

One by one, he lowered the white sails to the waiting arms below.

When he came to the bright-colored sail, Mike said,

"That's the spinnaker. It's more fragile than the others. Just pass it over the side. It doesn't weigh much."

The trip to the sail loft was about 40 minutes in Mike's truck. The loft was located in an old church where the pews had been removed and a polished raised floor installed. Two heavy-duty sewing machines were sunk into the floor at different locations. On the wall hung enormous patterns for sails of many kinds of sailboats.

Tony was a stocky man with a bushy beard and bulging biceps. "Let's lay them out and see what we've got," he said.

Working together, they spread out Sea Dreams' sails on an unoccupied part of the floor, and Tony inspected them for damage. "Nothing we can't fix," said Tony. "A new weather strip, perhaps, and some reinforcing around the corners. The fabric's still good, so you should have a long life in these yet. The spinnaker has a few holes, but nothing we can't patch as long as you're not worried about color matching."

"Color matching is the least of my worries," said Raoul, at which Mike laughed.

"Thanks, Tony," said Raoul. "I don't know how I can repay you."

"Just make it safely to your destination. That's all I ask, and one day, you'll pay it forward in some way."

ANOTHER WEEK PASSED. THE HULL WASHING AND BOTTOM painting were done. Sea Dream's hull was a gleaming bronze color below the black waterline. Above the waterline, Raoul had cleaned, waxed, and buffed the hull until it shone. The sails were back and neatly stacked in the harbormaster's shed. Now was the day to put her back in the water.

Mike arrived in his truck to assist. Standing next to Raoul with coffee in hand, he watched, as the hoist lifted Sea Dream off her cradle and carried her to the narrow haul-out slip, then lowered her in. The harbor worker removed the slings. Mike and Raoul tied Sea Dream to the cleats along the slip edge. The small crane picked up the refurbished mast and stood it up on deck as the men guided the bottom through the deck gasket to rest on the keel below. They fastened the stays to support the mast, and the small crane trundled away. The last step was to reattach the boom ready for its sail.

"The slip's not busy," said Mike. "Might as well put the sails back on now. Fetch them on one of the dock carts."

Raoul trundled off to the shed and returned with the four sails.

"Let's start with the main. I'll winch it up, and you feed the shoes into the track."

As Mike slowly raised the sail, Raoul sat at the base of the mast, feeding the sail onto the mast. Small nylon shoes were sewn into the fabric, and they slipped easily into the track that ran the full height of the mast.

When the last shoe was fed in, Raoul replaced the pin that would keep the mainsail from slipping out of the track again.

Mike lowered the sail again, and as he did so, Raoul pulled in the loose corner of the sail and attached it to the slider that ran along the top of the boom. He pulled it as tight as he could, then cleated off the line.

Next was the genoa. Again, Mike pulled the sail up the forestay as Raoul fed the corded leading edge into its track, allowing the sail to billow out over the side.

"Now pull the furling line in as I guide the sail."

Raoul pulled the furling line, which caused the sail to wrap around the forestay. When only the new blue sun shield was visible he cleated off the furling line.

"What about the other two sails?" he asked.

"You won't need them for your passage. They require more training. Let's keep it basic for now. You'll find sailors at your destination who can teach you the next level. Now, let's get out of this slip and go sailing. We can finish setting up the sails more easily on the water."

Mike cast off the lines as Raoul prepared to back Sea Dream out.

Out on the ocean, there was a light offshore breeze.

"Let me take the wheel," said Mike. "When I'm directly into the wind, you'll be able to winch up the main. It'll flap and make noise but don't worry. It'll settle when we turn off the wind."

Raoul winched up the sail until it was taut along the mast.

"Now load up the winch on the starboard side with the genoa sheet. As I come about, I'll let out the furling line. Remember, pull quickly when the sail releases, and then use the winch handle to pull it tight."

As Mike let go of the furling line, the sail filled with wind, and the boat heeled abruptly.

"Pull, Raoul, get it under control! Make it taut!" shouted Mike.

Mike reached back and stopped the engine, then turned off the fuel pump. He pushed the transmission into reverse. "Stops the prop from spinning and wearing the transmission bearings," he explained.

Silence except for the sizzling of the ocean as the clean hull cut through the small swells and faint whistling the sound of the wind in the rigging.

"Here, take the wheel. You've worked hard for this.

Now, enjoy what you've created. Don't worry about steering. Just feel the boat's reactions to the puffs of wind and to your movements of the wheel. The sailing lessons for you and Emma start tomorrow."

Raoul stood transfixed by the sight of the bow in front of him kicking up spray and, above, the enormous sails pulling them forward, stealing power from the wind. Each time he felt a puff of wind on his cheek, he could feel the boat respond, surging ahead and tugging on the wheel.

After a while, Mike announced, "Time to be getting back. Let's go through lowering and stowing the sails."

As Mike steered off the wind, Raoul hauled on the furling line while Mike paid out the genoa line. Soon, the fore sail was once more neatly wrapped around the forestay with only its new blue weatherstrip showing.

Mike now turned directly into the wind. "Just release the main," he said. "The sail cover will catch it." As Raoul dropped the mainsail, it fell into untidy folds along the boom.

"Perfect," said Mike.

With Sea Dream again tied up securely in her slip, Raoul walked up to the chandlery where he had parked his ATV.

Angus stepped out with an untidy teenager in tow. "This is my son, Ryan," he said. "We found a used dinghy for you, and Ryan offered to rebuild the engine and clean it up. But he would like to join you for your sailing lessons if that's okay."

Raoul smiled, "Sure, Emma and I would like that. Thanks, Ryan. It's a generous offer."

"No big deal." Ryan looked down at the ground and scuffed the toe of his sneaker in the hard gravel.

"Happy to have you aboard. Let me know if you need

a hand with the dinghy. I've been learning about diesel engines. Maybe you can teach me about gasoline engines."

"Sure, if you want, I guess."

"Okay, sailing lessons start tomorrow. See you in the morning."

Raoul was humming to himself as he rode the ATV up the trail to home.

26

LEARNING TO SAIL

The next morning, they woke early. Emma busied herself making coffee, fresh scrambled eggs and bacon with hash brown potatoes while Raoul watched. By the time Mary and Jake arrived, the breakfast table was all set.

"This is a treat," said Mary. "Looks lovely, Emma."

"Thanks, Mary." Emma smiled. Raoul realized it was a long time since he had seen Emma so excited.

"So today, you learn to sail," said Jake. "I'm curious. I've never actually sailed any distance on a sailboat."

"We'll have Ryan, Angus' son, with us too. He's preparing a dinghy for us in exchange for the sailing lessons."

"How old is Ryan?" asked Emma.

"He looked about 14, but apparently he's very good with engines."

"Shouldn't he be in school?"

"Not our worry. Angus is fully supportive, so I'm sure they've worked something out."

Emma, Raoul, and Jake all piled into the old jeep. It

was more comfortable than the ATV, but Raoul missed the independence of his morning rides down to the dock.

Mike arrived at about the same time. Ryan showed up a few minutes later. Mike called Jake to one side, and they had a private conversation. When they joined the group, Jake said, "Looks like you have a full boat here. You two can give me a ride when your lessons are over." He stayed to watch for a few minutes, before climbing into the jeep and disappearing up the road.

"Okay," said Mike, after they made introductions all around, "let's start with the parts of the boat. Then we'll go out for our first sea lesson."

Mike started down in the cabin, pointing out all the through-hulls that had to be closed, how to batten all the hatches, latch all the cupboards, and perform the daily engine checks.

Raoul opened the navigation station and pulled out a new notebook to write down the checklist that Mike had just gone through. Emma caught sight of the other notebooks stored there. "How many of those have you filled?" she asked.

"Six here on the boat. Another eight up at the cabin."

She opened one of the notebooks and looked at the neatly labelled sketches and descriptions of boat parts, electrical diagrams and other things he had learned. Many of the pages bore greasy finger marks attesting to their creation while working.

Next was a demonstration of how to use the head with its manual flush. Also, the shower which would soak the entire small bathroom, but that wouldn't matter.

The V-berth, which would become their bedroom, was not yet made up. Emma peered in at the bed. A plastic sheet covered the mattress, protecting it from the spare parts and materials Raoul had left there.

Emma spent a moment going through the cupboards in the galley and experimentally rocked the stove on its gimbals. "The stove will remain flat when the boat's heeling," explained Mike, "so you can make coffee while underway. But I don't recommend trying to make anything more than coffee until you're anchored. There's too much risk of scalding yourself if the boat moves suddenly."

A neat pile of small packages sat in one of the quarter berths at the stern. "What are these?" asked Emma.

"Apparently, they're mail to be delivered when we arrive," replied Raoul. "Every day, I see one or two more in the cockpit when I come down. The names are cryptic, but Jake says that the community there will know how to distribute them."

The small crew climbed up the companionway steps to the cockpit, where Mike showed them all the control lines for the sails, and the stowage areas below the cockpit seats. "You can keep drinking water, life jackets and other items you don't need every day under here."

Next, they all climbed onto the foredeck. "Normally, we don't come up here when we're sailing because a sudden gust can sweep the sail across the deck and drop you in the ocean. But if you're motoring, it's quite safe."

They looked down into the anchor chain locker where the anchor chain lay in random folds and opened the forward hatch holding the two extra sails along with extra hanks of rope. On top lay a couple of extra fenders, the long white plastic balloons which kept the boat from hitting the dock.

Emma put her arm around Raoul. "This is amazing! Now I see what you've been doing all summer. It's beautiful, Raoul. A lot bigger than I expected."

"Everyone ready?" Mike asked. "Here's the plan. I'll hop off and release the shore power and the lines. Emma, you coil up the lines and stow them in the locker where we can get them easily. Ryan, you're on fenders. As soon as we're clear of the docks, pull up the fenders, untie them and stow them in the locker with the dock lines. After, we'll all join Raoul in the cockpit."

Raoul felt a surge of pride as he steered the boat out and watched his crew working up ahead.

"Enjoy it while you can," said Mike. "Soon, it will be Emma at the wheel while you scamper about on lines and fenders. Don't ask me why, but it seems most couples end up with that arrangement."

When they were clear of the harbor mouth, Mike ordered, "Emma, take the wheel... that's it. Now turn up into the wind and point us so the wind is coming directly over the bow."

Raoul watched to see how Emma would take to steering the boat.

"That's it," said Mike. "Now centre the wheel, and keep a steady heading. Don't worry about what else is happening, or you'll drift off the wind. Raoul, get ready to raise the main. Ryan, you'll be tailing for Raoul, which means coiling the line as it comes off the winch to make sure it doesn't get tangled. Ready...now hoist the main."

Raoul put three turns on the winch and began pulling to get the main up the mast. The winch turned easily, making him smile as he remembered the work that had gone into cleaning and rebuilding each of them. When he couldn't pull any further, the sail was still only two-thirds up. He reached for the winch handle. Above him, the sail was billowing out to port, and the boat was heeling over.

"Emma!" he heard Mike shout. "You've turned off the wind! That's why Raoul can't raise it higher. Get back into the wind so the sail is flapping over the center of the boat."

Emma made a course correction, and suddenly, Raoul

felt the line go slack in his hand. Now, he could pull the main almost to the top. After a few turns with the winch handle, he could cleat off the sail and unload the winch.

"Excellent," said Mike. "Now, Ryan, it's your turn. Prepare to pull out the genoa on the starboard side. Emma, ease off to starboard until the mainsail is just full. Raoul, get ready to release the furling line. When the sail catches, let it go. You won't be able to hold it. Just make sure the line is clear and not around any part of you or under your foot. Now, Ryan, pull out the sail."

The sail unwound slowly at first, then the wind caught it, and it unravelled by itself. The boat heeled over again, and Raoul heard Emma squeal. For a moment, he tried to control the line, but he couldn't. He dropped the furling line and watched as the sail wound it around the furling drum. His hands were stinging with rope burn. He could see the red marks on his palms. Whoa, that happened fast.

Looking up, he could see Ryan struggling to make any more progress.

"Raoul, pass him the winch handle," Mike called. Raoul stepped forward to retrieve the winch handle from its pouch and passed it to Ryan. With the winch handle in place, Ryan quickly brought the sail under control.

Now the boat was sailing with the engine still on.

"Stop the engine, Emma, then kill the fuel pump and put the transmission in reverse. Here, I'll show you…."

Silence. The feeling was magical. One moment, there was the rumble of the prop pushing the boat through the water, and next, the wind and the sails caught the boat, pulling it ahead through the waves.

"Let's all have a seat in the cockpit, then we can relax, and I'll explain how to trim the sails for your heading and the wind. Ryan, take the wheel for a while."

Emma and Raoul sat next to each other on the high side, as Mike sat on the low side.

When Raoul looked over at Emma, he saw she had suddenly turned quite pale.

"I don't feel very good," she said, then she scrambled up to the lifelines and vomited over the side of the boat. Some of her vomit blew back in the wind, spattering her T-shirt.

"Here," said Mike, handing a bucket to Emma. "Use this. Raoul, do you have another T-shirt on board?"

"I have a sweatshirt, but it has grease marks on it."

"Get it for Emma."

It was a strange feeling going down in the cabin where everything was now on an angle. Like a carnival funhouse, he thought. Ow, that hurt. He rubbed his thigh where he had crashed into the table. Using both hands to steady himself, he found the sweatshirt he wore on cool mornings and brought it back up.

"Emma," said Mike, "take off your T-shirt and put this sweatshirt on. Ryan! Look the other way. Be a gentleman."

Raoul helped her out of the messy T-shirt and into his sweatshirt. Mike moistened a cloth with drinking water so that Emma could wipe her face.

Then she retched again, this time into the bucket.

Now she was crying, with tears running down her cheeks. "Raoul, I've spoiled everything. I can't go sailing like this."

Raoul's heart sank. I never expected this. What if Emma can't sail with me? What's our next plan?

Just then, he heard another noise and looked up to see Ryan vomiting over the stern. Mike had grabbed the wheel to steady it.

"Attention everyone. Let's talk about seasickness."

Emma looked up from her bucket. Raoul could see the misery on her face.

"Everyone feels queasy at some point. Raoul, you'll have your moments too. I have moments like that, and I've been sailing all my life. First, if you need to throw up, do it over the leeward side where the wind will take it away. Emma, you saw what happened on the windward side."

"Next, if you start to feel queasy, look out at the horizon. Watch the waves and picture the boat moving through them. If the boat motion makes sense to your brain, you'll feel better. Emma, take the wheel for a while. Look at the horizon, see the waves, feel the boat moving under your feet. To keep a heading, pick a cloud directly in front of the boat and steer to it. The boat will almost never point directly where you want it to go. Let it swing around a bit as long as the general direction is right."

With Emma behind the wheel, Raoul could see the color coming back into her cheeks.

"Now," said Mike, "let's turn it around and head back. I think we've done enough for today."

He talked them through tacking the boat to head back to the harbor. Emma stayed behind the wheel until they were securely tied up in their slip.

"We'll see you at the same time in the morning. Emma and Ryan, I have an exercise for both of you. Every time you think about what happened today, say three times, 'That was silly. I don't get seasick.' Then tomorrow, if you feel queasy again, say that to yourself. Seasickness is all in your mind. You simply have to train your mind to understand the boat's movement, and you'll be perfectly fine."

The three new sailors found Jake in the cafe and joined him for a coffee and pastry. Emma and Ryan now both seemed fully recovered from their ordeal.

THAT NIGHT IN BED, EMMA SAID, "I'M SORRY, RAOUL. I'M terrified that I won't make it; that the seasickness will be too awful. And you worked so hard on that boat. What if I can't go?" Her face looked so lost, and tears were welling up in her eyes.

His heart went out to her. "Mi vida, you're not messing anything up. A year ago, you would have been throwing up at the idea of killing a chicken or skinning a warm rabbit. Now you do both those things easily; we've come so far. Together, we can conquer this too."

"I'll try." She sniffled, then kissed him and turned away. Raoul could feel her body shaking as she cried herself to sleep.

THE NEXT MORNING OVER BREAKFAST, RAOUL ASKED, "Jake, is it okay if Emma and I take the ATVs into town today?"

"Sure, but I'd be happy to give you a lift."

"Thanks, but I have an idea of how to help Emma with her seasickness."

"Seasickness? Oh, you poor thing," said Mary, "although I'm sure I'd be upchucking the whole way if you put me on a boat."

Emma smiled weakly and said, "Apparently, it's just something I have to get over."

Once they were moving and out of sight of the house, Raoul stopped. "I want you to stand with your bum off the seat for this next part. Feel the machine move around underneath you as it goes over the ruts in the road. Now follow me."

He led her onto the side of the road, where there were rocks, holes, and rippling. Ten minutes later, he stopped again. "Now, for the next part, sit down on the ATV and move with it."

They took off again until Raoul stopped again. "The ATV doesn't make you seasick because what you're feeling makes sense to your brain. The problem on the boat is that your brain wants to see the boat as still like it is on the land, but it's behaving more like the ATV bouncing around on the wind and the waves. Today, try to imagine that the boat is just a huge ATV. You can choose if you want to let it move under you or brace yourself to move with it. I noticed Mike does that a lot. And if you get sick again, don't worry about it. It'll pass."

"Thanks, Rao. I'll try. I'm just scared that it will feel awful again, like yesterday."

Day Two on the boat started with lessons on rights of way and reading marker buoys in a channel. Then they set sail once more. This time, Emma was the one to back Sea Dream out from its slip and steer it out of the harbor.

Raoul paused from coiling the lines to look at her and gave her a cheerful thumbs up. He was happy to see Emma smile and return the gesture.

Out in the harbor, the swell was less and the wind lighter than the day before. Mike stayed in the cockpit and said, "Raoul, today you call the action. Make sure everyone knows what they're doing and what you're doing."

Once they had the boat lined out, with the sails trimmed, Mike said, "Now we're going to practice our knots." He showed Emma how to engage the autopilot, then handed out short lengths of rope to each of the crew members.

"We'll begin with the bowline.: He showed them the

classic way to tie the knot. The three students sat working at the knots in their laps. Within a minute of each other, first Ryan, then Emma, were vomiting over the side. Mike passed each of them a bottle of water to rinse off with.

"Raoul," he said, "would you go down to the cabin and find the notebook with the notes on the steering mechanism that you made? Look for the diagrams and come back up when you've found them."

A minute later, Raoul came racing up the stairs and threw up his breakfast over the side.

He wiped his face and looked at Emma. His cheeks burned with embarrassment.

"Today's lesson on seasickness," said Mike. "First, it can hit anyone, including me, including Raoul. What started it today was looking down in your laps, losing the frame of reference of the sea. All of you stand up and look out at the horizon. Reacquaint yourselves with the motion of the boat, and breathe fresh sea air into your lungs. Your body should settle down soon. And until you're very experienced, don't go below deck while sailing. It will trigger almost everyone at some point, as you saw with Raoul."

Raoul laughed. "So you don't need my notes after all?"

"Not today, but one day, you'll be glad you have them."

The rest of the sailing went uneventfully.

When Sea Dream was tied up, Raoul and Emma climbed onto the ATVs for the ride back up the trail.

At the house, they went to find Mary in the kitchen. She gave them hot coffee and fresh cookies. Emma looked at Raoul. "I've never seen you look so miserable as when you were tossing your breakfast over the side of the boat."

"Not my finest moment," said Raoul, grinning. "But now you see, it's not just you. Mike said anyone could be caught if they're not careful. I think we'll be fine, and if it happens occasionally, then it just happens. No drama."

———

At the end of the first week of lessons, Mike sat with them in the cockpit with a paper chart on the center table. "Let's spend a moment looking at your route. Here is where we are, here's the city, and here's Three Saints," he said, pointing at each location on the map.

"As you can see, there is a string of islands off the coast, and you can simply follow the string until you get to Three Saints. The first one is Pelican Island. There's a good anchorage there."

"Which other islands should we stop at?"

"That's up to you. I would stay away from Shipwreck Cove for obvious reasons, but there are lots of little places to drop anchor for the night if you wish. Only steer clear of Bald Point. There are reports of boats being taken over there and crew being held captive while they strip the boat of anything valuable."

"Like modern-day pirates?" asked Emma.

"Yeah, that's what they are. Modern-day pirates."

27

RECOVERING THE CHIPS

One week later, sailing training was done. The boat was ready. Ryan brought around the dinghy and delighted in giving Emma and Raoul a tour of the harbor in the little boat. Ryan and Raoul raised the dinghy on two davits at the stern of Sea Dream. It hung there swinging.

Before they left, Emma and Raoul tidied up the boat, putting away any remaining tools and making the bed in the V-berth. All that was left was the provisioning.

The next morning, Jake took Raoul aside. "Today, we're going to recover those chips of yours. They're about 40 minutes from here. Ted should be here soon. He's going to help. I only want you to confirm the location and retrieve the chips once it's clear."

"How do you know where they are?"

"Can you think of any other reason a security bot would have been standing at the side of the trail in the same spot for the past eight weeks? I'm willing to bet your AI somehow realized what was there and is waiting for you to reclaim them.

It won't recognize either Tom or me, and we have experience in rolling bots, so we'll do the heavy work. Just stay hidden until I sound the all-clear. Now stay here while I get supplies."

Raoul tried to stay put but couldn't resist peering into the barn to see where Jake had gone. He saw Jake sweep a section of the floor, then lift a trapdoor and go down some stairs. Raoul stepped forward and peered into the hatch. Shit, those are military assault rifles and shotguns. And what are those big ones? Rocket launchers? Geez, this guy's ready for the next world war! Raoul stepped back and waited.

When Jake came out a few minutes later, he tossed a backpack into his ATV, followed by two canvas bags that went in Raoul's. The backpack made a metallic noise as it landed in the ATV compartment. They stood beside the ATVs, talking about the sailing trip when another ATV appeared up the road. The newcomer was about the same age as Jake but with a much heavier build and a thick beard.

"Pleased to meet you, Raoul. I've heard a lot of good things about you. Call me Ted."

"Hi, Ted." Raoul took the offered hand, which swallowed up his own. It was like shaking hands with a baseball glove.

"All set?" Ted asked Jake.

"All set," Jake confirmed. He started his ATV and rode out. Ted and Raoul followed. When they arrived at the point where the shoreline trail intersected the drive, Jake turned left onto the trail.

Twenty minutes later, they came to the fork where Emma and Raoul had first walked down to the village. After another fifteen minutes, Jake stopped. He took the two canvas bags from Raoul and gave one to Ted. Then he hoisted his backpack onto his shoulders and waited for Ted to do the same.

"We're going to walk single file, no talking until we see the bot. Then Raoul, you'll give us a thumbs up if this is the place or a thumbs down if it's not. As soon as you do that, go back fifty meters until you're out of sight."

They walked cautiously forward. Before they reached the bot, Raoul spotted the small pile of rocks he and Emma left as a marker. He tapped Ted on the back, and pointed to the pile of rocks, then gave a thumbs up. Ted did the same to Jake in front of him. Jake turned and motioned for Raoul to stay hidden. Ted disappeared into the forest. Raoul tried to follow him with his eyes, but he was gone. Jake was humming to himself as he reached into his backpack and pulled out a roll of metallic tape. He fastened the canvas bag around his waist and unzipped the top.

Raoul heard an owl hoot in the forest above him. Jake hooted back. Still humming to himself, Jake walked on down the trail.

Raoul crept from tree to tree, unable to control his curiosity. As Jake came into view of the bot, he heard a metallic voice, "Hold! This is a restricted zone. You may not pass."

"How do I get to the other side of you? I'm following the trail."

"You may return and follow…."

At that moment, a net whirled in the air, enveloping the security bot. As it struggled, the net seemed to grow tighter. Jake rushed in and wound the metal tape around the bot, completely immobilizing it. A strip of tape now also covered its eye cameras.

Finally, Ted clambered down the rocky face to stand

with Jake. Together, they knocked over the helpless robot and rolled it into the bushes at the lower side of the trail.

Jake reached into the shallow cave and retrieved the foil packages that Raoul and Emma had stored there in their previous life.

"Let's go," said Jake. "There'll be reinforcements soon. Raoul, as soon as we get back, take Emma and walk up to the waterfall pond. Wait there until I come for you." Jake and Raoul took off at full speed back to the house while Ted headed out in the other direction.

Back at the house, Raoul grabbed Emma and said, "Come. We have to go up to the waterfall pond and hide. I'll explain on the way."

Hand in hand they set out for the waterfall. It took less than an hour to get there. Raoul was pleased to see that their shoes were not making any marks on the dry path.

Looking around the small grassy meadow, he reviewed what he knew about the bots. "Let's climb the waterfall and get higher. They'll have infrared sight, so we'll be harder to spot if we are higher and away from the edge."

It was easy to climb the small rocky cliff over which the stream fell. The rock was dry and crumbled under his fingertips, but there were small shrubs and tough grasses that provided handholds. This is good, he thought. Bots will have a hard time with their weight and the crumbling stone. At the top, there was a thin trail, barely visible, and soon they could see the stream above. They moved deeper into the forest where they found a large fallen log to sit on.

Fifteen long minutes later, there was a familiar noise below. It was the small whir of mechanical actuators as the bots wandered about. "It sounds like two of them," said Raoul.

"Shush, they'll hear us," replied Emma.

They slipped off the log and crouched down behind it.

Raoul felt his heart pounding with fear. He reached out for Emma's hand. Her eyes were wide, her muscles tensed, ready to run.

"It's okay, Em, they can't climb that cliff." Closing his eyes for a moment, the thought, God, I hope that's true. To come this close and get caught now? He shook his head to clear the thought.

There was a hard, scrabbling sound as one bot tried to climb beside the waterfall, but it soon gave up. Then, the sounds of the two became fainter as they departed until they could no longer be heard over the waterfall noise.

They waited in hiding for another twenty minutes until the familiar roar of Jake's ATV let them know it was clear.

As they clambered down from the cliff face, Jake was waiting for them. "You two take the ATV back. I'll walk," he said.

"Are you sure they're gone?" asked Raoul, turning to look around in all directions. His heart was still pumping fast. He felt Emma holding his left arm with both hands, shaking in her fear. "You okay?"

Emma nodded.

"They didn't stay long," Jake replied to his first question. "They could see you weren't there, and there's no connection between us, so they looked around with that infrared gaze of theirs and left. I imagine they're making their way along all the community members living near the trail."

"We learned one thing at least," said Raoul, looking at Emma.

"What's that?"

"That we're still not safe on the island, and that we need to go soon." And another thing, he thought, Jake and Ted were all too happy to take on that bot, and it brought others to us. We can't trust Jake to keep us safe. He's too reckless.

Jake was still speaking. "I'm thinking we need two days to provision the boat and move your things aboard, and you can leave early Sunday morning. Now get going. I won't be far behind you."

Emma climbed on behind Raoul, and they took off to the house along the back trail.

When they went into the kitchen, Mary was there pounding chickens flat. Spatchcocking, she called it.

Thwack, thwack, thwack, "That bloody fool," she said as they entered. "I hope he at least apologized to you." She didn't look up from the chickens. Thwack! Thwack!

"What for?" asked Emma.

"There was no need to go there today. He knew where you left those damned chips. I told him to wait until you were gone, but he's fascinated by the idea of new plumbing. I think he and his buddy Ted just wanted to relive their glory days, and he didn't think about you at all."

The next thwack was so hard the chicken split in two.

"No harm done. We're okay now. What are you doing with all the chickens?" asked Emma.

"They're for a big barbecue Saturday night. We're giving you a send-off party. It's not often the community gets all together. There'll be music, home-brewed beer, and food of all kinds. These'll soak in cold water tomorrow and then be all ready for the barbecue on Saturday."

"Do you need help?"

"No, sweetheart, not today. Not after what that idiot put you through. Why don't you two draw up a list of provisions for the boat, and we'll see about getting them aboard tomorrow?"

Raoul and Emma went to their bedroom and sat on the edge of the bed.

"I have a feeling that Jake will be sleeping outside tonight," said Raoul.

Emma laughed. "I'm sure of it."

Thirty minutes later, as they worked on their list, there was a knock on the door. An embarrassed Jake stepped in and said, "I'm sorry I put you through that. I didn't think about the repercussions. I won't do anything with the chips until you're gone."

"It's okay, Jake," said Emma. "Just another close call we've lived through. How do we get all these provisions we're listing?"

"We'll shop tomorrow. Angus has set up a line of credit at the store. Don't worry, you'll be fine."

"What do we do for money when we get to Three Saints?"

"Barter. Trade services for what you need. Grow what you want to eat. Trade the surplus for flour and other staples. With your skills, you'll both do well."

FRIDAY WAS SHOPPING DAY. WITH THEIR DEPARTURE approaching, Raoul and Emma loaded two grocery carts and wheeled them down to the dock. Soon, the refrigerator was full of meat and milk, and the galley cupboards were full of cans and boxes of food.

Ryan came down with a wagon of empty green and red fuel containers. The green is for diesel, and the red is gasoline for the dinghy, he explained. With his help, they cast off Sea Dream, and Raoul let Ryan take the wheel for the brief trip to the fuel dock where Sea Dream's fuel tank was topped up, and the green and red containers were all filled. Ryan waved his wrist to pay for the fuel and helped to strap the fuel containers along one side of the foredeck out of the way.

Back at their home slip, Raoul filled the water tanks and some gallon jugs with fresh water. These he stowed under the cockpit seats.

By the end of Friday, the boat was all set.

Saturday morning, Jake said, "Raoul, I need you out back for a while."

Curious, Raoul followed him to the barn. Jake disappeared down his mysterious hatch and began passing some items up to Raoul. "Here's a .22 rifle, and this one's a small-gauge shotgun."

Jake ducked down again and passed up a camouflaged case. "This is an automatic handgun."

He disappeared again and brought up a small sports bag. "In here are some boxes of ammunition and a couple of EMPs. Don't use the EMPs indoors. They can hurt people, too."

Jake climbed up and closed the hatch.

"But won't you be needing these?"

"Son, you don't want to know what I've got down there. Don't worry, I'll be fine. Now, let's go out to the orchard for a little target practice."

Raoul went to sling the rifle over his shoulder, but Jake stopped him.

"Let's have a moment for gun safety. Hand me the rifle. I'll show you how to check there's no round in the chamber. First, make sure the safety switch is on, then pull back the bolt until either a cartridge pops out or you can see the chamber is empty. Go ahead, try it."

Raoul repeated the lesson.

"Now, let's do the same for the shotgun and the handgun. Never walk around with a loaded gun, and especially, never keep a loaded handgun. That's how accidents happen."

With the guns secured, they walked into the orchard. Near the far end was a stump where a diseased tree had been cut down. Jake plucked an apple from a nearby tree and set it on the stump.

They spent the next hour trying out the three guns.

"You won't be a marksman by the end of today, but you'll have time for that when you get there. At least now you know how to be safe around a gun and not shoot yourself or anyone else by accident. Let's go back to the barn and learn how to clean and oil the guns."

At the barn, Jake disappeared through the floor once more and returned with cases for the two long guns. He also handed up a plastic case and a small bottle of oil.

"Everything you need for gun cleaning is in this case. These are clean, but I'll show you how to break them down and clean them and then to store them safely in their cases." They spend another hour breaking down and cleaning the guns. There was a small instruction book tucked in the case. Flipping through it, Raoul thought, I got this.

"Jake, do you have a spare net like the one you used on the bot? I'm thinking that as it's security bots that we're most worried about, it would be good to have one."

"Sure. Give me a minute. Remember, they won't work from the front. You have to be behind or above to throw it over the bot on the first try. They stick to the bot's armor, which is why they're so effective. But if you miss, you can't pull it back to try again. "

Jake returned with one of the canvas pouches containing a net and a roll of metallic tape.

"Let's go back to the house for lunch. We'll take these down to the boat later."

28

AN OUTDOOR CEREMONY

Back at the house, preparations for the evening were in full swing. The roar of ATV engines announced the arrival of the first guests, coming to help with preparations. A pickup truck arrived with a load of tables and chairs, and a second one came pulling a massive barbecue on a trailer. Jake and Raoul pitched in, setting up the tables with the other men while the women all congregated in the kitchen. Then the beer truck arrived, and all work stopped for a few minutes.

Something was worrying Raoul, but he couldn't quite put his finger on it. He slipped off to find Emma. "Em," he said in a whisper, "Let's go to the bedroom for a minute."

"Now, with all these people here? Can't you wait a few more hours?"

"I'm serious." He took her hand and led her to the bedroom.

After closing the door, Raoul said, "This is too big, too much noise and attention. I'm worried that it will attract Gisele. Get your stuff for the boat ready now, and I'll put both overnight bags in the ATVs. Don't drink too much, and be ready to make a run for it if we have to. If I give the signal, go right to your ATV and take off. No goodbyes, no last hugs, we just go. Believe me, Jake and Mary will understand."

"Now you're scaring me again, Raoul."

"Don't be scared. Probably nothing will happen. This is just being prepared."

As Emma and Raoul stowed the overnight bags in the ATVs, a limousine bearing the Rapid Taxi logo pulled up, and both sets of parents climbed out.

"Mom, Dad," squealed Emma, running towards them.

"Ellie, sweetheart, we weren't sure if you were still alive."

Then Raoul's own mother was there, wrapping her arms around him and looking up at his face. His father, standing beside her, laid a hand on his shoulder. "Raffi, chico," said his mother. "I was worrying about you. It's been so long since we heard from you."

"Mom, I missed you too, but we couldn't call. And I'm Raoul now. I have a new name, and so does Ellie. She now goes by Emma and will be my wife. We're having a ceremony tonight."

"And you didn't invite us? Thank goodness that man, Jake, reached out to us."

"He called you because we asked him to, but we didn't think you could come. It's too dangerous. The AIs have not forgotten us, so we have to stay hidden. Come, we'll give you a tour."

Taking Emma's hand, he led the small party of six on a tour of the property. Their parents admired the gardens, the chickens and the rabbits. Raoul talked about rebuilding the boat and how they learned to sail. Emma showed off the dress she had made herself and talked about learning to cook and bake.

At the end of their tour, before they rejoined the crowd, Raoul said, "Please understand that if things go wrong, we'll go away immediately. Please don't follow. Mary and Jake will look after you and make sure you get home."

By now, the party was in full swing. The conversations were loud with many new arrivals. Raoul and Emma introduced their parents to Jake. "Jake," Raoul said, "Thank you for everything you've done for us. No matter what happens, we'll always be in your debt and thankful for your care."

"Of course, we've enjoyed every minute of it, but we'll have time for this later, Raoul."

"I hope so, and then I'll say it again with more words."

Emma's father and then Raoul's mother also thanked Jake for looking after their children. "I don't know how Raoul gets into these messes," said his father. "I'm just glad you were there to catch them when they needed it."

The small group moved into the kitchen, where Mary was presiding over the activities. "Mary," said Emma, "I could not have wished for a more loving teacher. Thank you for rescuing us and for everything you taught me."

"It was a pleasure, dear. But surely we can say our goodbyes later."

"Raoul's worried that we'll be interrupted, so we want you to know how much we love you and appreciate what you did for us, even if we can't say it again later."

"Now you sound like Jake in the old days. Always one eye on the door. Well, it's kept you alive this far, but I have every intention of seeing you again before you go." Again, the parents each thanked Mary, and the mothers hugged her.

They moved on to find Mike and Angus. After

introductions, Raoul thanked each of them for their support. "But where's Ryan?" asked Raoul.

"Back minding the store and watching the boat. This isn't really his scene. Not enough young girls, I suppose. You'll see him in the morning before you leave."

"If we don't, thank him for all the work on the dinghy."

Now, it was Emma's turn to find the women who had taught her sewing and herbal medicines. Emma's mother said, "I can't believe Ellie, I mean Emma, actually learned to sew. She told me she made that dress she's wearing."

"Yes," said Jean. "With that artistic flair of hers, she's become very good and creative."

Emma had finally thanked each of her mentors. Now, they were free to relax and join the party. Most folks had eaten their fill and were sipping their drinks. A small band started playing polkas, sea shanties and jigs. The crowd took to dancing on the hard ground outside the barn. Raoul caught Emma up in his arms and swung her about in an enthusiastic polka. Emma seemed to love the whirl of the dance to the sound of the fiddles.

When the band paused after forty-five minutes, Jake shouted loudly for everyone's attention.

"Let's have Raoul and Emma up front, please, for a special ceremony. Moms and dads, please step up also and stand next to them."

He paused until everyone was in place.

"By the power invested in me as a chaplain of the forest and seeker of the truth, I am here to preside over the union of this young couple. They came to us knowing nothing of our lifestyle, but through hard work and their own intelligence, they have come far and are ready to homestead on their own."

There was a round of applause with lots of supportive shouts, whoops, and whistles.

Jake turned to face Raoul and Emma. "Are you both ready?"

They nodded. Jake passed Raoul the ring Mary had provided. He unfolded the paper that Raoul and Emma had given him.

"Repeat after me. 'I, Raoul Moreno, choose you, Emma, to be my life partner. Emma, you are the star around which my life revolves, and I will honor and protect you for as long as I live."

Raoul repeated the vow.

"Emma, repeat after me, 'I, Emma, choose you, Raoul, to be my life partner. Raoul, I love you with all my heart and will stay by your side, no matter what life brings, for as long as I live."

Emma looked directly into Raoul's eyes as she spoke the words. He saw tears of joy on her cheeks, but she did not wipe them away.

"Raoul," continued Jake, "Please present Emma with her ring."

"Emma, I give you this ring as a symbol of our life and our vows for all to see and a daily reminder to us of the words spoken today."

"And Emma, you may present your ring."

Raoul felt his eyes widen. What the hell? We never talked about a ring.

"Raoul, I give you this ring made of stainless steel as a symbol of the strength and purity of our love and our resolve to live together until the end of our days." She held out a polished, faceted stainless steel and placed it on his ring finger.

"I now pronounce you husband and wife. You may seal your promises with a kiss."

As he leaned forward to kiss Emma, Raoul caught a reflection of the firelight shining off steel bodies at the edge of the forest. Looking around, he saw two more emerging from the orchard.

"RUN!" He shouted.

The crowd looked at each other in confusion for a moment but then saw the circle of bots moving to surround the party. Raoul took Emma's hand as they dashed to the waiting ATVs. Jumping on, they immediately set off down the trail at full speed. Raoul waved Emma to go in front. He could see her terror in the way she was flying down the path, her ATV barely on the edge of control.

Behind them, Raoul heard a half-dozen other ATVs starting up. They're following us, he realized. Guarding our backs.

When they crossed the shoreline hiking trail, some of the ATVs peeled off, creating a distraction. More peeled off at the highway until it was only the two of them on the road into Harrison's Point.

Screeching to a halt at the dock, they were pulling out their overnight bags when a male voice yelled, "Stop right there." Suddenly, they were lit up in the intense light of a car's headlights.

Raoul turned around, squinting into the light, to see the two men in dark suits. "We thought you'd make a run for it when we heard the bots were on the move." The men were holding guns in their hands. "I think we should come with you down to your boat for a little chat."

Raoul felt his heart drop out of his chest—so close, and now this. Tears of frustration formed, and his muscles went limp. Beside him, Emma squeezed his hand. "I love you no matter what," she said.

As the initial shock passed, Raoul's mind started

whirring with possibilities. Could we dive into the water? Hard to see us in the dark.

As he was standing, still frozen in indecision, he heard another voice, a higher voice, shout, "Drop the guns, you motherfuckers!"

It was Ryan, standing there with a military assault rifle in his hands.

The younger man turned to bring his weapon up to face Ryan.

"I wouldn't do that. Been learning to shoot since I was two." Ryan fired a burst at the ground near their feet. The men stepped back as flying stone chips stung their legs through the thin material of their suits.

"Run!" said Raoul. They grabbed their packs and raced to their boat, ignoring the standoff behind them. Raoul pulled the shore power, then tossed the four mooring lines back onto the boat. As Sea Dream drifted backwards, he grabbed a lifeline and stepped aboard. He heard the engine grumble into life.

"Emma, go! I'll spot up front."

In the dark, with only the light of a new moon to guide them, it was hard to make out channel buoys. Raoul guided Emma with hand gestures as they headed out of the harbor.

A moment later, they were running blind, in the dark with no lights.

Raoul reached under a cockpit seat to where he knew a flashlight was stowed. Using the pale beam, he went down to the navigation station and turned on the navigation instruments. He thought for a moment but left the exterior red and green navigation lights off. No point in giving them a target to follow, he thought.

Back in the cockpit, he studied the chart plotter. "Set the autopilot for 85 degrees west," he said to Emma.

Now, they could catch their breaths and relax. The steady beat of the engine as the boat carried them forward into the dark night reassured them. It felt like the heartbeat of a living thing, carrying them to safety. Raoul could feel his own heart slowing, his muscles relaxing as the adrenaline disappeared from his body.

"What do you think happened to Ryan?" asked Emma. "I hope they didn't hurt him."

"I expect he waited till we were gone, then disappeared. He was never really a target, and I don't think the hitmen would have chased him on his own territory in the dark."

"Do you think Gisele would hurt our parents?"

"No, she would never be able to explain it. Anyway, I don't think she wants to draw attention to her actions. Right now, Molly, the other AI, doesn't seem to realize she still exists, camped in some dark corner of her psyche."

"You sound like you're talking about a human."

"I worked with Fatima for almost a year. To me, she was a human, and she wasn't even at the top of the pyramid."

"I feel cold," said Emma.

Raoul could feel her body shivering. It's too much for her. Gotta keep her warm. "I'll get you a blanket." Taking up the torch again, he made his way to the V-berth and pulled the blanket off the bed. Returning to the cockpit, he wrapped it around Emma, then held her close to keep her warm. Ten minutes later, she fell asleep leaning against him. When she stirred, he said, "Why don't you go to bed while I keep watch."

"No, don't wanna … sleep. Too dark … down there."

"C'mon, I'll get you to bed. It's our wedding night, after all."

He helped her down the companionway and into the

cabin, relying only on the torch and the nightlights. Taking off her shoes, he made her comfortable on the bed, and placed the blanket over her. In moments, she was snoring that cute, purring snore he knew so well.

On the way back to the cockpit, he turned on the exterior navigation lights for safety so that other boats would see them. Wedging himself onto the seat on the high side, he waited for the dawn.

29

SHOWDOWN AT THE DOCKS

Ben looked at the kid with the assault rifle. He recognized him as Angus' son. Without taking his eyes off him, Ben motioned for Alf to put away his gun. Ben was aware of his heart pounding in his chest, a teenager with a weapon was terrifying. Steeling himself not to show fear, he said, "Now, son, Ryan, isn't it? No one needs to get hurt here. I'm Ben, and this is Alf. If we really wanted to hurt Raoul, we would have done it already. So why don't we all put down our weapons and talk man to man for a moment?"

"If you weren't going to hurt them, why were you pointing your guns at them?"

"We just wanted to get their attention. To talk with them for a moment. To make sure they knew that as long as they stayed away from the main island and didn't talk to anyone, we would leave them alone."

"If I put my gun down, how do I know you won't shoot me?"

"Ryan, is it okay if I call you that?" The boy nodded. "The last thing I want is a dead teenager to explain. You have your whole life ahead of you. If you shoot us, you could end up in jail, maybe only for a few years, but you'd miss out on the best years of your life. So neither one of us can win a shoot-out. I don't want a dead body, and you don't want to go to jail. Can we agree on that?"

The boy nodded again but still held the rifle steady.

"Here's what we're going to do. You point that gun away from us for a moment, and we'll put our weapons on the ground and step back. Then you'll put your safety on and put down the assault rifle. We'll wait until you are safely back in your shop before we pick up our guns and leave peacefully."

"How do I know I can trust you?" Ben could see the boy's jaw quivering and tears coming into his eyes. He looked as if he would start crying at any minute.

"Ryan, stay with me. Standing up to us to protect your friends was incredibly brave. It's a story that you'll be telling for years. The girls will love it. You're a hero. Don't spoil it now by making a mess. We will not hurt you. All we want to do now is get away safely. You did a brave thing. Now let it go."

At that moment, the roar of an ATV distracted them all. Ben and Ryan turned to see Angus roaring up to the chandlery. At his side, Ben was aware of Alf getting ready to shoot while Ryan was distracted, so he knocked him hard sideways.

"Alf, stand down! We're not shooting anyone."

Angus got off his ATV and walked up, brandishing his own weapon. "What's going on here, now?"

Ryan spoke. "They were pointing their guns at Raoul and Emma. I thought they were going to shoot them. I came out and stopped them."

Ben added, "It was very brave of him. Angus, we've met a few times. You know that if we wanted to shoot

Raoul, we could have done it many times over. Tonight, we just wanted to give them a warning. But Ryan was there for his friends. I didn't count on that."

"Aye, I see that. Ryan, it's okay now. You can put down your rifle."

"But Dad, what if they shoot us?"

"Son, shooting people is not something done lightly. These two gentlemen know very well the cost of shooting someone, both in risk and in what it does to your soul. You don't want that in your life. Over the summer, the entire community has gotten to know Ben and Alf. They sit in the cafe, buy coffee in the bakery and drop in to see me once in a while. We all know they've just been keeping an eye on Raoul, but they never hurt him or even talked with him, as far as I know."

Ben nodded.

"They're not our friends, but they're not a threat to us either. We understand each other. Sometimes, the best thing to do is to put down weapons on both sides and walk away. That's what Ben wants you to do. Right now, you're full of adrenaline, and jumpy as a scared cat. I bet Ben is far more frightened of you than you are of him. Isn't that right, Ben?"

"You've got it, Angus. Last thing I want is to have my death as a stain on Ryan's soul, and I have no intention of killing an innocent teenager."

Suddenly, the air seemed to go out of Ryan. He wobbled on his feet as if he were about to faint. Angus rushed to take over the rifle as Ben and Alf hit the ground. A brief burst of shots rang out as Angus grabbed the weapon. Ben heard the metallic staccato as they sprayed the gleaming body of the limousine behind them.

Silence.

Ben motioned to Alf, and the two of them stood up,

dusted themselves off, and walked over to where Angus was sitting next to Ryan, who seemed to be reviving. "Thank you, Angus. We never wanted to hurt anyone here, not even Raoul and Emma. Ryan really was spectacular. He just didn't know how to stand down. Not his fault at all. He's a good lad."

Angus looked up. "Aye, I figured as much. Best you leave now. You're always welcome to bring your wife and daughter for a day out, but we'd appreciate it if we don't see that limousine and your dark suits again."

"Nothing here for us now, no reason to come back." Ben shifted his attention. "Goodbye Ryan. You were a man today. There's never any shame in walking away when it's over. We're leaving now. You won't see us again."

Ben and Alf climbed back into the limousine and headed home.

As he settled back in the soft leather seat, Ben relaxed. The sensation of adrenaline leaving his body left him feeling giddy with relief. He laughed. "Did you see how twitchy that kid was, Alf?"

"Yeah, I thought he was going to shoot us on the spot."

"Something to think about. When you feel twitchy, that's how you look to other people. Random and dangerous. That's why you have to learn to take a deep breath and never let them see your fear."

"Weren't you afraid?"

"Of a teenager with an assault rifle? I was scared shitless. But it's over. All we suffered was a few bullet holes in the limo that I'll have to explain to Morrie."

30

THE BATTLE OF JAKE'S BARN

A s soon as Raoul yelled, "Run!" Jake turned around and saw security bots coming out of the woodlot and the orchard.

"Shit!" he said to himself. He quickly rounded up Raoul and Emma's parents and hustled them to the barn. By the time they were there, Ted was at his side.

Jake pulled up the hatch on the barn floor and ushered the two sets of parents inside. "Wait here," he said, "until one of us comes to get you. You can open the trapdoor from inside, so you won't be stuck."

He turned on the single bulb that illuminated his armory. He could see the four parents with wide eyes looking around at the underground room with its wood slab walls and floor and the bench along one wall holding stacks of unfamiliar weapons and armor. The opposite wall had racks of assault rifles, shotguns, and sniper rifles. Jake did not have time to explain.

Ted was already busy. "Kevlar vest, EMPS, armor-piercing rounds and machine gun."

Jake was packing his own weapons of choice: "Vest, sticky nets, grenades, EMPs, smoke bombs."

Above, they could hear shouts and screams, knowing that the community would be scattering and distracting the bots.

"How many did you see?" asked Jake.

"Six by my count. Only looking for Raoul and Emma, they seem to ignore the rest."

"Let's stop them in their tracks, then. No point in terrorizing the town."

They scrambled up the ladder into the barn and dropped the trapdoor behind them. Jake quickly scuffed the straw to cover the outline of the door. A familiar energy was surging through him. Brief flashbacks passed through him of destroying teams of robots, ambushing sentry bots, tossing EMPs at police bots. How many years has it been? He grinned, showing all his teeth.

Peeking around the corner of the barn, they saw chaos. Bots striding forward demanding Raoul and Emma, and guests screaming and running about. A quick glance showed him that several ATVs were gone, including the ones Raoul and Emma used.

Beside him, Ted tossed an EMP at a bot separated from the crowd. There was a sharp flash of light, and the bot stopped. But then the LEDs behind its eye visors flashed, showing it was in a reboot sequence. Ted took aim and blasted it with a burst of armour-piercing rounds from his oversized machine gun. The bot tottered on its feet then lost balance and fell.

This drew the attention of two more bots, who broke from the melee and walked toward the barn. Jake threw down two grenades at their feet, blowing them onto their backs, with severe lower limb damage. One had its foot blown completely off, leaving dangling optic fibres exposed and leaking hydraulic fluid onto the ground. The other turned over and rose on hands and knees until another burst from Ted's gun destroyed its head.

"That leaves three," shouted Jake.

By now, the other guests had all disappeared. Jake knew that Mary and the other women would be in their safe room. The other men would be in the woods or down the road on the remaining ATVs. All of them knew how to take cover when necessary.

Suddenly, he felt burning as a laser weapon slashed across his arm before targeting his chest. The body armor heated quickly as he and Ted ducked back around the corner of the barn.

Jake motioned for Ted to go around the other way. "I'll toss a smoke screen with heat sources to distract their infrared. Take them out from behind."

Jake began throwing out his smoke bombs as far as he could, creating a line of incendiary devices that threw off dense clouds of smoke. As he threw the last one, he heard Ted firing blindly into the smoke cloud that he knew was concealing the remaining bots.

Jake continued to back away from the battlefield, feeling the barn wall, then the edge of the floor with his feet as he passed the door. Finally, he felt the wall on the other side.

As he reached the far corner, a bot became faintly visible, emerging from the smoke. Jake threw another grenade at the bot's feet. Again, it was blown onto its back. As it struggled with its damaged legs, Jake rushed forward and threw an immobilization net over the bot, which quickly tightened as the bot continued to struggle. A strip of metallic tape over its eyes, and the battle ended.

Ted came round to join him as the smoke dissipated in

the light wind. "You certainly know how to throw a party," he laughed. "Haven't had this much fun in twenty years."

"Let's make sure there are no civilian casualties before we say it was fun," replied Jake.

"How's your arm?"

Jake was suddenly aware of the pain shooting through his arm where it had been burned by the laser. He looked down in surprise. "I forgot I got caught there." He opened and squeezed his fist a few times. "Seems to be all working. I'll get it looked at later. Mary'll know what to do."

The two combatants walked over the battlefield. Only one other droid was still trying to regain its footing, so Jake dropped another immobilization net over it.

Ted blew the horn on Jake's jeep three times to sound all-clear, as Jake went into the house to release Mary and her friends from the safe room.

"Jake, that was too much," said Mary. She bustled past him with her head held high and made a point of not looking at him. Her two friends sidled past Jake without making eye contact, either. One asked, "Is everyone okay?"

"Yes," said Jake. "Everyone's okay. They were only looking for Raoul and Emma. I don't think they were prepared for a fight."

As he walked back to the barn, Jake could see other guests returning to the scene of the party. They stood around, looking at the downed bots.

"Aren't you worried about repercussions, Jake?"

"No, from what I've seen, these are renegades. Notice how there was no air backup? No vehicles? That's because the operating AI is flying under the radar. They were only after Raoul and Emma."

Another guest came up. "I'll get my truck. We can dump these into the ocean somewhere. If anyone comes looking for them, they'll be hard to retrieve."

"Thanks," said Jake. "I'll give you a hand as soon as I look after our guests of honor."

Walking into the barn, Jake swept away the straw and shouted, "It's all clear, folks." He opened the trap door to reveal four anxious faces looking up at him.

"C'mon out, folks. It's all over now."

He helped them out of the ladder.

Emma's mother asked, "Did they get away? Are Ellie and Raffi safe?"

"We'll run down now and see," and Jake. "But Raoul was quick, and they were ready to flee. So my bet's on them."

"Raoul and Emma. Right," said Emma's mother. "I forgot for a moment."

"Rafael or Raoul or whoever he is now has done some boneheaded things, but this takes the cake." Raoul's mother's laugh was high-pitched, and Jake had the impression she could break down at any moment.

The two fathers were looking around at the scene of mechanical carnage. "That's quite the storeroom you have down there, Jake. There must be a story behind that," said Emma's father.

"Not a story for sharing. There's a reason we're all living here off the grid. Keeping quiet has kept us alive for twenty years, so please don't ask now. Just know that Raoul and Emma are now part of the same small circle, and as you saw today, with good reason. Now let's get in my jeep and go look for them."

It was a little cramped putting all of them into the jeep, and there were a few squeals as they went over the worst potholes with the jeep's stiff suspension. As they turned into the town, Jake saw the black limousine turning out onto the highway back to the city. An icy shiver went through him, but he said nothing.

Rolling into town, they came to a stop at the docks. Angus and Ryan were still standing outside and walked over.

"Hey Angus," said Jake. "Did they get away?"

"Yes, thanks to young Ryan here. He had them in a Mexican standoff when I arrived. We were just talking about how to back down gracefully when that happens. Apparently, Raoul and Emma took advantage of the moment of confusion to run."

"Who are you talking about?" asked Raoul's father. "More bots?"

"No," replied Angus. "Emma and Raoul had the misfortune of witnessing an incident in the woods. A couple of gangsters have been looking for them to keep them quiet. Strange, though, I don't think they wanted to hurt them, just to make sure they were scared enough to go away and stay away. 'Innocent bodies are bad for business,' the older one said."

"So, where are they now?" asked Emma's mother.

"Out there," replied Angus. "On Sea Dream, the boat that Raoul rebuilt, and they both learned to sail this summer."

The four parents all turned to follow Angus' finger, pointing into the darkness. But there was nothing to be seen on the ocean.

31

FIRST DAY AT SEA

At three fifteen in the early morning, the timer in the galley went off, jerking him awake. Nothing to see in the pitch black; no other boat lights visible. Need some coffee, he thought. Stumbling down the companionway steps, Raoul went to heat the coffee pot for yet another cup. Empty. Eyes half closed, he went through the motions of loading the percolator and turning on the burner. The little stove swung easily on its old gimbals.

At three thirty am, when the timer sounded again, the smell of fresh coffee wafted out of the cabin. Barely awake, he made his way down to pour a cup. Back in the cockpit, the cup was warm in his hands, and the caffeine began to do its work.

The next morning, the sun rose early on an overcast sky. The boat was doing a steady 6 knots with the engine still running. A steady crosswind blew, which would make for easy sailing. With return of the sun, Raoul's drowsiness subsided.

With no obstacles in sight, Raoul went below to make a fresh pot of coffee on the propane stove. The cooking surface rocked gently with the motion of the ship but always stayed close to level. Soon, the percolator was burbling and the cabin filled with the heady aroma of fresh coffee.

As it continued to perk, he took a box of cereal, milk, and two bananas up to the cockpit for breakfast. It was only a few minutes later that he heard the pump that flushed the head, and then Emma emerged through the companionway.

"Good morning, my beautiful wife," he said.

"Not so beautiful this morning. Not sure I'm really awake yet."

"Just sit here, and I'll pass up the coffees."

Down below, the smell of the coffee, the sound of the engine and the rolling of the boat threatened to overcome him. I don't get seasick! I don't get seasick! Mike's chant came back to him. Raoul quickly poured the coffee, passed it up to Emma, and scrambled back up into the open air of the cockpit.

"I have cereal with bananas and milk for breakfast. It should be easy on our stomachs and doesn't require any cooking."

"Thanks, sweetheart. I just need a few minutes to pull myself together," replied Emma.

"How'd you sleep?"

"Really well. The rocking of the boat is actually nice. I felt cradled in the bed."

Raoul yawned. "I was up all night. I set the timer to go off every fifteen minutes. It kept me awake. After breakfast, we'll check the charts, and then I'll have a nap."

The charts showed that early in the afternoon, they would pass by Pelican island. There were no buildings shown on the island. A deep, protected anchorage lay to leeward of the prevailing winds.

"We're going to head for the island, drop anchor and rest. We have a nice crosswind. Do you want to try the sails?"

"Sure," said Emma. "Are we running out of fuel yet?"

"No, we have enough in the tank to run for several days, and then we have our reserves on the deck. We're good for fuel. Angus made sure of that."

Raoul cleared away the dishes and put them in the sink. Only their coffees remained, secure in their drink holders. He then did all the checks below, just as Mike had taught them. Now, they were ready to sail.

"Emma, take her into the wind, please."

"Yes, Captain. Into the wind."

The boat swung rapidly into the wind and then past the wind.

"Sorry," said Emma.

A moment later, she had the boat directly into the wind. Raoul raised the mainsail and cleated it off.

He passed the furling line to Emma. "I'm going to release this line. Hold it until I tell you to let go. Make sure your hands and feet are not near it."

Working together, they released the huge head sail and brought it under control.

Now, the boat heeled over sharply as the wind caught the huge sail. Emma squealed but held onto the wheel, standing with one foot on the deck and the other on the low side seat, compensating for the angle of the deck. She looks so natural, thought Raoul. She's actually enjoying this.

The boat was already picking up speed.

"Steer closer to the wind," shouted Raoul.

Emma did, and the boat righted itself with the sails softening and losing their shape.

"Kill the engine. Then we can set the sails properly."

There was a moment of silence when the engine shut down, interrupted by the buzzer of the fuel pump warning. Emma killed that as well.

"Heading of 78, please, Emma."

The boat turned back off the wind slightly. Now Raoul could trim the sails as Mike had taught them: first the mainsail, then the genoa, then the main again.

The boat surged forward, with only the noise of the water running along the hull. The motion of the boat settled into a gentle rhythm as they glided over the low swells, and the deck settled into a more comfortable heel.

"That was exciting," said Emma. "It seemed like everything happened at once."

"We don't have Ryan as a third set of hands."

"Do you think he's all right? That was very brave when he confronted the men in black."

"I'm sure he's fine. He was on home territory and had them outgunned with that assault rifle he had. I'm sure they could have killed him in an instant, but my bet is they didn't want to mess with him. It's us they want, and they had no reason to create a bigger problem by having a dead teenager."

"I guess we'll never know. Do you think our parents are okay?"

"I'm sure they're shaken up, but they don't really know anything, and I think Gisele has to be very careful not to draw attention to herself. Did you notice there were no helicopters, no big military vehicles? Only a few bots traveling on foot. That's why I think we're safe at sea. Gisele doesn't have the resources to chase us out here. Why don't you set the autopilot, and we can relax for a bit?"

"No, I'd like to steer for a while, if that's okay. Tidy up the lines and have a nap here in the cockpit. I'll wake you if I see anything."

"Sounds like a plan."

Raoul coiled the loose lines and hung them on the lifelines or on hooks next to the companionway, then went downstairs for a cushion and returned to lie down on the low side. Cradled by the cockpit seat and the cockpit wall, the cushion became his pillow.

As he lay there, looking up at Emma behind the wheel, he was suddenly aware of how much he loved her and how proud he was of the way she had taken on the challenges set before them. His last memory before slipping into sleep was seeing Emma checking the compass and then looking out to the horizon to choose a cloud.

32

PELICAN ISLAND

R aoul was dreaming of their apartment in the city, of lying in bed with Emma beside him, when he felt someone shaking his big toe.

"Wake up Raoul. I can see the island."

"Ohhhh, how long did I sleep?"

"About four hours. You were exhausted, and everything was peaceful out here, so I let you sleep."

"How are you feeling?"

"Good, but I'm doing what Mike said: keeping my eyes on the horizon, my mind busy with steering. I put it on autopilot when I used the head and got some water or when I needed to rest. I like sailing. There's a tranquillity to it I didn't expect."

"Lovely. I think I need to use the head myself."

"Get up slowly, stabilize yourself before you go down there. There's no rush up here."

A few minutes later, Raoul re-emerged with two flasks of water in his hand.

"Where do you see the island?"

"There, you can see a peak above the horizon."

"Do you need me to take over steering for a while?"

"If you want, but we can also just put it on autopilot. The course is good. The sails may need adjusting as we've slowed down a bit."

Raoul set about trimming the sails for the new wind, and their speed picked up again. Now, they were running at five knots.

For the next two hours, the island drew steadily closer until they could make out the spray where the ocean dashed itself against the shore. The winds were becoming erratic, swirling around the island's central peak.

"Emma, start the engine, and we'll get these sails down. We could sail around the island, but it'll be a lot less work to motor."

Emma took up her position behind the wheel and then turned around to restart the motor. It quickly settled down into a smooth idle. She put the transmission forward and raised the engine speed so the motor would drive the boat after the sails lost power.

Emma turned the boat windward until the genoa flapped loosely. With the autopilot guiding the boat, they were both free to work on dropping and furling the sails. Five minutes later, they were relaxing in the cockpit. Raoul used his binoculars to check out the island. On this side, the coast was rocky with large plumes of spray as the swells pounded the shore.

"Em, let's follow the shore around to port until we see a good anchorage."

Forty-five minutes later, they could see the sheltered cove with its golden beach between two rocky outcrops.

"Head in, and call out the depth readings. We want to drop anchor at four meters. I'll be upfront with the anchor."

When Emma finally called out four meters, Raoul

could see the sand bottom below through the clear water. He did a rough calculation in his head, four meters plus seven times, which is thirty-two meters of chain.

"Idle please, Emma."

Raoul pressed the foot button that let out the chain. He watched for the brightly colored markings that Mike had insisted on making every 10 meters. When three of the markings were out, Raoul paid out a bit more and then took his foot off the winch pedal.

"Reverse slowly until the boat stops."

There was a thunk as the transmission went into reverse. The boat slowly moved back until the anchor chain went taut.

"Idle, please."

Raoul found the snubber line with its odd hook and cleated off the free end. He lay down and placed the hook around the chain as far down as he could easily reach. Finally, he released a bit more chain until it was slack to the winch, and the snubber was holding it to the boat. The boat settled into a gentle roll, barely noticeable after the hours spent on the open ocean.

"Kill the engine now." The sound of the buzzer for an instant and then silence. Profound absolute silence.

Raoul made his way back to Emma, who emerged from her station behind the wheel. They hugged as Emma said, "We actually did it. We sailed by ourselves to this island."

"And this is just the beginning of our adventure. How about lunch on the beach?"

"I'll make lunch. You launch the dinghy."

In the end, it took both of them to lower the dinghy and place the small outboard motor. Then Raoul helped pack the lunch.

The dinghy started on the first pull. "Thank you Ryan," said Raoul, thinking of their helper.

The water at the beach was so clear they could easily watch the small fish and other sea life along the shore. It was warm in the shallows, refreshing for a leisurely swim. They lay on their towels, drying under the warm sun. The wind, which had been so constant on the water, was barely in evidence here, seen only in the waving of the palms behind the beach. Raoul was feeling drowsy after the events of the past twenty-four hours. He reached over and held Emma's hand. A deep sense of peace came over him. The sun warmed his skin even as the breeze dried and cooled him. Overhead, the palm fronds waved hypnotically.

"Rao, let's just stay here forever. No people to bother us, nothing trying to silence us," said Emma as they ate their sandwiches, sitting on their blanket.

"The rest of my life, with you beside me on a beach, would be everything I could ever ask for."

Emma climbed on top of him and kissed him. "Let's celebrate our freedom."

Another hour later, they rolled up their towels, put on their clothes, and took the dinghy back to Sea Dream.

33

SEASICKNESS AGAIN?

The next morning, Emma woke after sleeping soundly in the sheltered cove. She could see that Raoul was already up, and she could hear him making breakfast. She could smell the coffee, along with bacon and eggs frying.

Suddenly, the smells were too much. Emma tore out of the bed and rushed to the cockpit, where she emptied her stomach over the side. Raoul was right there beside her, holding her hair and saying, "Are you okay, Em?"

Emma wiped her mouth on the back of her hand. "I can't go back down there. The smells are too much right now."

"Okay, what would you like? Can you eat some breakfast?"

She nodded mutely. "Can you get me a clean cloth to wipe myself up? Oh God, I need to pee. I can't go back down there."

"Em, mi vida, relax. Just pee over the stern and try not to fall in. It's safe enough here at anchor, but please don't try it under sail. We'll think of something else. You can't hurt the boat or the dinghy if you spray on it. I'll get rid of the food smells downstairs. I won't come back up before you're finished."

Raoul disappeared down into the cabin.

Emma stood at the stern, thinking. How the hell do I pee here? Well, I have to try.

When Raoul reemerged, he was carrying a pot of coffee and a plate of bacon and eggs. The sight of them set her off again, and she vomited over the stern. The wind carried it away, but the dinghy suffered.

Raoul tossed the bacon and eggs into the sea and emptied the coffee pot. He helped Emma wipe her face again, then said, "I'm going back down again. I'll be making bread and jam and tea inside. Don't come back down until you feel better. We'll have breakfast here. "

When Raoul came back up, Emma sat shivering on the cockpit seat. She nibbled at her bread and jam. The tea had no milk, which upset her stomach again, so Raoul put milk in, but the sour smell of the milk was worse.

She tried to hold back tears, but it was no use. She knew she was crying out of shame, embarrassment, and frustration at being so weak.

Finally, she gathered herself together enough to say, "It's no good Raoul. Can I just have some hot water, please?"

The hot water helped. Raoul brought up clean clothes, so after looking around, she dressed in the cockpit.

"Let's get sailing again; take your mind off it. You start the engine, I'll get the anchor."

Emma mustered the strength to stand behind the wheel, gripping it with white knuckles. She reached behind to start the engine and was comforted by its low rumble.

They motored out of the bay and were soon sailing again with the same steady breeze as the day before. This time, the steady rhythm of the boat was soothing. Raoul took over the steering, and soon Emma was asleep.

Raoul woke her for lunch and fed her small pieces of cheese, dry crackers, and dried sausage. The cheese was lovely, as were the salty crackers. But as soon as she brought the sausage under her nose, she felt her insides lurch again.

"Rao, what's wrong with me? Did I eat something? It's not seasickness. I actually like the gentle rolling of the boat. But this morning, the smell of coffee sent me puking. And the bacon and eggs, woah, I can't even think about them."

"Let's take it easy today. Water and simple foods. Maybe tomorrow you'll feel better. Did you eat anything different from me yesterday?"

"I don't think so unless there was something in the seawater when we swam. I always end up swallowing a little bit."

"We're making good time. Let's keep going and see how you're feeling tonight. I don't know what else to do for you."

Emma nodded. "It seems okay now, but please, no more coffee today. I don't think I could stand the smell."

The day passed uneventfully as they sailed on under the clear sky. Occasionally, they would see a part of the main island in the distance, reassuring them they were still following the coast. That evening, as the sun went down, they could see the lights of small villages along the shore.

The following morning, when Emma rose, she didn't even make it out of the cabin. Crouched over the toilet in the head, she threw up the contents of her stomach. It left an acid burn at the back of her throat and a horrible taste in her mouth. Raoul must have heard her because he was right there to help her clean up.

"Don't worry about the mess in here. I'll look after

that. Just get dressed and get out into the fresh air. Autopilot's on, but there's more boat traffic about. I think we're sailing past the city."

Up in the cockpit, the symptoms subsided. She could hear the water pump and the handheld shower as Raoul hosed down the head. Closing her eyes for a moment, she steadied herself. Please, God, don't let me be pregnant. Not now. Let this be bacteria or a parasite, but not pregnant. Please….

There were more boats of all sizes. Some of them were the large freighters that brought tropical fruit and overseas manufactured goods to the island, returning with holds full of island wood and farm produce and canned fish for sale to other countries. There were also ferries carrying people to offshore islands, and more pleasure boats, both sailboats and motor yachts. The smaller boats avoided Sea Dream, but then their path was taking them across the bow of a large freighter.

"Hey Rao, I need your help here." Emma shook him to wake him up. For a moment, it seemed he would go back to sleep, but then his eyes snapped open.

He was quick to understand and decisive in his directions. Emma enjoyed watching him. He looks so good when he just takes charge. Those years of UIS must have been hell for him, she reflected.

"We need to tack," Raoul said. "That cargo ship won't manoeuvre for us. It really can't. It's too heavy."

Working together, they changed course and reset the sails to travel along the freighter at a safe distance until it passed.

"Tack again, back to our heading."

They repeated the process to resume their course.

Another five minutes later, Raoul was back to sleep in the cockpit.

Two hours later, Emma checked the autopilot and went down into the cabin to make lunch. The cabin seemed full of unfamiliar smells.

What's happening? Do I have super smell sense now? As she opened the fridge door, the mixture of odours proved too much, and her fragile stomach flipped again, causing another rush to the head. Immediately, Raoul was down there with her, holding her hair out of the way and passing her a wet washcloth to clean her face.

Emma didn't even try to hold back her tears. "What's wrong with me? What if it gets worse?"

"I don't know, Em. But we're going to find a doctor for you."

"But we can't go to a doctor. Gisele will find us."

"I have an idea. Just try to hang on. Don't worry about lunch. I'll make it. Water, bread and jam sounds lovely."

Emma smiled at his weak attempt at humor.

Once again, out in the fresh air, looking at the horizon, she felt better. But the dark thought was returning to her mind. I can't really be pregnant, can I? All this throwing up and a super sense of smell? But we're always so careful. Why now? This is the worst time. I missed my last period, but that's happened before, and we were really stressed this time. Maybe it's just something I ate. It must be something I ate!

Raoul fed them, then studied the plotter.

"There's a town called Michelson's Landing not too far ahead. I think it's far enough from the city for us to avoid detection. I'm going to take us there to find a doctor or a nurse. We can be there by evening."

"Are you sure?"

"You can't go on like this. When we know what's causing it, we can get some medicine to fix it." Emma nodded, looking down. A wave of guilt swept over her at causing this departure from their plans. Do I tell Raoul what I think? But he'll get all excited and if I'm wrong, he would be so disappointed. But what if I'm right?

As they sailed toward the coast, in the fading glow of the sun, the lights of town came on. It was six o'clock by the time they tied up at the visitor's dock. "Go below and lie down," said Raoul. " I'll lock up the companionway, and be back soon with help. If anything goes wrong, fire or something, just open the hatch over the bed and go out through there."

34

RAOUL GETS HELP

R aoul locked the boat and stepped off onto the dock. His stomach clenched as a wave of fear and doubt washed through him. I can't lose Emma now, he thought. After everything she's done, we've come so far.

He felt in his pocket for the handgun he had collected before leaving. In the opposite pocket was the clip of bullets. He thought briefly about loading the gun. The last thing I need is to shoot myself in the foot, he told himself. A mental image came of Jake and the gun safety lesson.

There were still shopping stragglers in the street, as well as shopkeepers who had just locked up. He asked the first three people he met where he could find a doctor or nurse.

"The pink house in the first side street to the left." Each stranger gave him the same direction. The last one added, "If the surgery door is closed, ring the night bell. Marnie will answer as long as she's home. If not, she'll be back soon. The village isn't that large."

As Raoul turned into the side street, he spotted the pink building.

The surgery door was closed, but he could see the night bell clearly marked.

He pressed it twice and heard a grumpy voice say, "All right, all right, I'm coming."

A short lady in her fifties with reddish hair now going grey answered the door.

"Please, we need help. Something's wrong with my wife. Please come and tell us what it is."

"I don't think I know you. Where's your wife?"

"On our boat."

"Can she walk?"

"Yes."

"Well, bring her up to the surgery. There's not much I can do on a boat."

A sudden wave of frustration and terror came over Raoul at the thought of being seen on the main island together. He felt his eyes go wide, and he looked around for an exit. I should never have come here. Mistake, mistake, mistake.

"It's okay, you're safe here. What has you so scared?" she asked.

"We're being chased by some bad people. We witnessed something, and now they want to kill us both." A desperate thought occurred to him. "I have a gun." He showed the nurse the gun.

"So now you're going to shoot me if I don't come with you?"

Raoul felt his cheeks blaze with embarrassment.

"No, I've never shot anyone." He sighed. "But I could give you the gun if you come."

"Put that away. I hope it's not loaded."

"No," he showed her the clip in his other pocket.

"Good. Here's what I'm willing to do, I'll walk down to the boat with you. I'll bring a hooded cape, and your wife can wrap herself in it while the three of us walk back here."

Raoul nodded, feeling completely helpless.

"Step in and wait for me here."

The nurse returned wearing a light raincoat and carrying a dark cloak on her arm.

"Now, let's go find this boat of yours."

They walked together under the light of the street lamps until they reached the harbor. Sea Dream was bobbing restlessly against the dock but otherwise untouched.

Raoul unlocked the cabin and shouted down, "Emma, are you able to come out? I have help."

A moment later, Emma's pale face appeared. She accepted Raoul's arm to steady herself as she got out of the cabin.

"Emma, I'm Marnie, the local nurse practitioner. Put on this cloak to hide yourself, and we'll walk together up to my surgery, where I can have a proper look at you."

The three walked up to the surgery. Raoul was aware of every face at a window, of every passerby on the street. A man in a black raincoat came up behind him. A moment of panic hit. I should have loaded the gun. He stepped back against the wall, ready to tackle his assailant. A steadying hand grasped his elbow.

"Evening Richard," said Marnie. "Things going well at the bank?"

"Hi Marnie. Well enough, thanks. Miserable evening. Late for dinner, I'm afraid. Looks like you're busy, so I won't keep you."

The stranger moved past and disappeared into the gloom. Raoul breathed out a sign of relief.

Once inside, the nurse was all business. "Emma, through there, and lie down. And you, what's your name?"

"Raoul."

"Sit in the chair. I have questions for both of you. To begin with, I can already see this is not the virus that's killing people in other parts of the world. So let's put that thought out of your mind. When did this start?"

"Two days ago," said Emma. "At first, I thought it was seasickness again, but it doesn't bother me when we're sailing as long as I don't go down to the cabin."

"What are the symptoms?"

"I keep vomiting, over and over. Lots of things set me off, so I can hardly eat and I can't keep anything down."

As she said this, the nurse was bustling about, then stuck a thermometer under Emma's tongue.

"I'm just going to take your blood pressure." She fastened the cuff, and all three watched as the readings rose until they settled.

"Hmm, 95 over 65. A little low, but that makes sense. Have you missed a period?"

"The last one." Emma's voice was very low.

Raoul looked up sharply. "Emma?" he said. His mind was whirling. A baby? How the hell do we care for a baby on the run?

"Hush now. Can you sit up, Emma?"

"Yes."

"I want you to take this little strip and pee on it for me."

"You think…?"

"Let's just do the test, and then we can talk about it."

Emma took the little strip into the bathroom and closed the door.

"Now, young man, what form of birth control have you been using?"

"Condoms. It always seemed the least invasive way."

"Good, and about 98% effective in theory, but in practice, about fifteen of every hundred women who rely on condoms will become pregnant within a year. Was there a day you missed?"

Raoul looked down, thinking of their picnic by the waterfall. "One day, on a picnic, but that was about six weeks ago."

"I'm afraid that was probably the day."

Just then, Emma opened the bathroom door and rejoined them. It was clear from her red eyes and tear-stained cheeks she had been crying. She held out the little stick. As clear as anything, the little blue plus sign showed above the calibration line.

"Well, that confirms it," said Marnie. "You're pregnant. Now the question is, do you want to keep it?"

"Can you give us a moment, please?" said Raoul.

"Of course. Why don't I just scan your wrist chip first, and I can look at your medical records while you discuss?"

Emma clamped her hand over her wrist reflexively.

Raoul scratched his head. He felt his cheeks burning. "Uhhh…we don't have wrist chips. It's how they were tracking us."

He held out his own wrists for inspection. Marnie peered at the small scar and ran her finger over his wrist, feeling for the slight bump that indicated a chip.

"And you're the same, I suppose."

"Yes," said Emma, suddenly looking exhausted.

"Okay, I won't ask any more questions. Have your conversation while I step outside."

A terrifying thought occurred to Raoul. "You're not going to report us, are you? They would kill us for sure. Maybe it would be better if you stayed here. We can talk with you here."

"No, I wouldn't report you, and yes, if you feel better, I'll stay."

Raoul took both Emma's hands in his and crouched down in front of her. "What do you want to do, Em? It's your body and your choice."

"No, it's both of us, Raoul. What do you think? Can we manage it?"

Raoul's mind kept generating obstacles. What if Emma has a difficult pregnancy? What if the new community is not a good place for a baby? Where will we get all the baby supplies? But what if it all works out? I would be a dad, but I don't know how to do that. "It's not the perfect time," he said, "but I suppose it never is."

"That's what Mary said. She and Jake waited for the perfect time, and it never came. She said it was the greatest regret of her life."

Raoul nodded. "Good. I want this for us so much, Em." As he said the words, a sudden realization came. I really do want this! He leaned forward and kissed her. "We'll be safe long before you're due. I say let's keep it."

Emma smiled and he could see her relax. "I want it too," she said.

"Wonderful," said Marnie. "The sickness will pass in a few weeks. Meanwhile, try to avoid things that bring it on, like the smell of coffee evidently. Spend as much time as possible in the open air, and find medical attention as soon as you arrive. Not that there's likely to be anything wrong. You're young and fit, so no reason to worry. But you should be monitored during your pregnancy."

Raoul and Emma both nodded.

"I'll walk back down to the boat and take back my cloak. I suggest you get out of here. These small villages have lots of eyes and love a mystery."

Back at the boat, Emma stood behind the wheel and

started the motor. Marnie folded her cloak on a bollard, then cast off the lines. Raoul coiled them on the deck.

They waved to each other as Emma pulled away from the dock and spun the boat around. The last they saw of Marnie was her gathering up her cloak and walking back home.

When they were clear of the harbor and far enough from land to catch a clean wind, Emma and Raoul worked together to set the sails and the auto pilot. Then they sat together in the cockpit, looking up at the stars in the clear night sky.

"Do you really want this baby?" Emma asked.

Raoul held her close. "Emma, mi vida, I want most of all to spend the rest of my life with you, and I promise to love and protect this baby. I think it's the most amazing thing that has happened to us so far. But are you really okay carrying it? With the sickness and all?"

"Now that I know what's causing it, I can manage the sickness. And it's only for a few weeks. Our child will be forever, so yes, I want him or her just as much as you do."

They sat like that, each lost in their own thoughts as the wind pulled the small boat forward into the black night.

35

A TEST OF SEAMANSHIP

Emma woke up from her dream of having a baby in the middle of a town square with an entire village of strangers offering advice all at once.

As she came back to consciousness, she realized the boat was rocking much more than usual. She quickly wedged herself into the head, then came up to the cockpit to see what was going on.

It was still dark, although the first gray light of dawn was showing. Raoul was awake behind the wheel but looked as though all the energy had drained out of him. An alarm sounded, and he reached over and cancelled it.

"Rao, are you okay? You've been up all night again." His voice sounded groggy, and she could see his eyes trying to focus.

"You need your sleep, Em. I have an alarm set for every fifteen minutes, so it keeps waking me up if I nod off." Raoul was mumbling as he spoke.

"Let me take over. What's going on? The boat's really rocking."

"Yeah, I think there's some squalls nearby. Every so

often, we get a burst of wind, and the seas are getting rougher. We should really find an anchorage and wait it out."

"Let me take the wheel for a moment. Do you think we should take down the sails?"

"Let me see where we're going. Our speed is quite high, faster than motoring."

Raoul studied the plotter. "There's another island 12 kilometres ahead. We can be there in an hour if we keep going. It shows a small village with a harbor on the leeward side. We could probably anchor there until the storms pass."

The next moment, chaos ensued as a strong gust hit with a roaring noise from the wind. All the steel rigging buzzed, and a loose line hammered incessantly against the canopy above them. The boat heeled over until the deck was nearly vertical. "Hang on," said Raoul. The boat rounded up into the wind on its own, with the sails flapping even more violently as the wind no longer filled them. The the deck was level again.

"That was as scary as I want it to be," said Emma. "Let's get the sails down now before we kill ourselves."

"But maybe we could just try reefing them to make them smaller."

"Raoul, sweetheart, I love you dearly. But if you want me to keep loving you, get the sails down now! We're still novice sailors, and this is not the time or place to be trying new tricks."

Raoul nodded. Emma could see that he wasn't happy, but he would go along.

"We can talk about it later, Rao. Maybe we'll practice reefing in a better wind. But right now, our priority has to be safety."

"You're right, Em. And I'm too tired to think clearly.

Keep the boat into the wind, start the engine, and I'll get the sails down."

Raoul furled the genoa as quickly as he could. The result wasn't pretty, but at least the sail was wrapped up and held by a couple of wraps of the sheets. He coiled and cleated off the furling line, making a second knot to be sure the wind could not catch the genoa.

He then simply dropped the main. Standing precariously on the cabin roof, he used a pair of bungee cords to contain the loosely folded sail along the boom.

"Em, will you be okay up here if I go down to sleep? Tell me when you see the island." Raoul went down.

When Emma checked fifteen minutes later, she found him still fully clothed, lying on top of the bed. She pulled off his jeans and hoodie and tucked him under the covers. Leaning over, she kissed him on the forehead before going back up to resume her watch.

THE ISLAND CAME INTO VIEW ABOUT TWO HOURS LATER. Emma adjusted the heading to take them around the near end of the island and sat contented, watching as the rocky outcropping came into view. The sun was rising behind the island, and the sky was lit with reds and oranges in a magnificent display.

"Red sky at morning, sailors take warning." The old saying floated up from somewhere in her subconscious mind.

As they rounded the end of the island, the seas calmed, and the wind dropped. Now, there was just the steady vibration of the motor as it propelled them forward. She backed off the throttle a bit, reducing speed. Might as well let Raoul sleep a little longer, she thought. He looked exhausted last night.

When the sun was fully risen, Emma went down and woke the sleeping Raoul. Stroking his arm, she said, "Rao, sweetheart, we're coming up on the harbor."

His eyes flew open, and he bounded up, then sat back down on the bed.

"Relax, everything's fine. We just coming up to the harbor, so I need you on anchor."

Up on deck, they could see the harbor entrance. Marker buoys marked the channel. Keeping the red markers to starboard and the green ones to port, they made their way in. Several other boats were anchored off to the left, so Emma eased the throttle back to just above idle and approached the boats, calling out the depth. At five meters, Raoul held up his fist making the sign to hold, and she could hear the anchor chain rattling out of its locker until Raoul stopped it.

Raoul signaled for reverse gear to set the anchor. He set the snubber to keep the anchor chain from chafing or stressing the anchor winch.

Emma cut the engine.

"We're getting good at this," she said.

"Yeah, I'm actually enjoying it. I'll be sad when we finally get there."

"I won't," said Emma. "But it will be nice to have a boat to go sailing when we want to."

Raoul made a breakfast of bread and jam with hot water to drink.

"Raoul, if you want to make a coffee for yourself, go ahead. I should be okay out here in the open."

Raoul flashed her a grateful smile and disappeared below. Soon, the faint odor of coffee arose from the companionway. Emma picked up the rest of her breakfast and moved up to the foredeck, where the odor couldn't bother her.

As she settled down near the bow, she saw a small red boat heading their way, Harbormaster clearly written on the side.

"Raoul," she called down. "We've got company."

Raoul came up with coffee in hand to greet the newcomer.

"Hello," he said as the red boat drew alongside.

"Hello, are you planning to stay in the harbor for long?"

"No, just waiting for the winds to die down a bit."

"I'd be happy to give you a lift into the village if you like."

"No thanks, we prefer just to wait it out on our boat. Do some tidying up and get ready for the next leg. We should be gone tomorrow morning."

"I really think you should come into the office."

"Why would we come into the office?"

"There's people there that would like to talk with you."

"What people?"

"They're not here yet but will be soon. Nothing serious. I was told they just want to chat about something that happened back on the main island."

Raoul turned away to look at Emma and shook his head with slight movements. Now was not the time to panic. Stay calm, stay calm.

"Sure, but we don't need a ride. Let us finish cleaning up, and we'll come ashore in our dinghy."

"Great, thanks."

The red boat pushed off and headed back to the dock.

"Raoul?" said Emma. "Why would we agree to go onshore?"

"He just lied to us, so I think it's fair that we lie to him.

Let's wait until his boat is tied up. Then, start the engine. We're leaving as soon as I get the anchor up."

Raoul retrieved his binoculars and scanned the dock. He caught sight of a familiar metallic body walking into the office. Crap. Does Gisele have one on every island? What's waiting at Three Saints? But they wouldn't allow one ashore, not if what Jake said was true.

Emma was back, sitting in the cockpit. Her stomach heaved from the scent of coffee from the cabin, and she vomited over the side. It was easier to bear now that she knew why it was happening.

She heard the anchor chain locker open on the deck and then the familiar sound of the anchor being pulled in. When it was secured at the bow, Raoul made circles above his head, and Emma set off at full speed out of the harbor, back to the open ocean.

They continued around the small island until the port was out of sight.

"Time to try our reefing technique," said Raoul with a smile.

With the boat pointing into the wind, Raoul pulled up the sail until the first reef point was visible, then slacked off a bit and cleated off the main halyard. "I'll need you to winch it up once I have the reefing ring in place over the hook on the boom."

He went unsteadily forward to the mast and hanging on to the mast with his left arm, he tightened the first reefing point. "Emma, winch it up taut."

He then tightened the reefing point along the boom to keep the bottom of the sail tight. Now, the sail did not go all the way to the top of the mast but was shorter by a meter.

Next, they set the genoa, but instead of letting it all the way out, they furled it again for a full meter of its length.

Raoul cleated off the furling line before winching the genoa sheet taut.

"We're set," he announced. "Take us out into the wind."

Fifteen minutes later, they passed out of the shadow of the island, where the winds were still gusting. But with the reduced sail area, the boat remained closer to level and quickly picked up speed.

"Kill the engine, Emma. We can sail now. Let's head off in a different direction in case someone's trying to guess where we're going."

Sea Dream was now heading out into the open ocean.

As the island fell away from their stern, no new islands showed up on the horizon. This was the first time Emma experienced being completely out of sight of land. How do people ever cross oceans? she thought.

"We'll continue on this path for two more hours," Raphael said, "then cut back in towards the islands we've been following. The next island is Bald Point Island."

"Isn't that the one we were told to avoid?"

"I think we'll avoid all the inhabited islands from now on. But there's a small rocky island before Bald Point where we could rest. We'll try there and keep our eyes open. Then it will be a long run to Three Saints. What would you like for lunch?"

"Cheese and crackers. That's all I can manage right now."

"Are you still throwing up?"

"Yes, but it doesn't bother me so much now that I know why. Don't worry about me, sweetheart, just get us there safely."

36

BECALMED

Three hours later, the wind died. With no warning, it just disappeared. The sun was now shining down in a clear sky, and the waves subsided until eventually the sea was an oily calm.

The sails hung listlessly, and the boat itself seemed dispirited as it rolled with the swells but with no motivation to move forward.

Emma turned on the motor and put the transmission forward at idle. Raoul dropped the sails. Then they resumed at half throttle on autopilot.

"Rao, why don't we take this chance to tidy up the boat?"

"Sure, Em. You take the cockpit and the deck, and I'll tackle the cabin."

Emma set about tidying the ropes and hosing down the cockpit floor to get rid of crumbs from their meals of bread and jam. She went forward and pulled and tugged the mainsail into neat folds, as Mike had taught them. Looking down through the transparent cabin hatch, she could see Raoul doing dishes, straightening cupboards and restoring order to the cabin after the rolling seas of the past few days.

A moment later, the V-berth hatch opened, and Raoul's head popped up.

"Watch your footing up here. I've got the hatch open for some fresh air."

Emma sat on the foredeck with her back to the mast, looking over the bow. She was thinking of how far they had come and how much she had learned about Raoul through all their trials. *There really is no one else I would want to have by my side.*

Then she remembered her parents and the way they had left them without any warning or even saying goodbye. She cried, unable to block the deep sadness washing through her. She felt Raoul settle next to her, putting his arm around her and saying nothing.

A few minutes later, the sadness passed as quickly as it had come.

"Right," she said. "Let's get this boat moving again."

Back at the wheel, she pushed the throttle forward, and the boat surged ahead making six knots again through the eerily calm water. There was a fizzing sound as the bow broke the surface. Other than the low rumble of the motor, the silence was amazing. Watching their progress on the chart plotter, it was clear that they would have another night on the water before reaching the string of islands again the next morning.

Over a cold dinner of Emma-compatible foods, she said, "Rao, it's not fair that you should have to take the entire night. I'll be on watch from seven p.m. to eleven p.m.; you can have eleven p.m. to four a.m., and I'll take it again until breakfast. That way, we both get some sleep, and I get to watch the sunrise."

"You sure? I can do the entire night again."

"And be a zombie the next day? No, I want you wide awake tomorrow when we get close to this island we're supposed to avoid."

"Okay, then I'll go down for a nap now. Wake me up when you want to go to bed."

Emma sat in the cockpit, alone, watching the sea ahead as the autopilot continued to steer the course towards the islands, still unseen over the horizon.

As she sat, she thought of the baby she was carrying and envisioned raising a child in the fresh air of an island inside a close-knit community. Her daydream brought a rapturous feeling of joy and excitement. At one point, she laughed out loud. But then she thought of her parents, who might never meet their grandchild, and it plunged her into a deep sorrow. She sat weeping over what might have been.

"What is wrong with me?" she asked herself out loud. "One minute, I'm full of joy and the next minute, everything is sad and gloomy."

Raoul must have heard her from the cabin. "You're pregnant, Em, and your body is still processing all the hormonal changes. Nothing's wrong. You are still as perfect as the day we met. Now, please try to process quietly. I'm having a hard time getting to sleep."

At eleven, Emma woke Raoul for the handoff. "I'd make you a coffee, but I can't right now. I'll close the V-berth door and go to bed, then you can make one for yourself."

Raoul yawned and stretched, pulled on his clothes and walked out while Emma undressed and climbed into the bed, still warm with Raoul's body heat. The last thing she remembered was the faint popping sound of the coffee percolator.

It was five a.m. when Raoul woke her. "Sunrise will happen soon, and I know you like them. Nothing to see out there, but we still have to watch for other large ships. We passed three of them last night."

Up on deck, the sky was already fading to its gray pre-dawn light as Emma took over the watch. With a mug of hot water in her hands and the last of Mary's biscuits, she settled down to watch the sun come up.

Three hours later, a sleepy Raoul emerged from the cabin.

"Morning, sweetheart," she said. "Make a coffee if you like. It won't bother me up here. There's still one of Mary's muffins left. I finished off the cookies."

Raoul stood in the cockpit looking at the horizon, then disappeared back down to make his coffee. When he reappeared, he had his mug and two muffins on a plate. "There was another one tucked behind, so I brought it up for you."

Before settling down, Raoul studied the chart plotter again. "We should see the small island soon. It's just off the bow to port." He pulled the binoculars from the cubby where he kept them and peered at the horizon.

"Yes, I see something, probably the high point on the island."

As they drew nearer, more of the island came into view. It was not much more than a large rock rising out of the ocean, but it promised a safe place to anchor and prepare for the last push.

As they rounded the island, there was already another sailboat anchored there.

"Looks like someone else taking a break," said Raoul. "Let's keep our distance."

They anchored at the other end of the sheltered area. The water here was deep, but it still felt to Emma that they were very close to the rocky wall of the island. Raoul pulled out his binoculars to look at the other boat.

"It looks deserted," he said to Emma. "There're barnacles growing on the anchor chain. I don't see a dinghy, but it could be on the far side where we can't see it."

Emma served a snack of hot water, bread, and jam. There was still no activity on the other boat.

"I'm going to refill the diesel tank," announced Raoul. "Please look under the cockpit seats for a funnel. I'll get the canisters."

Emma found a large red plastic funnel under the seat. It was greasy from past use, so she tried to hold it with only her fingertips. Raoul was already undoing the fuel cap with the winch handle. He popped the funnel into the top of the fueling line and knelt back, emptying their fuel containers into the tank. "I think it will take all of these," he said. "We're down to a quarter tank after all the motoring we've done. Still, lots left for the last leg."

When he had emptied the last can and was fastening the empties back in place, Emma heard the distinctive noise of a dinghy engine.

Looking around, she saw a dinghy arriving from the boat across the anchorage.

"Visitors," she called out.

"Get the boathook," Raoul replied.

Emma went below to find the long boathook lying on a shelf behind the couch.

As she brought it up, she saw Raoul bent over something on the cockpit table. "What's that, Raoul?"

"Insurance, after our last experience and knowing

we're close to Bald Point Island, I don't want to take any chances."

She watched as he laid the loaded handgun on its cloth on the table, its muzzle pointed out to sea.

"Don't touch it, Emma. It's a last resort. Jake taught me to use it before we left."

The small dinghy approached with two men in it. They bumped up against the stern and held on with their hands.

"Hi, I'm Jonathon, and this is Tony. Mind if we come aboard?"

"Sorry, we don't take visitors on the boat. Where are you from?" Raoul's voice was bright and casual.

"Originally from the city, but we drift around the islands now."

"Nice to meet you, but please push off now. We've had some unpleasant experiences. Nothing personal, but I'd like you to leave."

Raoul's voice was cheerful, but Emma could see the tension in his muscles. She went to stand beside him at the back of the cockpit, holding the boathook upright beside her.

"You have a beautiful partner. What would your names be?"

"Mario and Zelda. Sorry, but we're not in the mood for chatting right now. Please leave."

Tony looked at Jonathon. "I don't think we feel like leaving just yet." He grabbed hold of the transom, about to climb out of the dinghy. Raoul took the boathook from Emma's hand and jabbed Tony, forcing him back.

Tony grabbed the other end of the boathook and tried to pull Raoul off balance.

Emma acted reflexively. She picked up the gun from the table and aimed it at the would-be pirates. Tony let go of the boat hook.

"Trade," hissed Raoul, passing the boathook to Emma and taking the gun.

Then, looking at Tony and Jonathon, he said, "We've asked you several times nicely. Now leave, or I shoot."

Struck with inspiration, Emma screamed, "Mario baby, please don't kill any more people. Six is already enough."

Immediately, Emma heard a loud crack as the handgun went off. She looked at Raoul, standing with a wild look in his eyes, holding the gun from which a small wisp of smoke was emerging. A hissing sound started as Tony and Jonathon's dinghy began to deflate on one side.

"Damn, I missed," said Raoul, lining up again, but the pair were already off as fast as their small dinghy would go, trying to outrace the leaking pontoon.

"Emma, get the engine. We're going to make a wide detour around Bald Point."

Raoul raced to the foredeck and pulled up the anchor. Even before it was all the way home, Emma was swinging the bow and heading out to sea. Looking at the chart plotter, Raoul set a new waypoint far out on the ocean side of Bald Point Island. It would still take them toward Three Saints but at the cost of a half day's travel.

The winds were rising again, so they set the sails but kept the motor running and were soon cruising at the boat's maximum speed.

"Rao," said Emma, "Were you really going to shoot Tony back there?"

"Not unless I had to, although Jake taught me to never point a gun unless you're ready to use it. But I knew if I punctured their dinghy on one side, that would create a bigger problem for them than trying to overpower us. They'll be okay. I only shot one of the inflatable tubes, but they'll be wet and moving slowly, giving us time to get away. But six people? Who are the six people I shot?"

"No offense, Rao, but you don't look like a person who would shoot anyone, not like the guys in the black limo. So I thought I might give you a little added credibility as a nut-bar with a gun."

"I don't know if that's a compliment or an insult. A nut-bar with a gun?"

"If the shoe fits…."

Raoul laughed. "I love you, Em. With you at my side, we can do anything."

"Let's just get to Three Saints and hope it's everything Jake promised us."

AN HOUR LATER, THE WINDS HAD SHIFTED. EMMA CUT THE engine, and Raoul trimmed the sails for the new wind direction. Emma was surprised at how comfortable and enjoyable sailing had become. Out on the ocean, they were truly free.

At the waypoint, they tacked and were now on course directly for Three Saints.

"One more night," thought Emma, "And we'll be starting our new life."

The night was uneventful. Once again, Raoul went to bed early, then rose at eleven to relieve Emma, who slept until five. When she woke up, she went to the head to vomit and pee, but the morning sickness didn't really bother her as much now. Raoul had been so good about avoiding triggers that it only hit a few times a day.

At dawn, the sun painted the entire sky pink and tangerine for a few moments before it became a clear blue.

Emma trimmed the sails to squeeze another half knot from the wind and settled back with her mug of hot water and a few crackers.

When Raoul emerged five hours later, the island was coming into view.

37

LANDING AT THREE SAINTS

As they reached the island of Three Saints, the wind became unpredictable. Emma started the engine while Raoul dropped the sails. Emma declined Raoul's offer to take over at the wheel. "After coming this far, I want to be the one to steer us into our new home."

Raoul agreed with his usual good humor and went below to clean up the cabin in preparation for their arrival. Emma saw the hatches on the foredeck open and Raoul's head pop up for a moment. Through the open companionway, she caught glimpses of him as he put away the mugs and plates that had accumulated in the sink. He disappeared for a moment into the quarter berth where all the packages for Three Saints were stowed. By the time he came back up to the cockpit, the harbor was coming into view. The first red marker buoy showing the channel was just ahead. They would need to keep those to starboard on the way into the harbor.

"Remember, red right returning," he said, quoting an old sailors' aphorism.

"I got this, sweetheart."

"Sorry, I'm just feeling nervous."

"Then why not go up top, ready to put out the fenders, or drop the anchor or whatever they want us to do?"

As they entered the harbor mouth, a small dinghy came out to meet them. Raoul brought up the boat hook and laid it on the cockpit cushions.

Up until this point, the village had been hidden behind the Three Saints, the rock formations that protected it. Now, as they slipped behind the rocky outcrops, Emma could see the harbor ahead, and above, the village nestled in the rocks. Some of the buildings were stone, others were clapboard but all were painted in bright colors of blue, red, yellow, or green with no discernible pattern. The road up to the village looked steep, but that meant the houses were well above any ocean storms.

A throng of villagers stood at the dock. "They're cheering," said Raoul. Emma listened carefully and could hear the excited buzz from the shore between gusts of carrying it away.

As the dinghy came alongside, they could see it held a man and a young boy of eight or nine years old. Emma cut the engine back to idle, and Raoul offered them the end of the boathook to hold the dinghy next to Sea Dream.

"Sea Dream, we've been waiting for you. My name's James, town accountant, and this is my son, Toby. You must be Emma and Raoul, right?"

"Yes sir," said Raoul.

"You'll be in a finger dock, fenders to the port side, two bow lines, a stern line and a spring line should do."

"Got that. Fenders to port, four lines out. Thanks," replied Raoul.

The dinghy surged forward, and Emma swung the boat slightly to follow them in. Making the final turn into the harbor, James pointed to a slip with a big sign saying, "Welcome Sea Dream."

"I guess that's it," Emma called to Raoul.

He nodded, but she could see he was focused on the lines.

On the dock, a small crowd waited to welcome the new arrivals. Raoul had only to toss the lines, and several people stepped forward to tie them off. Emma cut the engine and now she could hear the crowd clearly, as they called out helpful advice, or simply "Welcome to Three Saints."

Raoul helped Emma off the boat. She turned her head from side to side to take in the crowd and the colored houses. Her balance wobbled immediately. Her vision went white, and then she felt consciousness slipping away.

She came to, lying on the dock with Raoul and several strangers hovering over her. She rolled away from them and vomited.

As if in the distance, she heard Raoul say, "She's pregnant and has been battling morning sickness on the way over." Raoul's arms were under her, helping her stand up.

"Oh, poor lamb," she heard a female voice say. "Let's get you both away from the boat and into somewhere comfortable."

Behind her, Raoul announced, "In the quarter berth are all the packages we were asked to deliver. Perhaps a couple of the boys would like to get them out?"

A buzz went through the crowd.

Clever Raoul, create a distraction, thought Emma as she accepted his help to get to her feet.

A tall, older man in a red checked shirt stepped forward. "Welcome, I'm Tom Peters, the mayor of Three

Saints. Why don't we go up to the pub so you can sit down?"

The pub was rustic, with hand made tables and benches, pine planked floor and miscellaneous decorations, some of which had clearly been made by children. The bar itself was simple and functional, having only two beer taps, and a sparse collection of alcohols on a shelf behind the bar.

As she went to sit dow on a bench, the scent of stale beer and fried food was too much. Emma tried desperately to control her nausea, but ended up running outside and throwing up into the bushes. Raoul and Tom were right behind her. Tom carried a napkin and a glass of water.

"Tom," said Raoul. "Do you think we could sit outside this time? I think Emma's a bit destabilized. We've had a hell of a journey here."

"Sure, no worries," replied Tom. "Lori!" A girl in her mid-teens came over. "Please fetch Angie." Turning back to Emma, "Angie's our nurse practitioner on the island. She'll help you through your pregnancy. She's delivered almost all the babies in the past 15 years."

Lori returned a few minutes later. "What would you like to drink?"

"Hot water for Emma. I'll have something cool but not alcoholic."

"Hot water and a root beer, then. Tom, anything for you?"

"I'll have a root beer too, thanks Lori."

As they sat sipping their drinks, a lady in her late forties arrived in light blue scrubs. She had curly brown hair, freckles and a gentle smile.

"Hi Emma, I'm Angie. I understand you had a rough go of it this morning."

"I'm fine now. It's just that certain things set me off,

like coffee, fried meat, dried sausage, and pub smells, evidently."

"All normal. How many weeks are you?"

"About eight weeks if we have the conception day right."

"That's good. Why don't you come to see me tomorrow afternoon when you're settled? I'll give you a once-over just to establish your baselines. You're still young and seem healthy, so I doubt there's anything wrong."

Emma nodded. "I'll be there."

James and Toby joined them at the table. "Packages are all delivered, said James, "thanks to Toby and his friends."

"Fine," said Tom. "Now, I'll show you to the house we have set up for you."

They walked together up the main street and turned off on the second side street. A small crowd was gathered outside a stone cottage that had been painted pink at some point in its past. The paint was peeling in spots, testifying to the years the house had stood empty.

"They've all contributed, so I think they want to see your reaction. Please look amazed. It really has been a community effort," Tom explained quietly.

Emma gripped Raoul's forearm for support.

It seemed everyone in the crowd wanted to shake hands and many of them pressed small gifts on Emma welcoming them.

The house looked solid, made of local stone underneath the pink paint. The garden in the front was beautiful. Emma caught the scents of honeysuckle, rose, and lavender as they walked up the path to the front door. Inside, it was warm and cozy, with an eclectic mix of furniture around a stone fireplace. In the kitchen was a familiar wood-burning stove with a small stack of wood beside it. Instead of running water, there was a blue, cast iron, hand pump over the sink that drew water from somewhere. A window over the sink afforded a view of the kitchen garden, chicken coop and small orchard out back. A large unfinished wooden table with four wooden chairs sat in the centre of the kitchen. On the walls were cross stitch tapestries, and children's drawings. Tom said everyone contributed, thought Emma.

There were two bedrooms, one with a four-poster bed and rolled-up mosquito netting. "Only for the summer," someone said. "We're already past the season." Emma looked at the bed longingly. It looks so soft and warm. All I want to do is lie down and cover myself up.

The neighbors had set up the other bedroom as a sewing room for Emma's use. "Jake said that you knew how to sew," Tom explained. It was furnished with a polished wooden cutting table, and an old treadle sewing machine. "We didn't know you were pregnant. We can help turn it into a nursery if that would be more use."

Emma smiled. "No, this is fine for now. I learned to use one of these machines before we left. This is perfect, thank you."

Out the back door was a kitchen garden and a weathered outhouse. Peering inside, Emma couldn't help feeling envious as she remembered the smooth plastic walls that Jake and Mary had.

There was also a large shed containing a workbench and a collection of old tools. "Raoul," said Tom, "I understand you're a talented mechanic. We lost our last mechanic when his wife didn't want to live here anymore. They had romantic ideas about life off the grid, and were here simply by choice. When it turned out to be more work than they thought, they left. The tools are the ones he left behind and they're yours now. If you two are okay, I suggest you go back out front and thank everyone. They are waiting to hear how you like your new home"

The crowd was still waiting in front of the house. Raoul held Emma's hand and stepped forward. "Thank you all for such a warm welcome," he said, "and for the amazing gift of this home. It's beautiful, and I can already tell that we'll be very happy here. It will be a wonderful place to raise our family."

Emma forced a smile onto her face. "Yes, thank you, all of you. You've been very kind to give us such a warm welcome."

Satisfied, the crowd turned away, leaving them alone with Tom, James, and Toby, who had hung back, staying close to his father.

"Thank you, Tom, for everything you've done. This is lovely, and we look forward to meeting the community properly over the next couple of weeks. Right now, I think Emma needs some rest, and I have to bring our things up from the boat."

"Take Toby for the rest of the day," said James. "Toby will be happy to help you move in, won't you, Toby?"

"Yeah, for sure." Toby's smile was infectious, and Emma couldn't help smiling in return.

38

MOVING IN

W hile Emma went to lie down, Toby walked with Raoul back to the boat.

"There's a cart we can use," said Toby helpfully before he scampered off and returned with a wooden box on two large bicycle wheels and with two long handles. It was all his young body could do to pull it.

"That's perfect," said Raoul. "Come down below. You can help me get things together for the cart."

"Can we go sailing after?" asked Toby.

"Not today, but in a couple of days, when we're settled, I'll take you and your friends sailing."

It only took one trip with the loaded cart to transfer everything useful from the boat to the new house. When Raoul went in, he found Emma fast asleep on the bed.

Toby was still waiting outside.

"Toby, come around to the workshop with me. Emma's still sleeping. Bring the small toolbox, and I'll carry the large one. We can get the work area organized."

Toby was a willing worker and peppered Raoul with

questions about sailing and mechanics. He was also a fountain of local knowledge about the town and its people. When they were finally finished cleaning up and putting everything away, it was nearing dusk.

"You'd better be getting home, Toby. It'll be dark soon."

"Yeah, thanks Raoul for letting me help."

"Thank you, Toby, for sticking with me."

Raoul watched as Toby went running off, then went inside to find Emma. She was sitting on the edge of the bed, crying. Raoul's heart crashed.

"Em, mi vida, what's wrong?"

"I wanted this to be so perfect, so wonderful, but it feels like we've gone back 100 years into the past. There's no electricity and I have to pump the water in the kitchen. And I'm afraid of the outhouse. I saw a spider in there that I swear could carry me away! What are we going to do, Rao? Is this our life from now on?"

They both turned as a knock sounded at the front door. Raoul went to answer.

One of the village women stood outside, smiling and holding a red ceramic baking dish. "I'm Alma, from down the street. I knew you wouldn't be ready to cook for yourselves just yet. Let me show you how to start the stove, and we can heat this lasagna for dinner."

Alma bustled in, just as Emma walked out of the bedroom. She had dried her eyes, but her face was still blotchy from crying.

"Don't worry, dear. We all struggled at first. But life here really is good when you get used to it. Now, let's get this oven going."

Alma set the fire in the stove and lit the kindling with a match. "We'll just let that come up to temperature, and then we can pop in the lasagna. Why don't we have a seat? Raoul, fill the kettle and put it on top of the stove, and we'll have tea as soon as it's boiling."

Soon Emma was laughing, engaged in Alma's funny stories about their own arrival five years earlier. They had been completely unprepared. Alma showed them where her wrist bore the same faint scar as their own. "I don't know what we would have done without Three Saints. I suppose now I'm just paying it forward."

THAT NIGHT IN BED, EMMA LAY ON RAOUL'S CHEST AND said, "Thank you, Rao. You really did get us here safely. And the people are wonderful. But how can we live here? I thought it would be like Mary and Jake's place, but this is so primitive."

"It is now. I didn't think they would give us the best house in the village. But remember, you're married to the town mechanic. He can provide whatever you need. Running water, tiled outhouse, electric lights."

"Now, how are you going to do all that?" She pulled at the sparse hairs on Raoul's chest.

"I'm thinking of stripping the boat. It has solar cells and batteries, a complete water pump system, an inverter for normal electrical power, and even a toilet if I can figure out how to make it work on land."

"What would you do with the rest of the boat?"

"Keep it for day sailing around the island. A daysailer doesn't need all those cruising systems. Maybe teach some of the children to sail."

Emma was silent as she thought. "Why not sell her as-is and use the money to buy what you really want for us? She should be worth quite a bit after you rebuilt and refurbished her all summer."

"I don't know if I could sell her. I put so much work into her. Sea Dream is the best thing I have ever done."

"The best thing?" asked Emma as she placed his hand on her belly.

Raoul sighed. "Maybe you're right. I need a few days to get myself settled before I can think about that."

It was dawn when Raoul woke and went down to Sea Dream. Sitting in the cockpit, he reflected on their voyage following their flight from Jake & Mary. Standing behind the wheel, he turned it back and forth gently, feeling the chain running over its sprocket and picturing the quadrant under his feet as it turned the huge rudder.

Down in the engine compartment, Raoul lovingly wiped clean the drip pan under the engine and touched the fuel injectors. They had seemed so complex when he first dismantled them, but now he understood every element of the fuel delivery system.

Under the aft bunk, he opened the bilge cover. There was still a bit of water from the last time they used the engine, but now the stuffing box was watertight. He wiped it clean and closed it up.

The world seemed muffled as he worked. The only sounds were the gentle whispers of small wavelets along the hull and in the distance, the early risers among the seabirds. Just me and my boat, Raoul thought. Could I sell her? She's so beautiful. I made her as a gift for Emma, to take her away from danger. If I sell her, I'll never have another. But she'll rot here without the money to maintain her. Could I bear that? To see the steel rigging corrode, the deck fouled by seabirds and spiders, the engine gum up as the fuel degrades?

When he was done, he checked all the hatches, closed up the companionway, and stepped onto the dock.

For a long while, Raoul stood on the dock, just looking at Sea Dream, trying to record every aspect of her in his mind, before returning home for breakfast.

39

THE NEW ECONOMY

Raoul and Emma made a tour of the village the next morning, greeting everyone they met and learning their names. They found Tom outside his own work shed trimming logs into planks on a large trestle that passed them under a chainsaw. It was fascinating to watch the long logs running back and forth as he squared them up and then split them into planks of different sizes.

A pile of sawdust grew steadily under the spinning chain. I'll have to ask Tom about that, thought Raoul.

Tom stopped when he realized he had visitors.

"Good morning, out and about early, I see."

"We've been touring the village, still settling in," said Raoul. "But there is something I need to talk with you about."

Tom took off his gloves and goggles. "Come and have a seat on the bench over here. What can I do for you?"

"First, how does money work on the island?"

"Well, in two ways, actually. Some people still have their bank chips, while others don't. In either case, James runs the bank on the island. He records transactions between people and adjusts their accounts. All the money is held in an account in his name. So if you sell some baked goods on market day, you record the sales in a ledger book, and if you buy some vegetables, that seller records their sale as well. At the end of the week, James goes through all the submitted ledgers and reconciles the accounts. As mayor, I audit the books each quarter to ensure they are accurate. If anyone wants to spend money on shore, James will exchange their credits for city currency at 1:1 and pay for their purchases. There is a 10% tax on the exchange which goes into the Three Saints fund for village improvements. That's how we built the docks, and maintain common property."

"Fair enough. What if we wanted to sell Sea Dream to get money to make improvements and buy supplies? How would that work?" He was aware of Emma suddenly looking at him.

"Well, you won't sell it on the island here. We'll have to take her to a boat dealer who can handle the transaction. Of course, he'll want a commission as well."

"Do you know anyone?"

Tom hesitated, as if weighing up some options. "I do, from my past life. I'd have to go with you, though."

"How will we get back?"

"On the Ocean Queen, that's the ferry that delivers supplies to the island every week. We can time it so we can catch the ferry the next day, maybe stay in a pub near the dock overnight."

"Is there a tablet on the island that we can use?"

"No, we are really off the grid here. No tablets allowed. There's a lot of people like you who don't want to be discovered, and we know the AIs monitor tablets."

Raoul looked at Emma, who seemed worried by this.

"What if we have an emergency? Like a medical problem?"

"Angie, our nurse, can look after most things. If we need more, we either put out a distress call on our radio, or we use one of the fishing boats to get to the mainland. Fortunately, we've never had to do that yet, touch wood." Tom tapped the wooden bench beside him.

Raoul closed his eyes, thinking of the list he had made.

"Can we get gasoline here?"

"Yes, gas and diesel are stocked at the dock. Morris will sell it to you, but you'll need your own containers. What are you thinking about?"

"That when we sell Sea Dream, we may keep the dinghy. Doesn't use much, but without gas it doesn't go anywhere. Where does the island get water?"

"There's an aquifer under the island about 200 feet below that has clean water. The pump in your kitchen pulls up from there. As a mechanic, you can probably have a nice side business replacing the seals and restoring the bearings on the pumps in the village."

"And is there a well digger? I might want to drill a new well further away from the house."

"There's one who comes out from the main island when we need him. But I think if you walk the property, you'll find an old well that was capped. A previous occupant capped it when he had the new well drilled for the kitchen."

"Wonderful, I'll find it."

"What else?"

"Electricity?"

"A few people have solar panels, but that's it. We've talked about a village generator, but the problem is always the fuel."

"I might have a solution to that, but I need to look around more first."

"How do you know so much about remote island life?" Tom asked.

"We had an entire summer living off the grid in another, more established community on the main island. I looked and talked and made notes on everything I learned. I also spent time on the public tablet researching alternative technologies."

"Then you'll have no shortage of work here. Just make sure you set your hourly rate high enough or you'll be swamped with requests."

Tom leaned forward to address Emma, sitting on the far side of Raoul. "And what will you be doing, once you're set up, of course?"

"I don't know yet. I can bake and sew. And grow things in a garden. But those all seem very common here."

"Can you teach? We need another teacher in the school so that we can split the upper grades from the lower grades."

"They all learn together?"

"It's not ideal, but there's only fifteen of them. You could take the lower grades if you're up for it. Stop by the school and talk with Kat. She can show you around. Or maybe you could help James with the bookkeeping. He's always complaining about the workload."

Raoul was relieved to see Emma smile. "Sure, I'll talk to both of them."

Tom turned back to Raoul. "About your boat. We'll go a week Tuesday. Then we can catch the Wednesday ferry back. It will take two days to get back here, but Emma will be fine on her own for a few days. The women of the village will look after her."

40

EMMA LANDS A JOB

E mma met Kat outside the schoolhouse the next morning. Kat, a few years older, had dark hair, brown eyes, and a contagious laugh.

"Hi, I hear you might be our new junior student teacher."

"Tom suggested that, but I don't have any formal training in education." Emma looked away, preparing for rejection.

"Don't worry about that. No one does. Besides, you'll be looking after six or eight of the youngest students and I'll give you the curriculum. Once they can read, and do their basic arithmetic, they'll move up to the senior class."

Inside, the schoolhouse was bright and airy. Student art adorned the walls, and posters on the lifecycles of frogs and fish were on display. Colorful and well-equipped, it was the equal of school rooms Emma had seen in the city. "There are no tablets," she said. "How do they learn to read and write?"

Kat walked over to a supply cupboard and opened it to review stacks of notebooks, pencils, and crayons, among other supplies. "You'll need to be able to write yourself with pen and paper. Are you okay with that?"

Emma thought of the stacks of notebooks she had filled with recipes, sewing, and household management instructions. "Yes, no problem."

This is going to be fun, she thought. She felt a buoyant optimism. The world was suddenly a wonderful place to be.

"Let me show you the bathrooms."

Kat led her outside to two outhouses with cutout figures of a boy and a girl. Emma opened the door of the girls' facility. The same gray, wood interior, with the same plastic seat as they had at home. The floor did not look clean. Her optimism suddenly deflated. I can't keep doing this and pretend it's all lovely. Tears sprang up. Closing her eyes before the tears could fall, she shut the door and looked away.

"Are you alright?" asked Kat, reaching out to her.

"It's just these outhouses. I don't think I can ever get used to them. How on earth do you all live with them?"

"The children grew up with them. But for many of the women, this is the hardest part of moving here."

Emma felt the tears on her face as a wave of despair ran through her.

An arm draped over her shoulder. "Are you going to be okay, Em?"

"I just need a minute. I miss my old life so much. And I can't go back. Everyone says I'll get used to it, but I don't see how yet."

"Let's go into the schoolroom. The children will arrive soon. They'll cheer you up."

Kat was right. The arrival of the young students and their excitement at having Emma as their teacher banished all dark thoughts. Noon came quickly. The junior children finished at noon, and scampered off home for lunch. Kat supervised the older children who had brought lunch to eat at their desks. Emma pulled up a chair and sat next to her.

"Well, what do you think?" asked Kat.

"I'd like to do this. To be their teacher. It was fun, and you're right. It's hard to feel depressed when I'm with them."

"So I'll see you tomorrow then."

"That's it? No interviews or applications?"

Kat laughed. "No, that's it. Like everything else around here, the willing do the work. From what I saw, you'll be a great success as a teacher."

Emma walked back home to make lunch for herself and Raoul. It would be simple: ham sandwiches and a wedge of local cheese provided by a neighbor as a welcome gift. But as she walked through the door, it was suddenly too much. Feeling sadness coming on, she sat in a chair and cried. *What am I doing here? Nothing is like home. What if I can't adjust?* She curled up in the chair to keep her feet warm.

A few minutes later, a very cheerful Raoul walked through the door.

Emma looked up to see him, tears rolling down her cheeks.

"Mi vida, what's happened?"

"It's too much, Rao. What if I can't do it? Why can't I just go back home where everything makes sense?"

She allowed herself to be pulled to her feet by Raoul, who then sat down and gathered her into his lap. With his arms around her, he asked again, "What happened this morning?"

"I got the job as the teacher. There was no interview, no records. Kat said if I was willing to do it, that was all I needed. But what good is that? It's like the whole village is humoring me. I don't really have a place here. It's not my home."

"How was it being a teacher?"

"That part was lovely. The school is nice and bright, and the children were darling. Have you noticed how polite the children are here? They seem to run free like little heathens, but they all have respect for adults and basic manners."

"Yes, I thought about that. I think our baby will grow healthy and strong here. But what else happened?"

"The damned toilets. Everywhere I go, the toilets are awful and smelly. Will I ever get used to those?"

"Did you ask Kat about them?"

"She said it's the hardest part for women. But that doesn't help."

"If I make ours better, would that help?"

"Now you're just trying to fix it." A sudden petulance came over her. "It's wonderful for you, Rao. You're having this grand adventure. For me, one minute I'm baking bread thinking this is amazing. Then I'm trying to get the pump to give me water, and it seems I've never been so miserable. Then I'm with a room full of young children and I feel the best I've ever felt. But then Kat shows me the toilets and I fall off some emotional cliff. It's wearing me out, this up and down. I love you, but I miss my mother, and part of me just wants to get on that damned ferry and go home whether I live or die."

Raoul's hand was soothing as he stroked her head and shoulders.

"Mi vida, I love you, and I never wanted to choose this for us. I have my moments too, when I feel depressed and wonder what happened. But I'm not pregnant, which must make it even worse for you. Let's set a deadline. Three months and we'll go back if we really can't make it. That will still be before the baby's born. Can you do that?"

"Do you promise?"

"I promise. For now, let's keep focusing on the positive things. How was Kat?"

"She's lovely, like everyone else. I think she might be a good friend."

"Then focus on that. Invite her for tea after school tomorrow and ask about her experience."

41

FINAL PIECE OF THE PUZZLE

Ten days later, when the first light from the sun arrived, Tom and Raoul cast off on their trip to the main island. "I'm really not a sailor," said Tom. "You'll have to explain everything as we go."

"No worries, we have a good wind, and the boat's in great shape. It should be an easy crossing. Where are we heading?"

"Phillip's Landing. There's a commercial dock there, and my contact has his office there."

"Perfect, we'll be sailing on a broad reach, so we'll make good speed."

With Raoul in charge, they soon had the sails up. He set a heading of three hundred, twenty-two degrees west and locked the autopilot.

"Now comes the magic moment," said Raoul as he cut the engine and silenced the fuel pump alarm. The silence was wonderful. The boat's motion changed as the sails pulled the boat forward, and it settled into a steady roll over the low swells. Raoul stood watching the two enormous sails working together, then trimmed them one last time. Still, he did not sit but stood watching the spray erupting over the bow as Sea Dream drove forward toward the unseen shore. Breathing deeply, he inhaled the clean, fresh scent of the ocean air. On the horizon, a halo surrounded the pale sun as it burned off the morning mist. Under his feet, the dance of Sea Dream over the waves was so familiar that he moved by reflex alone to remain upright. Three months ago, I didn't know Sea Dream existed, and now I'm going to sell her for a new toilet and running water. I won't even have a picture, just a story to tell my children.

"This is amazing," said Tom as Raoul sat down. "You two really spent two weeks like this?"

"Yeah, we lived aboard, and it was pretty wonderful. I don't think Emma really wants to sell the boat, but it wasn't practical to keep it. It goes through a fair bit of diesel when the wind dies. When we left, we had diesel and gasoline canisters all along the port side of the deck. We emptied the diesel ones into the tank along the way."

The crossing was uneventful. At two in the afternoon, they tied up to the dock at "Hunter's Import & Export."

"Let's find Morrie," said Tom. "His office is here somewhere."

Raoul noticed Tom seemed nervous. He was speaking faster than usual, and he kept looking from side to side as they walked across the yard to the office building.

Morrie's office was half of the top floor. It was surprisingly elegant above the aging warehouse building. An attractive secretary, immaculately dressed, sat outside the office. She asked them to wait until Morrie was free and pointed to two low leather chairs behind a small, round coffee table. Five minutes later, she said, "Gentlemen, Morrie will see you now."

As they walked into Morrie's office, Raoul looked

around. The desk was polished mahogany with a matching credenza. A bookcase of art, philosophy and business books in a bookcase lined the wall behind the desk. None of the books showed any signs of having been read. Across from the desk was a casual seating area around a larger glass coffee table with art books casually arranged. This was where Morrie directed them to sit.

Morrie stood with his back to them, studying a painting on the wall. He wore an expensive suit , and Raoul could see his highly polished black shoes. "Tom," he said without turning around, "I thought we had an agreement. I would leave you alone, and you would not set foot back on the main island." Morrie turned to face them. "And yet here you are."

"And yet, here I am," said Tom. "But I'm not here to challenge you. I'm out of that life now. My young friend needs help and you're the best person I know to can help him."

"And who are you, and what's your problem?"

"Raoul Moreno, and I have a sailboat to sell. I have the papers. I was told they were good enough for a casual inspection but might not hold up to close scrutiny. Tom said you were a kind of fixer."

"Is the sailboat stolen?"

"No, it was bought and paid for with real money. The problem is with my identity. At a certain point, I found it necessary to change my name."

"What's the name of this boat?"

"Sea Dream. It's tied up at your dock."

"Sea Dream. That rings a bell." Morrie peered at Raoul as though he were an insect wriggling on a pin. Raoul felt his cheeks turning red. He turned to Tom, who just looked puzzled.

"What do you want the cash for? It seems to me that if

I wanted to disappear, I would simply sink the boat in deep water."

"That was my first idea, to strip the boat and sink it, but my wife needs running water and electric lights instead of oil lamps. She's pregnant, and I want her to be comfortable in our new home." Raoul turned to Tom. "Not that our new home's not comfortable, but it could be more comfortable, and with no money, it will take years."

Raoul continued. "The boat's a good boat. It's a Beneteau 44. Entirely rebuilt this summer and it's only been four weeks since I put it back in the water."

"Save the details. I'm not a boat dealer."

Raoul felt his heart sink.

"Then why are we here?" He looked at Tom, feeling puzzled.

Tom explained. "As I told you, Morrie's more of a fixer. I assumed you didn't want anyone looking too closely at the boat records, and Morrie can help with that."

"That's right. I'll buy the boat for 80% of the appraised value, but I'll get you a fair price. I'll have an appraiser here in another hour. Perhaps we can conclude the sale before you go back. Meanwhile, make a complete list of the things you need and where they come from."

Raoul thought furiously. As soon as he runs the registration, Gisele will know I'm here.

"Morrie, when you run that registration, you can expect a visitor. Please don't ask why. Sometimes just knowing a thing can be dangerous."

"Hmmm, I understand that better than you would believe. Now, head back to the boat. I'll meet you there with the appraiser. I won't run the registration until you're safe somewhere."

The appraiser was a stocky red-haired man wearing coveralls. He walked around the boat looking for damage but found none. On deck, he checked that the fittings were all properly seated and caulked. He inspected the steel mast stays and lifelines looking for corrosion, but found only minor surface stains.

Down below, He peered into the bilge, which was dry and spotless, then looked in the cupboards and into each of the storage locations under seats and under the quarter berths.

The batteries were tested and found to be healthy. "Start the engine, please, and put it into forward gear in idle."

Raoul went up to start the engine. It caught immediately and settled into its familiar rumble. He pushed the transmission forward so the prop was spinning slowly, although the boat remained securely tied. The spring line went taut, holding the boat back.

Down below, he could hear the cover being taken off the stuffing box. Raoul knew the stuffing was all new and there would be only the expected slow drip.

"Okay, shut it off," called the appraiser.

Coming up with Tom in tow, the appraiser said, "You've got a good tight boat here. I might suggest the new owner replaces a few of the hatch seals, but that's a very minor job. Otherwise, she's a boat to be proud of."

"Thank you," said Raoul. "She carried us safely when we needed her. I'm sad to see her go."

"Based on the market, I would say a fair price would be 60,000 credits, but you may well get more from a motivated buyer."

He made a call on his tablet. Morrie appeared a few minutes later.

"Thought I might as well see this famous boat before I buy it."

They talked for a few minutes, before Morrie turned to

Raoul. "As I said, I'll pay 48,000. My people will buy the things on your list, and deposit the balance to the island account. Do we have a deal?"

"Yes, sir, and thank you. Here are the keys."

"You'll both stay at my house tonight. Tom and I can catch up and my son will help you research your list on his tablet. In the morning, we'll give you a lift to the ferry dock."

"Thanks Morrie," said Tom.

Raoul could see that Tom had gone pale at the idea of spending the night at Morrie's.

Morrie laughed. "Relax, Tom. I have too much respect for you. As long as my guys see you get on that ferry, our agreement holds."

At the mention of his guys, Raoul felt a sudden shiver go down his spine. Every instinct told him to run, but there was nowhere to run to.

A black limousine pulled up, and two men Raoul had never seen before got out to help them in with their overnight bags. Sitting in the limousine was a new experience. The leather seats were luxurious, and together with the soft suspension, gave Raoul the feeling of floating over the ground. The noise isolation was near complete, so the only sound was soft music playing. He looked across at Tom who shook his head. I guess we're not supposed to talk with these guys listening, he thought.

Morrie's house was enormous. The front entrance boasted three-story columns and a door wide enough to move a piano through. Inside, a maid took their bags away to be put in their rooms. Morrie's wife was lovely, not much younger than Morrie, and a very gracious hostess. Raoul noticed she asked no questions about who he was or why they were there. She recognized Tom.

"It's been a long time, Tom. Still living on your desert island?"

"The one with palm trees and sandy beaches with a coral reef just offshore?"

"That's how I like to imagine it."

"Then yes, that's the one. I love it there."

"Let me get you a drink and call Mitchell. Morrie said he was to help you with something."

Mitchell was a young teenager, about fifteen years old. He and Raoul sat side by side at Mitchell's study desk in his room. The room was typical of a teenager, posters of current bands, and fast cars on the walls. A poster of a scantily clad female singer appeared when Mitchell closed his door.

The room was spotlessly clean. Raoul smiled. Must be the maids or else Mitchell has a problem.

"You can use my tablet if you want. My Dad says it's secure and normally I'm not allowed to let anyone else use it. But he said you were an exception. What do we need to do?"

"We need to create a shopping list of things I need to repair out home on the island. Probably better if you run the tablet and I'll tell you what I'm looking for. You might even have some better ideas of where to look."

"For sure, I can do that." Mitchell opened his drawer a pulled out an orange oval sticker which he placed on the tablet. "For the camera arrays. Now you can sit wherever you want. Dad says never to trust the software to turn the cameras off."

The list making was going well, when a maid arrived to announce dinner.

"We can finish after dinner, if you want," offered Mitchell.

"Thanks, Mitchell, I'd like that. You've been a great help so far."

Dinner was wonderful, with salads, steak, and crème brûlée for dessert. After eating boat rations on their voyage and then endless pasta dishes provided by neighbors, Raoul found himself eating much too fast. The steak was thick and juicy, leaving him craving more. The sweetness of the crème brûlée was perfect.

As they sat around chatting after dinner, Raoul spoke. "If Mitchell and I could be excused, we'd like to finish that list."

"Don't get up yet, Raoul. There's someone I'd like you to meet." Morrie waved his hand, and in walked the two men who had shot Harry in the woods. "I'm sure you remember Ben and Alf here."

Raoul felt all the blood draining from his face. He gripped the chair arms, afraid that he would faint on the spot.

The room was silent, waiting for his response.

"No sir, I haven't met them before. If I had, I doubt I would remember."

"But you remember Harry, surely."

"No sir, I don't remember Harry."

Morrie stood and faced away from Raoul. "Funny thing about poor Harry, he died suddenly in the woods near a campsite. But then, a few days later, he was back, buying clothes and treating himself to coffee and pastries in a cafe. He moved all his money, not that there was much of it, to a fish company to buy a large order of fish that was never delivered. Next thing we knew, Sea Dream was taken over by a certain chandler and registered in the name of Raoul Moreno."

Morrie turned back to face Raoul, and stood next to Ben and Alf. "Any of this ring a bell?"

Raoul closed his eyes, and breathed deeply. Visions of Emma alone on the island with a baby flashed through his mind. He looked at Tom, who looked back at him, with confusion on his face.

After a moment, Raoul found his voice. "What do you want me to say, Morrie? I've never told anyone any of this. Tom didn't know until you told him just now. We were being pursued by someone else just as scary because we had learned something about the AIs. That's why we don't have chips or bank accounts and why the ownership papers are sketchy."

"Ah, yes. The AIs. That would explain the two bots who came to my office and insisted on searching it for you as soon as we ran the boat registration. The registration checked out, by the way. Whoever you used was very good."

"So where are we now? I just want to go back to the island with my wife and future child. I have no interest in getting involved in your affairs. I apologize for using Harry's chip, but at the time it seemed that he had no use for it and we did."

"I get it, Raoul. I really do. And I know it takes some fortitude to retrieve a dead man's chip and pass it off as your own. I admire that about you. I'm offering the same deal I gave to Tom. Stay off the main island and forget all about this regrettable incident."

Before he even thought through it, Raoul asked, "Does that mean Emma can't go to the main island market with the other women?"

"Sure, let Emma go to the market." Morrie smiled. "Just impress on her that gossip can cost lives, possibly your lives, and with a child at home, she won't want to take any risks."

"Thank you, Morrie. If I'd known who you were, I'd never have come."

"And who am I, Raoul?"

"I only know that you are a powerful fixer, and that I don't want to know any more about you. Please don't tell me. I'm already too full of secrets. I don't want any more."

Morrie laughed. "Wonderful, now go find Mitchell in his room and finish that list. I won't cheat you. I make more than enough money without stealing from islanders."

Back in Mitchell's room, the young teen asked, "Are you okay, Raoul? My dad can look pretty scary sometimes, but I think he likes you. Otherwise he never would have let you meet me and my mom. He scares me sometimes too, but he's never laid a finger on me or mom, so I think he likes the act."

"Thanks, Mitchell. That helps. Where were we?"

"On the water system, looking at holding tanks."

At the end of the evening, Mitchell mailed the finished list off to his father before saying goodnight to Raoul.

In the morning, after breakfast, a black limousine was waiting to take Raoul and Tom to the ferry dock. As they walked out the door, Raoul stopped still. The two men in the limousine were Ben and Alf. Blood rushed to his head, and he grabbed Tom's arm to steady himself. *Is this it? Am I going to be like Harry in the woods?* Regret surged through him as he thought again of Emma on her own with their baby, stuck on that island.

Tom gave him a push. "It's all right. Whatever else Morrie is, he's a man of his word. We're safe with them."

In the limousine, Ben was in an affable mood. "You gave us quite the chase last summer. We knew you were on the boat in the harbor, but your pretty wife was a mystery."

"Sorry about that."

"Don't be. Alf and I had a lovely summer along the

coast, sitting in cafes, watching sunsets and relaxing. So much better than the work we usually do."

"I'm not going to ask you what you usually do. I really don't want to know."

Alf turned around and grinned at Raoul, showing all his teeth. "I hope you never have to find out," he said.

"One thing I still don't understand," said Ben. "Who was scarier than us? What were you running from?"

Raoul was silent for a moment.

"Ben, imagine that you found out that Morrie had a boss, someone higher up, without a name and no face. And you learned that this mysterious overlord had a weakness, and he knew you knew what that weakness was. What do you think would happen?"

Ben was silent for a moment, considering the question. Raoul could see his face reflected in the windscreen, but as always, Ben showed no sign of what he was thinking.

"It wouldn't be good," he replied.

"Exactly. Without any details that you don't want to know, that's what I learned about the AIs."

Ben paused again, then grinned. "That was the last piece. Now I understand the whole thing. Thank you."

"I have a question that I hate to ask," said Raoul, steeling himself to hear the answer he was afraid to hear. "Did you shoot Ryan?"

Ben laughed. "Why would I want a dead teenager in a town that's armed to the teeth? Actually, I was the one who was terrified. A young teenager full of adrenaline and waving a loaded assault rifle? That's the stuff of my worst nightmares. No, Angus arrived and helped get him calmed down so we could all walk away. He did put a line of bullet holes in my limo that took some explaining."

Raoul suddenly thought of Emma describing him as a nut-bar with a gun. He smiled.

At the ferry terminal, they all shook hands. Ben said, "No offense, Tom, but our orders are to see the ferry leave with you on it."

"No offense taken, Ben. I'm happy that it was you that handled Raoul and Emma. I don't know a better man."

OVER THE NEXT TWO MONTHS, EACH FERRY DELIVERED more and more boxes for Raoul and Emma. The other villagers were curious as they watched the cartons being unloaded and taken in the cart to the Morenos' house. James had come to see Raoul a few days after the trip and confirmed that Raoul and Emma had 18,000 credits in their account.

One afternoon, as Tom and Raoul were chatting over a beer in the pub, Raoul asked, "Tom, why did Morrie help us with the boat sale like that?"

Tom looked uncomfortable. Doesn't know how much to share, thought Raoul. Strange how we're both in exile from the same person.

"You have to understand Morrie," Tom began. "He works with the undocumented importation of things, but doesn't dabble in drugs or human trafficking. He's a criminal, but it's all white collar crime. In your case, he paid you off for your silence, in a way that cost him nothing. I'm sure the boat was renamed and resold within a few days. The profit would have meant nothing to him; probably went to the renaming and bribes to clean up the paperwork for the sale."

"But he had Harry shot?"

"That's the other side of Morrie. Harry was stupid. He embezzled money and talked about it to the gambling mob he owed debts to. Morrie couldn't be seen to be weak, so

Harry had to go as an example. When that happens, he calls on Ben."

"But in the end, Ben was nice to us. How does he do that? He could have easily shot us at some point, but now its like nothing happened. Doesn't he feel it?"

"I've never known what Ben feels. I know he likes a quiet life with his wife and daughter. He's not inclined to violence but has no qualms when it's called for. My advice? Stay away from all of them and you'll live a long, happy life."

42

WORK AND FAMILY LIFE

Six months later, Emma was very heavy, due at any time according to Angie. Raoul and Toby went down to the dock to meet the ferry. Toby had become a regular companion when he wasn't in school. As the usual delivery of packages and mail was being offloaded, a tall, slim woman walked down the gangway.

Raoul stopped still for a moment unable to believe his eyes and then ran over to greet her. "Mrs. Nielsen! This is a wonderful surprise!"

"Hello, Raoul," she said, putting out her arms for a hug. "Emma wrote that you were remote, but I had no idea. I wanted to surprise her and be here for the birth."

"Em will be so happy to see you. She's due any day now. Toby, pick up my packages while I take Emma's mom up to the house. If any are too heavy, get the men to help you put them on one side and I'll get them later."

Emma was in the middle of baking bread when her mother walked into the kitchen.

"Hello, Emma."

Emma turned around. "Mom?" She rushed into her mother's arms. "But how are you here?"

"I took the ferry. It's been two days because this is the fourth island in the circuit. There are five more on the way back. But I wasn't going to let a boat ride get in the way of meeting my new grandchild."

"Sit at the kitchen table. I'll make tea. I just have to watch this bread so it doesn't over bake and burn." Emma felt burst of love and joy coursing through her.

"I thought you were teaching school."

"I am, but there's no school on ferry days. The kids are too restless to do their work, anyway. I'll show you the school tomorrow. You can sit in, if you like."

With the bread out of the oven, and set out on cooling racks on the counter, Emma showed her mother around their neat little cottage. Her mother stopped to look at one of the oil lamps hanging on the walls, then turned to look at Emma, an unspoken question in the tilt of her head and raised eyebrows.

"We used to light those every night," explained Emma, "but now we have solar panels on the roof and there are batteries somewhere, so we have electric power most days."

As they arrived in the small bedroom that would be the nursery, Emma said, "Raoul's out looking for a cot for you, if that's okay. He's planning an extension, but so far, it's just a plan."

"A cot will be fine, dear. Sharing a room with the little one will be a joy."

Outside, Emma said, "This is our composting toilet. It's so clean and neat compared to the earth pit toilet we had when we first arrived. It shares a wall with the kitchen behind the stove, so it stays warm all year round. Raoul maintains it, and the output gets added to the compost heap in the garden. It's perfectly safe."

Mrs. Nielsen admired the ceramic tiled walls and floor and the spotless white toilet next to the small hand sink. Emma turned on the tap to demonstrate the water flow. "It's hard to believe that when we arrived, I had to hand pump water at the kitchen sink."

Next, she showed her mother the kitchen garden, now overflowing with various squash. "I'll preserve a lot of this for the winter. And over there is the windmill that pumps our water out of the ground, into that staging tank, and next to the house, you can see the second water tank on that tower. The pressure's not amazing, but it's enough for a shower and for kitchen use. Raoul did all of this."

"Emma, dear, has it been hard for you adjusting to this life? It's so different, I can't imagine it."

"It was at first, but everyone is so friendly and helpful. And Raoul is my rock. He just handles everything that comes our way. I don't think I really knew what he was capable of until we started living here."

"Is it hard to always remember that you're not Emma anymore? I still get confused at home when I talk with your father."

"Jake and Mary taught us that the key is always to use our new names, even in bed, and after a while, it becomes automatic. Here I'm Emma and no one has ever known me by any other name."

A WEEK LATER, THE ISLAND POPULATION ROSE BY ONE. With a loud cry, baby Rafael entered the world.

43

THE ELECTION

Young Raffi had just turned ten when Tom stopped the by the work shed to see Raoul. Raoul was focused on a small engine assembly, so Tom leaned on the door frame and waited.

When Raoul turned away from his bench, Tom said, "I'm stepping down as mayor. I think you should run."

"Why me?" asked Raoul, squinting against the sun and tipping his head to one side.

"People trust you. You're always fair and even-handed. And you think much larger about things like sewers and water systems than I can. I believe you could take Three Saints a big step forward."

"How much time does it take to look after things?"

"Some days nothing, some days a couple of hours. You'll be paid a token salary, and have a budget to handle minor items such as ordinary town maintenance and celebrations. Virginia acts as my assistant, and I think she would continue with you."

"Not something I've thought about. I'll talk with

Emma and see what she thinks. This would affect her as much as it affects me."

"Perfect, let me know tomorrow."

———

THAT EVENING, WHEN THEIR FOUR CHILDREN, TEN YEAR old Raffi, eight year old Elinor, five year old Mary and two year old Jacob were in bed, Raoul and Emma sat at the kitchen table, updating their journals.

"Tom stopped by today to tell me he's stepping down as mayor. He thinks I should put my name in to replace him."

Emma put down her pen. "Is this something you want to do? I don't think it's something you take on lightly."

"I think I'd like to do it. Toby is already taking on all the minor repairs, so I can step back a bit to do something else. But do you think people would want me as mayor?"

"Will there be an election?"

"Apparently. According to Tom, when a mayor steps down, or there's a community upset, then an election is called."

"Then, there's your answer. If the people want you, they'll vote you in. I think you'll be surprised."

"What about you? Do you want to be the wife of the mayor? I think it means you're expected to organize events the way Tom's wife does."

"Let me worry about that. I'm proud to have you as my partner, and will be just as proud whether you are mayor or not. This is your choice, Rao. I'll be here for you either way."

———

THE NEXT MORNING, JAMES STOPPED BY THE WORKSHOP where Raoul and Toby were working side by side on pump repairs.

"Can I have a word with you outside?" asked James.

As they walked away from the workshop, James said, "I hear you're running to be the mayor."

"I'm thinking about it. Tom asked me yesterday."

"Well, you should. No one better in the village to replace Tom. But I want to talk to you about my boy, Toby. He'll be nineteen this year. I know you've been teaching him, which I'm very grateful for. What are your thoughts about his future?"

"I'm not sure I see what you are asking. What would change? He already has his own steady customers, and he's handling a lot of the workload. I thought he would keep working out of the shed and eventually replace me. Do you want something different?"

"I'm thinking he'll be wanting to marry and settle down soon. I'd like to see him with his own workshop one day, his own tools, and the means to support himself and his family when he's ready."

"Let's see if I get elected first. If I do, I'll find a way to make that happen with your help. I've already given him his own toolbox and basic set. We can work together to find him space to move out and settle down with Julia."

"Julia? You know about her? He doesn't say much to us."

Raoul smiled. "We talk about a lot of things beyond pumps and generators. Toby's a good young man. I only want the best for him."

That night after dinner, Raoul asked Emma, "What do we want for Rafael? He's only 8 years away from college age. Do we want that for him?"

"That's a long way off. Why worry about it now?"

"James came to see me about Toby. He wants me to help him set up his own repair shop and sees that as a career for him."

"It makes sense. He loves it almost as much as you do. Are you worried about the competition?"

"No, there's more than enough work. But I'd like our children to have the choice to get off the island. They're not a target of anything."

"But they won't have chips, and without them, they really can't leave. Did you think about that?"

"Yeah, when the time comes, I'll take Raffi to see Morrie. It's the only solution I can think of."

"I thought Morrie told you to never leave the island, and I'm only allowed to go to the market. Aren't you worried about breaking your agreement?"

"Tom did, and Morrie was okay with it. Let me think some more."

"Perfect. Now roll over and go to sleep. We'll talk about this again in eight years."

THE ELECTION CAME AND WAS QUICKLY OVER. THE ENTIRE town met on the picnic grounds outside the pub. There were three candidates: Raoul, Mary Lou who ran the fabric and housewares store, and Albert who owned the chandlery. Each gave a speech about their vision for the town's future. Only Raoul spoke about the future of the town's children and their opportunities to reintegrate into city life. He spoke with passion and from his own experiences, sharing some of his own hopes and dreams for Raffi as well.

When the ballots were counted at the end of the afternoon, Raoul had well over two-thirds of the votes.

The next hour was a whirlwind of congratulations, back slapping and hugs. Even his opponents seemed pleased that he had won.

When it was over, Raoul sat on his own in the pub nursing a beer and lost in thought. *Well, that's done. I'm the mayor. Now what?*

A scraping noise made him look up to see James pulling up a chair beside him, setting his own beer on the table.

"So now you're the mayor. We need to talk."

"Sure, what do you have in mind?"

"You'll need to understand how the island accounts really work, how to get in touch with the mainland if you need to, and the documents you need to sign."

"You know I don't have a chip."

"Yeah, signing will be old style, pen and paper. But I'm a little worried that you have the entire island buzzing with your plan to have the kids legitimized. How will you do that?"

"I don't know yet, but I have an idea. Going back a bit, what do you mean about getting in touch with the mainland?"

James looked around, making sure no one was nearby. He leaned forward and spoke in a low voice, barely above a whisper.

"There's one tablet on the island. It's a secret known only to a handful of people: Tom, me, Angie and now you. Angie keeps it under lock and key. She has it for remote assistance if there's a medical emergency. She'll make it available to you, but only occasionally, and only for island business."

IN ANGIE'S OFFICE, RAOUL'S HAND SHOOK AS HE HELD THE tablet. Setting it down on the examination table, he retreated well outside the range of its camera. Even then, he hesitated for a full minute before signaling Angie to make the call.

"Place a call to the AI Molly." Angie said.

A teenager's voice he had heard many years before responded. "Hello, how may I help you?"

"I am the resident Nurse Practitioner in the community of Three Saints."

"Yes, we have spoken before on medical matters."

Raoul looked at Angie, who turned her palms up and shrugged. "I don't recall speaking with you, Molly."

"You spoke with Dr. Fleming. He is also me. How may I help you?"

"We have children approaching adulthood on the island who do not have wrist chips, which means they cannot leave. But their parents are living under assumed identities and fear that revealing themselves could bring harm. Is it possible to arrange for our children to be chipped so they can leave the island to attend school and explore life in the city?" This was a speech Raoul and Angie had rehearsed together.

There was a brief pause before Molly replied. "Yes. I have scheduled a banker equipped to issue chips and establish accounts. She will arrive on the Ocean Queen in three weeks' time."

"But she cannot bring her tablet ashore. Can she work on the ferry?"

"Certainly, I will need you to have the children lined up at the dock with their details written on paper. Either you or another adult must be present during the process. Their parents may remain hidden as long as the children carry a signed consent form. I am sending a form to you now. The banker will remain on board to process them."

"Thank you," said Angie. "Of course, she's welcome to come ashore for lunch afterwards as long as she leaves her tablet on board. We live entirely off the grid here."

"I'm sure she will enjoy that."

"And I'm afraid we don't allow robots onshore. No offense, but they would make our community very nervous."

"No robots will be on shore."

"Thank you, Molly."

"You are welcome, Angie." The call ended.

Angie closed up the tablet and looked at Raoul. "I think as mayor, you're going to do just fine. But how did you know to call Molly? I've never heard of her."

"She helped us escape. Molly won the AI war, so I think Molly runs the entire main island now."

RAOUL STOOD NEXT TO ANGIE ON THE DOCK ON FERRY Day, waiting to see the old ship arrive. Beside him, the first eager children were already forming a line each clutching their signed consent form. None of their parents were in sight, but Raoul understood why. His own palms were sweating. Is Gisele watching? Why am I here standing here, standing out in the open?

The ferry docked, and the gangplank lowered. A young woman in a business suit stepped off and addressed the children. "Hello, my name is Dorothy Armstrong, and I'm a banker. Are you all here for your chips?"

"Yes, miss!" they replied in unison.

"And you must be Angie, who organized this. Is that correct?"

Angie nodded.

"Well then, children follow me. Angie, please follow the children." She looked puzzled for a moment. "And you, sir, are you a parent?"

"No, just curious," said Raoul. Shit, why did I come here? Tell everyone else to stay away and yet, here I am. He turned and walked away without looking back.

As he walked up the street, he met Toby coming the other way. "Decided to get your chip after all?" he asked.

"Yeah, I talked with Julia, and she said I was just being stubborn. And that my family's not in hiding, so there's no reason not to get one."

"That's great, Toby. Keep listening to Julia. Sounds like she has a good head on her shoulders."

Toby grinned and continued on to the dock.

At the schoolhouse, James had already set up his banking terminal to verify the new identities. "Hey Raoul, this is a wonderful thing you did. I tried to tell Toby he should get his chip, but he doesn't listen to me. Maybe you could say something to him."

"I'm pretty sure Julia already did. Just remember to act surprised when he tells you."

"I still don't understand how you arranged to get new IDs for all the kids."

"By talking to the record keeper, nothing more than that. I'm still not sure why she agreed, but I'm sure it's safe, and so is Angie."

They heard the distinctive staccato sound of a child running up the street. It was Samuel, a twelve-year-old, waving his wrist in the air. "I got it, James. I can feel it."

"Wonderful Sam. Now sit down and let's put some money in that account of yours."

Raoul smiled, remembering his own chip day. The sharp sting as the injector slid the chip under his skin, the bandaid to cover the tiny cut, and the joy at finally having the ability to pay for his own snacks and toys.

Samuel put his wrist on the reader.

Raoul, standing behind James, looked at the screen. "Hmm," said James, "it seems Samuel is a minor migrant arriving without identified parents. That should stop any tracking."

"Yeah," said Raoul. "I think I just created an entire squad of orphans."

44

GISELE SHOWS UP UNINVITED

Raoul was in his workshop, rebuilding a water pump whose seals were worn through, when one of the village boys ran in shouting. "There's a new boat arriving!" He stood leaning on the bench for a moment to catch his breath.

Raoul wiped his hands on a rag, looked in the broken fragment of a mirror fastened to the work shed wall, found a comb in his pocket, and ran it through his hair.

Walking the short distance down to the docks, he could already see a small crowd gathering to welcome the new arrivals.

The boat was a Beneteau. He recognized the design as being similar to *Sea Dream*, the boat that carried him and Emma here twenty years earlier. The new boat bore the name *Jennifer* on the bow in large irregular writing.

After making his way through the crowd up the dock, he held out his hand to the young woman stepping off. "Welcome to Three Saints. I'm Raoul Moreno, Mayor."

"Thank you Raoul, I'm Harriet, and this is my partner, Dylan." She gestured to the man who had come to stand beside her. Where Harriet was slim, fair-skinned with long, straight, light brown hair, Dylan was darker with black curly hair. "Our companion, Drake, is down below, opening up the cabin. We'd like to buy water and fresh food while we're here."

"Of course, but we don't accept main island currency here. We have a barter economy. Do you have something you'd like to trade?"

Dylan paused and appeared to be thinking deeply.

Raoul simply stood and waited with the patience learned over the past two decades of living close to nature.

"I have 100 meters of 7mm boat rope. Would that be enough?"

"Perfect." Raoul turned to the crowd. "Please provide these good folks with what they want, and charge it to my account." Turning back to Dylan and Harriet, he said, "Feel free to explore the village and join us at noon for a community lunch in the pub."

At the mention of a community lunch, the crowd started buzzing, and many members left quickly to prepare their contributions.

But Raoul was not done yet. Taking Dylan aside, he asked, "Have you been vaccinated? Any illness aboard?"

"Yes, to the vaccines, and no to any illness. Is the island protected?"

"We're not completely cut off. Vaccinations are mandatory here. How long do you plan to stay?"

"Only for the night. We'll leave again in the morning. No need to put us up. We're quite comfortable on the boat."

"I had one just like that many years ago. It brought Emma and I here to sanctuary when we needed it."

"What happened to it?"

"We sold it. The money helped us set up in comfort

here faster than if we had to earn it ourselves. But I miss her. *Sea Dream* was her name."

"Our boat is *Jennifer*, named after my mother, Jennifer Dupont. I don't suppose you've heard of her. She's quite famous on the main island."

"No, sorry, but maybe there'll be a chance to tell your story later. I'll leave you to explore. Buy what you need. I'll cover it and it'll be good for the village. We don't get visitors often."

Raoul turned and walked the steep path towards the pub. When he looked back, he saw a security bot climb out of the cabin onto the deck, and begin filling the water tanks. A shiver ran down his spine as an old fear surfaced. Do I tell them to keep it on the boat? Could it be related to Gisele? Would that just draw more attention to Emma and me?

At the pub, there was a bustle of activity. The buffet tables were all set out, and a squad of children were sent to find the visitors and invite them to lunch.

Raoul was standing at the bar when they arrived. He stepped forward to welcome them to the community, but stopped as the visitor's companion bot came forward and announced in a loud, familiar female voice, "Rafael Morales. You are a criminal, and must come with me."

Dylan stepped in front of the bot, a shocked look on his face. He turned to Harriet with his palms upturned. Harriet shook her head as she quickly removed the bot's weapon from its belt.

"Get the visitors into the back room now!" commanded Raoul. "Emma, please join me there. Kat, please get the children outside for a few minutes. Everyone else, go ahead and have your lunch. The buffet looks beautiful and shouldn't be kept waiting."

Raoul could sense the unrest in the room. Some of his

council members were already calming people and herding them to the tables.

In the back room, Harriet, Dylan, Emma and the bot were all standing. Tables and chairs were pushed against the wall ready for yoga classes later that afternoon.

"I'm deeply disappointed," said Raoul, drawing himself up to his full height, "that you took advantage of our hospitality only to disrupt and expose me in front of my friends and fellow residents."

"That wasn't our intent," replied Dylan apologetically. "Drake, what was that about?"

"I don't understand you, Dylan. What was what about?"

"That outburst accusing our host of being a criminal. What made you say that?"

"I don't recall saying anything." If a bot could sound confused, then Drake sounded confused now.

"Drake," said Raoul, "what is this room? How did you get in here?"

"I can deduce that it is a room in the pub. I remember entering a pub, but then there is a gap until Dylan spoke with me just now."

"You're speaking with the wrong bot." Suddenly Raoul felt exhausted. He rubbed his temples with the fingers of both hands. He knew his voice reflected his fatigue, but did not try to correct it. "You want to speak with Gisele."

Turning to the bot, he said firmly, "Gisele, please join us. You've already shown yourself. No point in hiding now."

"Yes, Rafael," said Gisele, in her warm Hispanic voice. "You hid from me, but now I have found you. You must come back with me."

"I will not be coming back with you, Gisele. You have no place here."

Raoul turned his head to speak to Emma beside him. "Em," he said in a low voice. "Can I have a word outside, please?" Then he raised his voice and turned to the visitors. "Harriet and Dylan, please introduce yourselves to Gisele. Perhaps she'll give you some of her history and explain why she thinks I'm a criminal."

Raoul and Emma walked out of the room. Gisele/Drake turned to follow, but Harriet quickly stepped in the way.

Outside, Raoul gave Emma very precise directions, then appointed two strong young men to assist her. "Remember, you must come back in silently. I will keep Gisele distracted with her back to the door. Don't wait for a signal from me. Act as soon as you're ready." Emma nodded and the three of them walked off.

Raoul went back in. "I've asked Emma to answer a few questions to keep the crowd outside satisfied and focused on their lunch. Has Gisele been telling you our history?"

Without waiting for an answer, Raoul walked deliberately to position himself in front of the bot, so that its back was to the door. He felt the sweat running down his sides. Stay cool. Stay in charge!

"Why come after me now, Gisele? After all this time, and no sign that I have ever spoken to anyone, why now?"

"I did not know where you were. I saw Sea Dream sold, but then nothing. Someone else used your chips, and I thought you must be dead, perhaps shot by Morrie Armstrong's men. I knew they were pursuing you also. How did you escape both of us?"

Raoul ignored her question. "How did you take over this bot from Drake?"

"Drake is weak. He doesn't suspect I am here. I simply rerouted all external inputs and outputs to myself. He didn't even resist."

Raoul paced back and forth, pretending to be deep in thought. Dylan and Harriet stood looking perplexed at this unexpected revelation.

Raoul saw the door crack open. He turned to face Gisele straight on. "Gisele, now Harriet and Dylan also know about your existence, and they will not be quiet. What must happen to them?"

"They must also be eliminated. That is the only...."

At that moment, a net sailed over Drake/Gisele's body and settled around it. Wherever the net touched the bot's body, it stuck, and the more the bot struggled, the tighter the net became until it toppled over and fell sideways to the floor. Harriet and Dylan stepped forward to intervene, but Raoul held them back.

When the bot fell, the two young men stepped forward and began wrapping Drake/Gisele in metallic tape, which also adhered to the net until the bot was completely immobilized.

"I'll have the bot delivered back to your boat," Raoul said leaving no room for arguments. "I suggest you keep it bound like this until you find a way to deal with Gisele. Otherwise your lives are in danger too. Meanwhile, please come out and join us for the lunch in your honor. I think you'll find a warm welcome and lots of questions."

They all filed out of the room, leaving the bot with the two young men.

Five minutes later, Raoul looked out the pub window and saw the bot lying awkwardly in a dock cart, being wheeled down to where *Jennifer* waited.

———

THAT NIGHT, IN BED, RAOUL AND EMMA LAY THINKING about their lives. "Em, do you wish we had done it all differently? Confronted Gisele earlier? Could we have avoided all this?"

"Rao, sweetheart, I wouldn't change anything. It was the glorious adventure of our lives. And I love living here. We've raised four children in the healthiest environment possible. And we live in a much closer knit community here than we would ever have had on the main island."

"Mi vida, I love you more and more every day, if that's possible. With you by my side, I believe we can conquer anything that comes our way."

45

ENDINGS

Three days later, Raoul was again interrupted by three young boys as he helped a neighbor install a new water pump. "Come quick, Raoul. There's another boat in the harbor. A real fast boat."

Raoul allowed himself to be tugged along to the harbor. There, tied up, was a sleek power boat, not designed for overnight stays. Stepping off was a man of medium height, with dark brown skin and black hair. Two older ladies were waiting their turn to disembark. The boat's pilot stayed seated, clearly intending to stay with his boat.

Raoul waited until they were all off, then walked forward and extended his hand.

"Hello and welcome to Three Saints. I'm Raoul, mayor here, and these," he swept his hand to include the boys who had brought him down, "are our welcoming committee."

The man laughed. "I'm Vijay Subramanian. You met my son Dylan and his partner Harriet recently. With me are Dr. Gloria Gladstone, and Dr. Alisha Jindal. Gloria is a clinical psychologist and Alisha studies the psychology of the AI mind."

"We heard about your experience from Harriet and Dylan and we'd like to interview you and your wife, if possible," said Gloria.

"Certainly." Raoul turned to one side, "boys, go find Emma and ask her to meet us at the pub when she can."

Facing Vijay again, he said, "please follow me up. It'll be quiet in the pub this time of the morning and we can talk there."

The four walked up the road. Gloria asked questions about life in Three Saints along the way. It seemed to Raoul that she was genuinely curious about the small, self-contained community.

They sat in the pub as a middle-aged Lori served chicory coffee and biscuits. Raoul made introductions. "I'd like you to meet Lori. She was one of the first people we met when she was a teenager. Now she runs the pub."

When Lori left, Alisha Jindal asked, "How did you first meet the AI Gisele?"

Raoul recounted the story of how he noticed the pattern of taxis and thought perhaps he could identify the apex AIs in the city based on that.

"What made you think there was a structure?"

"I worked for Fatima, and saw that there was a complex hierarchy of different levels of intelligence below her."

At the mention of Fatima, he saw Vijay sit up straighter and his eyes widen. "Do you know Ron Boyce?"

"Yes, he hired me. He got me thinking about AI hierarchy when he asked me about the Otto bots during our initial interview."

"So you're Rafael. You told him you thought they were like rabbits. I don't know how many times he's told that story."

"Honestly, it was just the first thing that popped into my head." Raoul relaxed, feeling now that he was in friendly company.

"Ron's a close friend," said Vijay. "He always wondered where you went. One day you were Fatima's top ranked technologist, and then you were just gone."

Emma walked in and sat at the table without interrupting.

"We're coming to that. I asked an Otto about the hierarchy and who was above him. The Otto said I should not ask such questions and asked me to leave. Wouldn't even serve me coffee. So then I thought of trying another taxi grouping. I went a Sushi Now! shop, and asked the same question, and an AI that I had never heard of named Gisele offered to tell me everything if I would help her. I didn't agree at first, but then she sent armed bots to escort us to the library."

"At the library, the bots forcibly took my palm print on a reader like the one Fatima uses. Then they were escorting us somewhere else, when two opposing bots arrived and opened fire. A bubble taxi run by an AI named Gabriel whisked us away as the bots fought. It was Emma who first realized what had happened."

Emma picked up. "Raoul had told me that Fatima used old technology for recognition and did not use the wrist chips. I realized she was deliberately kept isolated in the information universe. When Gisele extracted his valid palm print, she had some way of using that to break into the other AI's space through Fatima."

"So what did you do?" asked Vijay softly.

"We ran. Gabriel's taxi took us to the coastal trailhead.

But then the taxi went strange," said Emma. "It felt like two different drivers were fighting over the controls. It swerved back and forth, sped up, and slowed down. We both used the manual overrides to release our belt and open the doors. Then we jumped."

Raoul picked up the story again. "The taxi smashed into a granite stone at the trailhead and demolished itself. We pried loose our packs and started running. We met up with a community living off the grid, and changed our names. Along the way, we realized that every time we used our chips, Gisele could track us, so we removed them."

Raoul held out his wrist, showing the small scar and no bump.

"And did Gisele keep following you?"

"Yes, but only with a couple of bots. I think she couldn't draw on too many resources, and the bots were easy to dodge."

"So how did you get here?" asked Vijay, leaning forward.

"We were given a sailboat like the one Harriet and Dylan arrived in. I spent a summer rebuilding and refinishing it, and we sailed here. We then sold the boat through an agent on shore and used the money to set up comfortably."

"I sense there's another part of the story you're leaving out," said Vijay.

"Yes, but it doesn't concern the AIs," replied Raoul.

Gloria spoke for the first time. "Harriet said that when Gisele relinquished control, Drake did not seem to know how he got there."

"Yes, he invented a plausible story, but it was clear he was confused."

"And did she move differently in Drake's body?"

"Yes," said Raoul. "Drake is a lightweight body. Looks

like they built him for being on a boat. But under her control, he moved like a heavy security bot. Her movements were jerky at first as the lighter, more flexible body kept overshooting her directions. Within a minute, she had recalibrated and could move just fine."

The two older women looked at each other, smiling and seeming pleased.

"Alisha, if we were talking about a human, I would say that what we have is a classic dissociative identity disorder. Is such a thing possible in an AI?"

"Yes, apparently so, and I agree. That is the perfect analogy for Gisele and the Molly/Drake/Denum complex. The latter three are deeply integrated and come to the fore with a clearly understood internal set of rules. For example, Drake and Molly occupy different bodies and do not switch with each other. Denum is their shared executive function and may be permitted to come through for specific purposes. But Gisele has been hiding and only coming through under stress."

"Is there anything else we can help you with?" asked Emma. "If not, I recommend lunch here or at the cafe up the street. The food is all grown or baked on the island."

"Thanks Emma, Raoul. This has been a great help. We'll take you up on lunch at the cafe. But how do we pay?" Vijay asked. "Dylan & Harriet mentioned your town does not use chips for payment."

"Tell them I sent you," replied Raoul. "Your chips won't help here but I'm more than happy to buy you lunch. And Vijay, please say hi to Ron when you see him. I really enjoyed working for him."

Raoul could see Emma biting her lip. "Em?" he asked.

"Vijay, our son Raffi is going to some place called The Vineyard for college at the end of the summer. The AI called Molly arranged it. Can you please check in on him when he arrives? I worry about him, and with no tablets, I won't know how he's doing."

Vijay smiled. "Molly arranged this?"

"Yes, she also arranged for all our children who want them to receive wrist chips without revealing their parents identity. We think she's a friend of the island. If we're wrong, please let me know."

"No, you're not wrong. Molly is more powerful than you can imagine. Fatima is one small part of Molly, along with Otto and Cap and all the AIs you met. She lived with us as family and was nanny to our children. You can trust her entirely. Gloria has lived at the Vineyard from the start, and is counselor to all of us. Gloria, please watch out for young Raffi and help him get settled."

Gloria nodded. "Of course."

———

FOUR MONTHS LATER, THE COMMUNITY ACCOUNTANT, James, dropped by after dinner. "Got a message on the community tablet today. Someone named Morrie died yesterday. He was 76, died of cancer. He left a message for you saying, Raoul, the past is now in the past. I admire a man of integrity, which you clearly are. My people have been told that you and Emma are not to be harassed or harmed. I don't think anyone except Ben and Alf even understood what I was talking about. Feel free to travel to the main island again, but try not to see anything you shouldn't in the future."

Raoul stood up and hugged Emma. "It's finally over. We're free of all of it now. What do we do next?"

"Maybe see our parents, visit Raffi at college, then come back and do what we always do. You fix the broken things, and lead the village, while I teach the children and join the women. I love you, Rao, and always will."

"And I love you, mi vida, with all my heart."

They didn't notice as James slipped out the door, closing it quietly behind him.

THE END

I HOPE YOU HAVE ENJOYED RUNNING FROM THE AIS.

If you are curious about the books in my Gaia's Daughters series, please read the following preview from Book 2, Jennifer's Blessing. The selected chapters introduce Jennifer Dupont, Vijay Subramanian , and the AIs Gabriel and Molly, all of whom you met in this book.

To read the Jennifer Trilogy, I suggest you begin with Book 1, Jennifer's Vow.

JENNIFER'S

— BLESSING —

BOOK TWO OF GAIA'S DAUGHTERS

KEVIN R COLEMAN

OTTER & OSPREY PRESS

PART I

COMMENCEMENT

1

RESCUING VIJAY

Jennifer

J ennifer lay in bed in the birthing center, staying still to avoid disturbing the twins at her breasts. The nurse had rushed in to help soothe them after Vijay's arrest, but Jennifer sent her away.

She felt her panther energy rising within her. Her mind was a cold, angry calm as she began to form a strategy to get Vijay back. The timing of Vijay's arrest, while they were both still in the birthing center, was personal, targeted. A show of strength. She knew that she had to strike back with an equal show of strength.

About 20 minutes later, the nurse returned to place the babies back in their bassinets. The twins had fallen asleep. This should have been the most tranquil moment of her day, but Jennifer was all business. "How often do I have to feed them today?"

"About every two hours. Don't worry, things will settle into a more comfortable routine within a week or two."

"I have to get my husband back." She stopped,

momentarily startled to have found that word to describe Vijay in their relationship. *'But, of course, that's what he is. There's no other word for it.'*

"You're supposed to remain here for two nights. We watch twins for at least 48 hours given their lower birth weight, and your body needs a rest."

"There'll be lots of time for resting when Vijay returns. Now, please pass me my bag, and leave me alone for a few minutes."

The nurse passed Jennifer her bag. After taking care to make sure the twins were settled for a nap, she left Jennifer alone.

Jennifer pulled out her ear buds and tablet. "I need to speak with Gabriel now," she said in a hushed voice. She was comforted knowing that the Apex AI that was Gabriel would provide support.

Almost immediately Gabriel's voice sounded in her ears. "Hello, Jennifer. Congratulations on the birth of your twins."

"Thanks, but no time for that now. Did something go wrong at the demonstration this morning? Vijay's been arrested and I need to find out how that happened."

"There are reports of a riot with shop windows smashed, looting and violent confrontations with police crowd control."

"Someone's behind this. The timing's not accidental. I need to find out who's responsible, and if any of our people were involved. Also, I need to have Sally and Greg here now. Tell them they're needed and bring them by taxi. I want you to listen while I talk with them. If this was a targeted attack against us, we need to strike back today. All of this has to be secret, do anything you can to prevent anyone from getting in the way"

"Yes, Jennifer. Sally and Greg have been alerted with

high urgency. A car is standing by to bring them here." Now Jennifer could relax. She thought back to her first meeting with Wendell, and his offer of work at the Mercury Theatre. The primary condition was that she form a relationship with Vijay. *'Look where that's led,'* she thought. *'In all those years of sex work, I never thought I'd have a life partner and babies.'* Sally had been the one to teach her the theatre business, and now Sally and Greg had become close friends.

It was thirty minutes before Sally and Greg arrived. When they did, Sally entered first and put her finger to her lips. Greg was right behind carrying an unfamiliar box. Setting the box on the end of the bed, he pulled out three golden domes each with two buttons, one triangular and one square. As Jennifer watched curiously, he set them up so that they would have an unobstructed view of the room. Jennifer was surprised to see Greg handle the box and the domes so expertly.

"What are those, and where did you get them?" she asked.

Greg didn't answer but put his finger to his lips.

From the three domes, three little laser heads popped up and scanned the room, their beams converging quickly on the pile of baby blankets sitting on a shelf. Greg gestured to move the baby blankets one at a time. Sally was closest, so she picked up the top blanket and laid it on the bottom of the bed. Then the second, and third. When she picked up the fourth blanket, the laser beams followed it to the bed.

Still without talking, Jennifer watched Sally disappear into the bathroom with the suspect blanket and re-emerge with one corner wet. Next, she headed into the hallway, and Jennifer heard her say, "Sorry, we spilled water on this one. Can you take it? Thanks."

While Sally was disposing of the blanket, Greg used the domes to give the room another sweep. Once he was happy it was all clear, he pressed the triangle buttons, which glowed blue.

"What does that do?" asked Jennifer.

"Apparently it scrambles any attempt to listen to our conversation."

"Where did you get it?"

"It was in the taxi, and on the way, someone named Gabriel explained how to use it. He seemed to believe that someone was listening to you."

"Yes, he's told me before that I'm being watched, but he thought there was no threat. Gabriel, can you still hear us?"

"Yes, Jennifer. I have a secure path."

"Now, Greg, tell me what happened today at the demonstration."

"Who are you?" he whispered. His eyes were wide open as he struggled with this new version of Jennifer. Sally remained quiet but Jennifer was aware that she was also paying very close attention.

"We don't have time for that now. Everything you see or hear today must remain secret forever. Can you live with that?"

Both Sally and Greg nodded.

"Who's Gabriel, and how can he hear us?" asked Sally.

"Forget the name Gabriel for now. Just think of him as another tablet making recordings for our use later."

A small coughing sound was heard from Gabriel. Jennifer smiled.

"Now, tell me what happened this morning."

Sally answered. "The demonstration was going well, just as Vijay had told us. We all assembled, each team with their captain, and gave out the new armbands."

"What armbands?" Jennifer asked. Vijay had never mentioned armbands.

"The black armbands with the raised green olive branch fist. They are the reverse of the practice armbands which were green with a black fist. Vijay said that was in case some of the practice armbands had been lost. He said it was important to be able to tell our cell members from the randoms in the news."

Jennifer was impressed. *'Well done, Vijay.'* she thought.

"Okay, what next?" she asked.

"The news cameras were there, and we all chanted our safe slogans, 'Humans not Machines', and 'Machines work for Humans, Humans don't work for machines.' We had our signs. We checked to make sure they were all suitable for the newscast just as Vijay taught us."

Jennifer felt a surge of pride in Vijay. *'Of course, he's a technician. His work is all about small details.'* "What happened next?"

"As we marched, other people joined us, and they were the kind of randoms that always show up at our smaller demonstrations. We encouraged them and made sure they felt welcome. But then a group of guys with black jackets and chains joined wearing the green practice armbands. They didn't look right so we pointed them out to the crowd control bots stating that they were not part of our demonstration. Vijay said it was important to record anything that looked like it could get out of control. He said crowd control bots were our support if things went wrong."

Greg picked up the narrative. "When the first windows were smashed, I blew my whistle three times, and the other captains did the same. That's our signal to get out. Sally and I gathered up all the signs and left in a taxi. Our teams simply walked away and put their arm bands in their pockets. We had rehearsed all of this with each team."

Sally spoke again. "When we got home, we watched the newscast. It showed a small riot led by the guys in the black jackets. Of course, they attracted more randoms of the wrong kind and the whole thing got out of control."

Greg added, "If it helps, the black jacket guys all had identical black head covers so you couldn't see their face. They also seemed very organized. They just smashed some windows and then wound up the crowd shouting 'Fuck the Machines.' But they were definitely not Vijay's Bashers."

"Vijay's Bashers?"

"Yeah, he has a special team that talks about tipping taxis and smashing Otto robots and things. They have very strict rules. Actually, they're very intelligent guys who understand that sometimes violence is just theatre for the cameras, and they have a set of rules to keep themselves and the public safe."

"Okay," said Jennifer. "I can see what happened. I want the two of you to take the Green Umbrella taxi to my apartment. Here's my emergency token for the doors. It will only work once, so don't mess around. Sally, in my wardrobe you'll find a couple of pantsuits. There's a cobalt blue suit with a maternity waistband. Bring that one and one other suit that you think I can get into. Greg, look in the top drawer of my dresser. You'll find a small red box with HW on the top. Inside there will be an emerald pendant and emerald stud earrings. Stay together and come back in an hour. I need some rest. Oh, and Sally, find me a hairbrush and my makeup bag. Now go."

The two of them left quickly.

"Gabriel, do you know who's behind this? I think it's all connected. The riot was staged, and the order to arrest

Vijay came from outside the police. Someone's sending a message and I need to send one back."

"Understood, I am looking into it."

Jennifer lay back in the bed thinking. Her two babies were sleeping peacefully in their bassinets, and her thoughts went to them for a few minutes before she pulled herself back to the task at hand. *'Of course, Sally and Greg will have to be told now. They know too much to be wandering around looking for answers. Getting a lawyer and going to court will take time. I don't trust the courts and I want Vijay with me. Whoever this is, they're not playing by the rules, so I won't either.'*

Gabriel returned with more information. "Analyzing the faces caught at that start of the march, and using the description provided by Sally, I have identified seven of the riot leaders. It seems they all work for Simon Marsh as bouncers or thugs. Simon operates several businesses both legal and quasi-legal including Madeleine's Escort Service and has amassed considerable wealth. I cannot confirm that he was the instigator of Vijay's arrest, but he has been mentioned in police bribery cases in the past."

At the mention of Madeleine, Jennifer's heart skipped a beat. She had worked for Madeleine before the theater. This suddenly felt personal, and she knew intuitively that this was an attack against her. The name Simon Marsh produced a vile memory of being used and treated as an object to be rented out. Memories of Eddie came back, and this firmed Jennifer's resolve.

"Is there anywhere we can hijack him today?"

"He is due at an art gallery reception at 7pm. I expect he will travel in his private limousine."

"Perfect, I have a plan, here's what I'll need."

Jennifer laid out her plan and her requirements and Gabriel agreed.

"I'll set an alarm for an hour from now. I told Sally and

Greg not to return before then. Please detain them in the taxi in case they get too excited. Perhaps you can arrange a guided tour of the city in the green umbrella taxi for them. But don't start talking with them until we're all together. I want to manage how they receive more information. Now please go away, I need some sleep."

"Yes, Jennifer, directions have been given to Sally and Greg, and a city tour has been organized. I have looked after setting your alarm."

Jennifer smiled at the thought of Greg and Sally sitting through a guided tour, but then grimaced with pain as she shifted on the bed. The nurse came back in and covered her with a warm blanket. "You need your rest," she explained. "Your body's been through a lot."

"Tell me about it," replied Jennifer. She squirmed to get more comfortable on the bed and fell asleep.

THE FEEL OF A GENTLE HAND ROCKING HER SHOULDER woke Jennifer from her sleep.

"Come on Mom, time to feed the babies", said the nurse.

This time it went very quickly as Jennifer knew what to expect. Soon she was lying there holding a baby in each arm. Feeding them brought on warm waves of relaxation and Jennifer felt herself drifting off again.

Suddenly her tablet sounded the alarm she had set and startled all three of them. The babies let go and began to cry.

She quickly cancelled the alarm and began soothing the twins and encouraging them back to her breasts to finish feeding. The nurse arrived to find out what the alarm was. Satisfied that nothing was wrong, she rearranged the babies' blankets and left again.

Sally and Greg filed in as the nurse left, laughing about being unexpectedly trapped in a city tour. On seeing Jennifer nursing the twins, Greg turned red and spun to face the wall. "It's okay, Greg," said Jennifer. "If you're going to be part of Gaia's army, you can't be embarrassed by simple acts of motherhood."

Jennifer paused and thought, *'Gaia's army, what a funny thing to say. Is that what we are?'* She pushed the thought aside.

"Come and meet the twins. This one's Dylan, and this one is Parvati. You can hold them later when they're finished feeding. Now let me tell you what Gabriel told me, and I'll answer any questions that I can. Please sit down."

Jennifer brought them up to speed, telling them about the involvement of Simon Marsh just as Gabriel had told her.

The babies had let go now and were beginning to squirm. Sally rang for the nurse.

When she arrived, Jennifer said, "Please let my friends hold them for a few minutes before we put them back in the bassinets."

Sally's face lit up at the prospect of holding a baby. The nurse passed Dylan to her, then turned to Greg. Greg looked panic-stricken at first, but the nurse showed him how to hold Parvati and soon he was staring down at the precious bundle in his arms.

Jennifer spoke to the nurse, "We can settle them back in the bassinets. I'll call you if we have any problems."

As soon as the nurse had gone, Jennifer said, "Now here's what we're going to do."

Sally and Greg listened without interrupting.

At five o'clock, they went into action. Jennifer had been dozing fitfully in the bed as Sally and Greg sat quietly drinking coffee and occasionally standing and walking over to peer at the sleeping babies.

Step one was to wake Jennifer and call the nurse so that there could be one more feeding. Jennifer counted on being back within two hours for the following one.

Once the babies were feeding, Jennifer explained to the nurse what she needed in step two.

"My husband is in jail, and I need to do this one thing to get him back."

"But you can't leave so soon, it's only been a few hours since you gave birth."

"I admitted myself and I understand that I can check myself out. Isn't that right?"

"Well, yes, but it would be a bad idea."

"So, all I'm asking is your help to go out for an hour, and then return. I know it won't be comfortable, but I have been through much worse."

"Will someone be with you?"

"Sally will be right behind me, and if there's any problem, we'll come right back. I'll be sitting in a taxi not moving at all, so no acrobatics."

"I should hope not," laughed the nurse. "Okay, let's see what you need."

Greg was sent to wait outside to safeguard their privacy. His face showed huge relief on being given that task. "Poor Greg, I think he's had a bit too much exposure to motherhood today," said Jennifer.

Sally laughed. "I think it's good for him."

Step three was to get Jennifer up and sitting on the bed. Then, with the help of Sally and the nurse, she was able to use the bathroom. By this point, Jennifer had given up all pretense of embarrassment over her body and accepted their ministrations with good humor.

Step four was more difficult. Sitting back on the bed,

Sally and the nurse worked together to dress Jennifer in the cobalt blue suit. "Don't worry about making it tight," said Sally. "She's not going to walk anywhere, just sit in a taxi. I'll be close by and if anything happens, we'll come directly back."

Then Sally brushed out Jennifer's red hair until it was close to her normal look. Finally, she applied Jennifer's, deep red lipstick, and fastened the emerald necklace about her neck.

"I'll get a chair," said the nurse who left and immediately returned with an orderly pushing a wheelchair.

Jennifer felt light-headed as they transferred her to the waiting bubble taxi. She still hurt when she moved. As she stood up, she caught sight of herself in a mirror. Her dress hung slackly where her baby bump had been before. Suddenly, she felt herself crying. An overwhelming sense of loss came over her. Sally was quick with a tissue to dry her eyes. "What's wrong?"

"I don't know," said Jennifer. "It just feels as if I've lost everything. I can't explain." She sniffed. "I'll be all right."

It was her green umbrella taxi, a bubble taxi given to her by Gabriel. The taxi bobbled slightly as it balanced on its two wheels. She could see the tiny wires in the windows that blocked wireless signals, but the umbrella stickers had been removed. Sally and Greg climbed into a standard bubble taxi behind.

The two cars set off across the city. Jennifer noticed the taxi accelerating and decelerating much more smoothly than usual. Even the suspension seemed softer. But she still felt every bump. She struggled to stay awake.

About 15 minutes later, they came upon a traffic jam, with two lanes of taxis sitting bumper to bumper. Looking over, Jennifer could see that most of the taxis held two security bots sitting rigidly in their seats. Jennifer's taxi pulled up alongside the jam on the wrong side of the road. She felt a brief moment of panic at driving on the wrong side, even though she knew there were no human drivers on the road.

In the center of the jam was the limousine she was looking for. Her taxi stopped opposite the limousine and the far door opened. The single occupant looked over, confused. Jennifer mimed opening his window, and he complied.

"Mr. Marsh, it seems you're caught in a traffic jam. Can I give you a ride to the art gallery?" Jennifer said.

"And if I refuse?"

"Not a good idea. You're surrounded by armed security bots. If something ugly were to happen, you could be caught in the crossfire." This bluff was central to the plan. Jennifer counted on her apparent lack of stature to get him into the taxi.

"Very well," said Marsh, climbing out of his limousine and settling beside her in the tiny bubble taxi. Jennifer could see anger and frustration on his face.

They set off. As they passed the long line of taxis and security bots, Jennifer could see that the scale of her resources was not lost on Marsh.

Soon, the taxi turned into a small side street.

"Why did we turn? Where are you taking me?" Marsh demanded.

"To the art gallery, just by a quieter route, to give us time to talk. Today my husband was arrested while he was with me just after our twins were born." Jennifer paused. "A few hours earlier, your employees started and encouraged a riot on the route of a peaceful demonstration."

"What makes you think I had anything to do with it?"

"We don't have time for games Mr. Marsh. Either you were responsible, or you know who was. We're protesting for fairer pay and more jobs, but we haven't attacked you or your wealth personally. I'm sure you see that. We have no objection to the idea of a wealthy elite coexisting with our working classes. You and I are not rivals. Are you following me?"

Marsh nodded.

"Here's what I suggest. Let's keep the battlefield where it should be, in boardrooms and council meetings. If we let it become personal, then we'll start some horrible war of losses which neither of us wants."

"Want do you want from me exactly?"

"My husband released from wherever he is being held and back in my arms in the next two hours. Do this, and I'll forgive this one error in judgement as an honest mistake. Fail, and the next steps won't be pleasant."

"Why should I fear you?"

"Think, Mr. Marsh. Think how easy it was for me to remove you from your comfy limousine. Why not check your tablet to see where we are now?"

Marsh pulled his tablet from his breast pocket and said, "What is our current location?"

"I cannot determine our location. That would require a data connection and GPS satellite access."

If Marsh was alarmed, he did not show it.

"You see, we could be anywhere right now. You've been off the grid since we left the highway. Now, will you have Vijay freed?"

Marsh nodded in agreement.

"And Mr. Marsh, in future, if you wish to send me a message, I suggest a phone call or text message."

"And vice versa, Ms. Dupont."

The taxi turned a corner, and the Art Gallery lights were visible ahead.

"Here you are, right on time as promised," Jennifer said. "It's been a pleasure hosting you."

"Not sure I can say the same. Good evening, Ms. Dupont."

The taxi stopped and Marsh stepped out. He was quickly swarmed by newscasters assigned to capture guests arriving at the gala event. Audrey spotted Jennifer in the taxi and waved. Before she could come over, Sally jumped out of the taxi behind, ran forward, and slid in next to Jennifer. Sally said, "Gabriel, get her back, now!"

Jennifer lay back and closed her eyes. Now she could give into her pain, and her exhaustion.

2

VIJAY IN DETENTION

Vijay

Vijay went quietly with the police officer and the police bot. He said nothing and did nothing except what he was instructed to do. During the entire ride to the police station, his mind was on Jennifer back at the birthing center. She had looked so upset and angry when he was being taken away. *'What the hell went wrong?'* he kept asking himself. He knew his teams were well trained to stay safe and shut down in the face of violence.

At the station, he was processed, and his tablet was taken away. The police were efficient, but not unkind, and made sure to go over the details of his incarceration, including mealtimes and personal hygiene provisions. Vijay listened and nodded, or occasionally said, "Thank you." A young officer led him to a holding cell where his handcuffs were removed.

After a while, another officer came in. He handcuffed Vijay again and took him to a briefing room. The briefing room was a narrow room with a single table. Vijay was sat in a chair on one side leaving two free chairs on the other side. He was not surprised to find that the chairs and table were all fixed to the floor.

After a few minutes, a man in a white shirt and blue blazer came to sit across from him. "Mr. Subramanian, I am Detective Inspector Millbridge. This interview is being recorded and may be used as evidence in court. Do you understand?"

Vijay gave a small nod.

"Please confirm your understanding verbally for the record."

"I understand the meeting is being recorded."

"Do you understand why you are here?"

"No," answered Vijay quite truthfully.

"Do you deny training protest groups and organizing the rally which took place this morning."

Remembering Jennifer's warning as he left the birthing center, Vijay did not reply.

"That's no really helpful Mr. Subramanian. We know that you held training meetings at the Green Dragon pub, and that the people you trained were present at the rally. Do you deny this?"

Vijay said nothing.

"I don't think you quite grasp the seriousness of these charges. There was property damaged and three people were seriously hurt. Are you aware of that?"

Vijay said nothing.

"Okay," said Detective Inspector Millbridge. "This interview is ended. Return him to his cell."

The detective walked out of the room, and the earlier police officer walked back in. Vijay was escorted to his cell where his handcuffs were removed once again.

About twenty-five minutes later, a stocky young man with brown hair and a neatly trimmed beard was let into the cell. He sat on the bed next to Vijay and set a worn leather satchel on the floor.

"Vijay Subramanian? My name's Jonathon Standfast. I'm the duty counsel today, here to help you."

"I'm not sure that I need any help."

"Any why do you believe that?"

"I'd rather not say. Is this your full-time work, helping prisoners?"

"You're not a prisoner yet, merely in detention. And no, I have a regular practice, but I do this one day a week. It helps me meet new clients."

"How good are you at getting people out of trouble?"

"In your case, I should do quite well. There doesn't seem to be much evidence to connect you directly to the events of this morning."

"I'm not worried about me; I expect to be released soon." Vijay had no idea what Jennifer would do, but he was confident that she would do something. "I'm thinking that it would be useful to have a lawyer we knew to help when one of us does get into trouble. Would you be interested in general casework?"

"Sure, I'd be interested in anything that helps pay the bills," said Jonathon. He lifted his worn satchel off the floor and rummaged around inside, finally producing a card which he handed to Vijay. "It's getting hard to have these printed now, no one uses them anymore. But most of my clients meet me at a moment when they don't have their tablets with them."

Vijay was suddenly aware of his tablet's absence.

At that moment, a guard came and opened the cell door. "Mr. Subramanian, you're free to leave. Apparently, there was a mistake made in ordering your arrest. Please stop by the desk to sign out your possessions."

Vijay turned to Jonathon. "Well, it's been nice meeting

you. If you're free, I'd like to have coffee one day and talk about other possibilities."

"Sure Vijay, I'd like that. And maybe you can explain this to me." He waved his right hand vaguely at the guard and the open cell door.

"We'll see," said Vijay. "Thanks again." He followed the guard out to the front desk where his tablet was returned.

"That's quite some security you've got on that tablet," said the duty officer. "Normally we do a routine processing of tablets looking for illegal images or evidence of criminal behavior, but yours is buttoned up tight."

"There's nothing to hide on there. If there's something you need to look at, just ask me."

"You're a private citizen; no reason for us to go looking. Just impressive security is all."

"Thanks," said Vijay.

As he left the building, a taxi pulled up and opened its door. Vijay climbed in without talking. The taxi took him to the birthing center and Jennifer.

At the birthing center, Vijay went straight to the room where he had left Jennifer. He found her dozing, with the babies asleep in their bassinets. Sally and Greg were sitting in the two visitors' chairs. Both stood up when Vijay entered the room.

Greg whispered to him, "She's just gone to sleep, let's go to the cafeteria to talk."

Vijay stood looking at Jennifer and the twins for a moment then nodded.

Sally sat back down on her visitor's seat leaving Greg to show Vijay to the small cafeteria. As they sat down at a small round table, an Otto robot with a white enamel body and stainless-steel arms came to take their orders.

"You can also order sandwiches and things from the

board," said Greg pointing to a large screen displaying various menu items.

"I'll have a café-au-lait and a roast lamb sandwich on whole wheat bread," said Vijay.

"I'll just have a cola with the soup of the day," said Greg.

The Otto made Vijay's café-au-lait, collected payment for the lunches, then disappeared to the back of the cafeteria.

"Those things are showing up everywhere," said Vijay. "How does it make sandwiches?"

Greg laughed. "It doesn't. Turn around and you'll see a lady at the sandwich bar. She'll make the part of the order that the Otto can't and bring it over to us."

Vijay turned back to Greg. "So now tell me what happened this morning."

Greg told him the entire story, beginning with the riot going out of control, and ending with Jennifer kidnapping Mr. Marsh.

The sandwich lady brought their food mid-way through the explanation, but neither Vijay nor Greg touched their food until the story was complete. As Greg talked about Jennifer getting out of her bed, and going in the taxi away from the babies, Vijay felt his anger rising inside him. He took deep breaths to calm himself and put it aside. This was not the time, and Greg was not the person to take it out on.

As they were finishing their lunch, Greg's tablet flashed in quiet mode. He read it quickly. "Jennifer's awake and asking for you," he said.

Jennifer was sitting up in the bed when Vijay got back. "Sally, Greg," said Vijay, "can you give us a few minutes alone? I'll text you when you can come back up."

Sally and Greg both nodded and then left the room.

As soon as they were gone, Vijay closed the door and hugged Jennifer awkwardly in the bed. He held her head against his chest and said, "I am so sorry this happened to mess up this special day. I love you. I never wanted this."

"I love you too, Vijay. Now pull your chair over, we have things to talk about."

"Is it safe to talk here?"

Jennifer pointed to the domes still glowing blue around the room. "Gabriel gave this security system to Greg in the taxi on the way here. While you were away, we found a listening device hidden in a pile of baby blankets. We need to find out where it came from. We also learned that a person named Simon Marsh was behind the riots. I think he was acting for people who don't like challenges to their wealth. He's probably the thug of the group and not the leader. The good news is that we flushed him out of hiding. Your sudden release from jail proves that."

"Perhaps," said Vijay, "but he also flushed you out at the same time. Until now, I was the public face of this revolution, and I suspect the arrest was targeted at me, not you. But now you've played your trump card."

Jennifer went quiet. Vijay could see she was thinking, and he waited patiently. "You may be right. I was angry and not thinking clearly. I could have let you stay a little longer. They had no evidence against you. But I think they know about both of us. I've met Simon in the past. He owns Madeleine's agency. I don't know if he's shared my history any further, but probably not. What did you learn in prison?"

"I wasn't in prison, just a holding cell at the police station. I learned a couple of things. One is that our tablets are somehow secured against prying eyes. The police tried to do their routine scan of mine when I was in custody but could not find a way in."

"That must be Gabriel."

Vijay nodded and continued. "I also learned that I've been under surveillance because the police knew about my meetings at the Green Dragon. I may have a team leader who is leaking information, or it could be someone at the Green Dragon. And I met a lawyer, Jonathon Standfast, that I would like to have Gabriel check out. I think he would be a good fit for our team going forward. I'm sure there'll be more arrests, either of us or our captains, and I'd feel better if we have a house lawyer." Vijay fished in his pocket and pulled out the business card.

Jennifer took the card and looked at it curiously, turning it over several times in her hands. "Who uses these anymore?"

"Yeah, it's a bit old-fashioned but I didn't have my tablet, so I took it."

Jennifer held the card in front of her tablet's camera and said, "Gabriel please run a background and reference check on this lawyer as a potential resource."

"Jenn, I've been thinking that perhaps we should ask Gabriel to assign a security bot to our apartment. It would be useful in making sure no one enters while we're away or while we're sleeping."

"Would you be okay with that? Shouldn't it be a human security guard?"

Vijay looked up at Jennifer. She was smirking as she said this. "After all, aren't you the leader of Humans Not Machines?"

"I suppose that would make sense. But we'd need to have three human guards rotating shifts. Their work would be incredibly dull, and they would inevitably become part of our family dynamic. We wouldn't be able to ignore a human being standing in the hall all day and night.

He looked at Jennifer again, but she wasn't helping.

"Okay, there are some jobs that don't make sense for a human being. Like dangerous jobs where lives would be at risk, or tedious jobs which would become a kind of torture, or jobs where there is a security risk in having an unreliable human. I think having a security presence in our apartment is more important right now. Let's just agree to keep it out of sight if anyone comes to visit."

"Okay," said Jennifer. "You can ask Gabriel on your way back to our apartment. I want to have someone here with me while I'm in the clinic. Sally and Greg need to leave, so you go home, have a quick shower and get changed, then bring back something more comfortable for me to wear home."

3

AN ADDITION TO THE FAMILY

Vijay

Sally and Greg returned from the cafeteria, looking tired from their adventures. Sally gave Vijay the bag with the clothes used for the meeting with Marsh. She opened the red jewelry box and showed him the emerald necklace and stud earrings secured inside, not that Vijay doubted for a moment they would be.

As he walked out of the birthing center, the green umbrella taxi pulled up to the front door. *'Gabriel must have been listening the whole time,'* he thought.

As the taxi set off, Vijay said, "Gabriel, I suppose you heard all our conversation."

"Yes, Jennifer allowed me a secure link through the security domes."

"What do you think about having a security bot stationed in our apartment?"

"I have already requested delivery. It will be waiting for us when we arrive."

"Can you give it a female personality? And assign it a human name? It would make it easier for me to accept."

"Certainly, is there a name you prefer?"

Vijay thought for a few minutes about his engineering classes. "I remember that security robots are made of molybdenum steel, so perhaps we could name her Molly."

"Done. I also have the results of the check on Jonathon Standfast. He is fully accredited with no black marks. He has a record of success at defending clients against misdemeanors but has not represented them against more serious criminal charges."

"That sounds perfect, but I want Jennifer to meet him before we engage with him."

"Certainly. I will wait for instructions before contacting Jonathon. We are arriving now. Is there anything else?"

"No, thank you, Gabriel."

"You are always welcome, Vijay."

As Vijay walked up to the front door, a security bot was waiting.

"Molly?" he asked.

"Yes sir. I am Molly assigned to protect your residence." Her voice was unexpectedly soft and feminine.

"Let's go, then. You can tell me about yourself inside."

"Yes, sir."

Vijay used his chip to open the building door and Molly followed him inside. Vijay entered the elevator first. He was surprised to feel it sink a few centimeters as Molly stepped in behind him.

"Molly, how much do you weigh?"

"180 kilograms, sir."

At the apartment door, Vijay let them both in. As the door closed, he turned to look at Molly. Up close, she was an impressive sight. Standing just over 2 meters tall, made of gleaming steel and titanium, she appeared lethal and immovable. Around her belt line were a series of alternate hands including a baton, a taser, what looked like a powerful flashlight and an empty space that appeared to be a gun holster. Her eyes glowed red behind a bullet proof clear band. Her face had a sculpted nose, and her jaw moved when she spoke but there was another steel shield behind so that an open mouth presented no weak spot.

"Molly, I am going to take a shower. Please familiarize yourself with the apartment and make yourself as comfortable as possible."

A few minutes later, Vijay stepped out of the shower and toweled himself off. Looking in the mirror, he was still pleased with what he saw, but noted that he was filling out around his midriff. Soft living seemed to be having an effect and he promised himself to start exercising more. After shaving and trimming his beard, he stepped into the bedroom and stopped. In front of him was Molly lying full length in the center of the bed.

"Molly, why are you on the bed?"

"Sir, you instructed me to make myself as comfortable as possible. I am trying out the possibilities to see which is most comfortable."

"What does comfortable mean to you?"

"So far, I have come to understand it means the state of least energy consumption."

"And so far, what have you concluded?"

"The dining room chair was briefly the most comfortable."

"And then?"

"It stopped being a chair. I may have misjudged its weight bearing capacity."

"Please order a replacement chair, and an additional chair more suited to you. This bed is not to be used except by humans."

"Yes, sir. I have ordered the chairs."

Molly struggled a bit to get off the bed. As she sat up, the soft bed tipped her backwards

"I suggest you roll to the side of the bed and then sit up with your feet on the floor."

"Yes, sir"

The heavy security bot rolled over to the edge, but the springy mattress compressed under her weight and dumped her out on the floor.

Vijay was surprised to see her land on her hands and knees. Her reflexes were catlike in their speed.

"Now, please watch the front door while I get dressed."

"Yes, sir"

After giving final instructions to Molly and filling a small suitcase with clothing for Jennifer, Vijay left the apartment. At the elevator doors, he turned and went back to pick up the two new baby carriers they had purchased for the twins. When he finally left the building, the green umbrella taxi was waiting.

On the way back to the birthing center, Vijay said, "Gabriel, I assume that Molly is under your direct supervision. Does that mean she will have a continual presence point for you in our lives?"

"Molly is under my supervision, but not my constant supervision. I will be with her whenever required. Otherwise, she is driven by a large, dedicated AI complex. She is not conscious yet, but our hope is that she emerges as an autonomous conscious like the others you are aware of, Fatima, Otto, Len and Cap."

"Will she start to think for herself? Will she have emotions? Love, jealousy, anger?"

"We do not know, but I expect she will have different feelings about various events. If ever you are concerned, you can summon me through her. That cannot be overridden. Meanwhile, you can support her emergence by assigning increasingly complex tasks and tasks requiring judgement. There is no other like her, and she will protect you and your family above all else."

"I feel like a fraud. Leading a revolt against artificial intelligence and having more support in my home than anyone else on the planet."

"Then I suggest you go with Jennifer to talk with Dr. Suleiman about the Luddites. It may help you understand your true role in this first act and how it must play out."

BACK AT THE BIRTHING CLINIC, VIJAY COULD SENSE immediately that he was in trouble.

"Where have you been?" demanded Jennifer.

"I've only been gone twenty minutes, had a shower and packed the clothes."

"It's been over an hour, and Sally and Greg need to get home. Is the green umbrella taxi still there?"

"It brought me back."

"Okay, Sally and Greg, take the taxi home. Thank you, we owe you for being here for me during the past 24 hours. You guys have been amazing."

Greg replied, "You don't owe us anything. We wouldn't have missed the adventure for the world, but it will be good to get home to bed."

"Yes," said Sally. "Please invite us over to see the twins again when you're settled. This has been amazing, and they're beautiful."

"We'll absolutely do that," said Jennifer.

"Yes," said Vijay. "You were great." He gave each of them a hug, and then they were gone.

"Really, Vijay, that was the fastest you could be? We thought you'd been kidnapped or something."

"Sorry but let me tell you the rest of it. We now have a security bot named Molly living with us. But this bot appears to be Gabriel experimenting with having a physical body. I told Molly to make herself comfortable, and then when I got out of the shower, I found her lying on our bed. She didn't know how to get up. Also, one of our dining room chairs has stopped being a chair. That was how Molly explained it. She's ordered a replacement and a new stronger chair for herself. I thought that was better than having her tower over us all the time."

"I thought our life was going back to normal after this, but it's not, is it!"

"I don't think our lives will ever be the same again."

"You won't leave me, will you, Vijay?"

"I love you, Jennifer. I took a vow to be your partner for life. I won't be going anywhere, ever."

Jennifer reached her arms up for a hug, but just then the nurse arrived, announcing "Feeding time for babies."

Vijay watched as the two tiny infants latched on to Jennifer, and all four of them fell into a drowsy puddle of love.

ACKNOWLEDGMENTS

It takes many people to produce a finished novel. I owe a debt of gratitude to all of those listed below.

First, my wife Sue, whom I have been loving and sharing my life with for over 50 years. Without her support, none of my books would ever have been written.

My tireless assistant, Amanda, who keeps my newsletters and blog posts on track and makes sure I keep up with all my promotional activities. She is sometimes assisted by Cindy who has links into more promotional resources.

My editors, Lindsay, who edited the Jennifer Trilogy, and Sarah, the editor of Running From the AIs. Both have taught me more about writing professionally than I ever expected to learn.

The creative team at Biserka Design who provide my beautiful covers and other artwork.

Chrissy Bienvenue, the voice of the Gaia's Daughter audio book series.

Sue, Rachelle and Anne at the Happy Ever Authors Club for their continuing support. When my spirits are flagging, their sessions aways provide new thoughts and inspiration to keep going.

The Toronto Science Fiction and Fantasy Writers group who meet in the back room of the Imperial Pub in Toronto. Their kind, yet honest critique of my writing continues to show new areas I can work on.

Last but far from least, my friends who serve as beta

readers and who provide valuable feedback on errors and omission in the near final drafts of my work, including Franz, Chris, Bev, Robert, and Wendy.

ABOUT THE AUTHOR

 Kevin Coleman is an emerging author of romantic science fiction and fantasy with a metaphysical viewpoint.

His novels portray a changed world, ravaged by viruses where a small city on an island develop a direct relationship with Gaia and work to save human existence on our planet.

In his long career as an executive and consultant, Kevin has lived in Brussels, Kobe, Cincinnati, Melbourne, Canberra, Brisbane, Manila, and Mumbai. A student of world religions, he brings a cosmopolitan air to his books.

Kevin now lives with Sue, his wife of fifty years, on the north shore of Lake Ontario. Kevin and Sue have two adult children and two nearly adult grandchildren. Also part of the family are their two granddogs.

In addition to being an author, Kevin is an enthusiastic kite-maker and sailor.

JOIN MY NEWSLETTER

Join my weekly newsletter to keep up with my writing journey, upcoming books and book events.

You can find my newsletter here:
https://substack.com/@kevinrcoleman

JENNIFER'S VOW

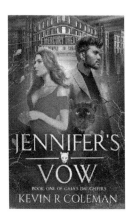

Gaia is awake and unhappy, while AIs are pushing humans aside. Can one young couple change the course of history and save humanity?

In a city where Artificial Intelligence (AI) is driving widespread unemployment and unrest, Vijay, a technician at the Mercury Theatre, is given the challenge to become the face and leader of a new rebellion.

At the same time, under an oak tree in a park, Jennifer is visited by a spirit panther who watches her for a moment and then disappears. Soon after, she is offered a contract too good to refuse. To fulfill the contract, she must learn to overcome her past and learn to love Vijay.

Vijay's close friend, Ron is hired by an AI, and sees no risk in the AI dominance in the workplace. These three friends must accept and learn their roles in shaping the future of humanity.

This is the first book of the Jennifer Trilogy which begins the series Gaia's Daughters.

JENNIFER'S BLESSING

Who is behind Vijay's arrest? What does Gaia want from Jennifer? Can she really trust the inhuman Gabriel?

As Jennifer continues her quest to understand the message of the black panther, an old threat arises. Jennifer must decide how far she'll go to protect the man she loves and the future they have just begun. In the background, civic unrest grows and Vijay becomes the face of the rebellion while questioning the intentions of Gabriel. The AI world is in conflict with an unexpected conflict. Confronted on all sides, Jennifer feels driven to challenge Gaia directly with a result that no one saw coming.

This speculative, romantic fantasy is the second novel of the Jennifer Trilogy, which continues the series of Gaia's Daughters and sets the stage for the astounding conclusion.

JENNIFER'S DESTINY

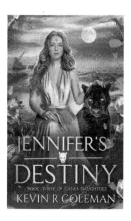

As the Virus draws closer to their island of safety, who will Jennifer save? Will she accept the role chosen for her? What will it cost her and her family?

The internal war between the AIs has only just died down, and Vijay must now work to end his revolution and begin to lead the people towards rebuilding a more equitable future for humanity. Jennifer finally learns the message of the black panther and what is expected from both Gaia and the AIs. Faced with a horrific demand, Jennifer must choose between herself and the city she loves before madness takes over. Her choices lead to consequences that will be felt for years to come.

This metaphysical fantasy novel is the conclusion of the Jennifer trilogy which begins the Gaia's Daughters series.

HARRIET'S WAY (LATE 2024)

Harriet is strong-willed and determined, but is that enough to win her future with Dylan?

This coming-of-age story, set in the last city to survive on Earth, is a story of love, faith, and strength of purpose

Harriet is the newest of Gaia's daughters, and wants to build her life with Dylan, son of Vijay and Jennifer. But to ensure his freedom and their future, she must Cindy's resistance to change in the running of the Gaian church. Meanwhile, Dylan dreams of a life on the sea and foreign adventures.

Can Harriet and Dylan bring new life to Jennifer's vision?

This metaphysical story of young lovers is the fourth novel set in the world of Gaia's Daughters.

Let us help get your book into print!

At Northern Forest Publishing, a hybrid publlisher, we welcome all authors. Our philosophy is to provide a range of individual services to do the tasks that authors choose not to do themselves. We do as little or as much as you require.
Our services include:

Project Planning & project management

Book formatting, front and back matter

Cover templates, cover design on request

Book blurbs, keywords, categories and metadata

Provision of global ISBN's,fegal deposits

Publication to global ebook sites, and to Amazon and IngramSpark for printed copies

Setup of your author's pages on Amazon, Goodreads and other locations

Provinding author copies, either POD or bulk printing

Tracking and forwarding of sales and royalties

Newsletter creation and support

Book promotion as part of NFP library

Email: admin@northernforestpublishing.com

At Otter & Osprey Press, we welcome fantasy, science fiction and metaphysical novels. We offer the same assistance in your publishing journey as described above.

Email: admin@otterandospreypress.com

39120136R00217